The Risky Busin

The Secret in the Grand Canyon

The Search for Kincaid's Cave

A Colten Burnett Novel

HEP ALDRIDGE

COPYRIGHT © 2025 HEP ALDRIDGE

Published by Hep Aldridge LLC.

All rights reserved

No part of this book may be reproduced, scanned or distributed

In any printed or electronic form without permission from the

author.

This is a work of fiction. Any resemblance of characters to actual

persons, living or dead is purely coincidental. The Author holds

exclusive rights to this work. Unauthorized duplication is

prohibited.

Cover Design by H. Aldridge

Special thanks to my editor Janell Parque

http://janelparque.blogspot.com

To be the first to hear about news, new book releases and

bargains from Hep Aldridge

GO HERE TO SIGN UP TO BE ON THE VIP LIST

http//mailchi.mp/b0c291dd854f/hep-aldridge

Learn more about Hep and his background on his webpage

http//hepaldridge.com

You can write directly to Hep and connect with him online.

EMAIL: cxburnett@gmail.com

FACEBOOK: https//www.facebook.com/hep.aldridge7

X: https//x.com/AldridgeHep

INSTAGRAM: https://www.instagram.com/hepaldridge/

CHAPTER 1

1971

Matt loved his job, with beautiful blue skies and not a care in the world, save for those pesky MiG-25s and the SAMs that he had to deal with. Major Matt Johnson sighed, just part of the day being a "Sled" pilot. On this run, his SR-71 had been outfitted with the latest sensors and recording instruments developed by DARPA, and it was his job to provide real-time evaluation of the system. The preliminary testing had gone well. Now it was "for real," and he was impressed. The system had been able to pick up energy readings from SAM missile sites much earlier and at a higher altitude than the previous system.

"Scotty," his Recon Systems Operator, had been updating him on the signals being received by "Eagle Eye" from the back seat. They were also able to pick up, along with the basic communication signals and radar, underground base power sources and numerous other interesting anomalies that had eluded them during previous systems missions. He was thinking that the boys at DARPA would have fun going over the data they were gathering when Scotty's voice came over the intercom, "Looks like things are about to get busy. I've got two fast movers in pursuit on our tail and closing fast, and the two SAM sites we're approaching have come alive." There was a pause, and then he continued, "Man, this system is cool. I picked up the bogies a hell of a lot earlier than with the old system."

"Good to know," I replied, "time to engagement with fast movers?"

"In max AB (afterburner) about four minutes; SAM's launch is imminent," Scotty said. "I have multiple missile launches, Matt... it's showtime, the clock has started." That meant he had started the timer on the missiles. Their fuel load only allowed for a maximum flight time of about 58 seconds, but they could cover a considerable amount of ground in that time at Mach 4 or 5.

Okay, I was going to have to worry about the SAMs first and deal with the MIGs after. I smiled, looked at my wife's picture taped to the instrument panel, and said softly, "No worries, honey, just another day at the office." The mental calculations sped through my head. We were operating at 65,000 feet at Mach 2.5. The MIG-25 Foxbat in maximum afterburner could reach our altitude and be within missile range in less than three minutes, with a top speed of somewhere around Mach 2.9. The SAMs were another story. Some had the capability to reach Mach 5, a speed that would make them difficult to outrun. However, they only had about 58 seconds of fuel to reach their target.

The chessboard was set. We needed to finish this final leg of our mission, and Scotty confirmed that it would take us twenty seconds before we could bug out. My move... for optimum data collection, we were supposed to stay below Mach 3 and a maximum altitude of 70,000 feet. I was easing the throttles forward when Scotty's voice came over the intercom, "Fast movers three miles and closing fast, missiles passing 25,000 feet, 30 seconds. Time to target 15 seconds."

I had reached Mach 3 and was approaching 70,000 feet when Scotty said, "Data run complete, fast movers are just within missile range, SAMs 60,000 feet, ten seconds of fuel left." Only time for one final move, as I pulled the nose up and shoved the throttles to their stops. The sudden acceleration shoved us back in our seats as I watched the Mach meter hit 4.2, and our altitude pass 80,000 feet. I smiled and said to myself, "Come on, baby, let's show 'em what you got."

"SAM's 70,000 feet and out of fuel, dropping away. Our ECM has jammed the MIG's missile lock, and they are slowly falling behind, but still coming," Scotty reported.

"That's their mistake," I replied as we hit Mach 5 and reached 85,000 feet. Two seconds later, Scotty laughingly reported, "They're done, falling away; I think the lead bogie just flamed out."

At this altitude and speed, we had surpassed their flight capabilities, another clean getaway, Matt thought. As the darkness approached, I could see the curvature of the Earth below, always a spectacular sight, and I slowly began throttling back. Our speed dropped from Mach 5.6 to 4.2, and our altitude began to decrease as I put us into a slow downward arc, heading for our refueling rendezvous with a KC-135 over the Arctic Circle.

The intercom came to life, and I realized how quiet it had been when Scotty said, not very convincingly,

"Well, that was fun."

I laughed, "Just another day at the office," I retorted.

"Many more of those days, and I can see why someone would want to take an early retirement," he quipped.

I scoldingly said, "Now, what kind of attitude is that? You know you enjoyed it as much as I did."

There was a silent pause before he said, "How many years have we been doing this?"

"A few," I replied.

"Well, I'm not sure enjoyable is quite the word I would use, but they are memorable."

I could hear the smile in Scotty's voice as I replied, "That they are."

Our flight plan took us over Canada and back into the United States, with a slow turn westward over northern Texas and across New Mexico. All was quiet until we were flashing across Arizona when the intercom squawked and Scotty exclaimed, "Holy crap!"

"What's going on?" I asked immediately.

"The readings on the new sensor cluster just went nuts."

"I thought it was performing perfectly," I replied.

"It was until thirty seconds ago, and now all readings are back to normal."

"A glitch?" I asked.

"I find that hard to believe with its flawless

performance so far," came the reply.

"So, what was it?" I asked.

"I don't know, but it happened as we were transiting Arizona in the Grand Canyon area."

Which, by now, was hundreds of miles behind us. I thought for a few seconds and then said, "Let's retrace our flight path and see what happens. If there's a problem with the system, we need to verify it before we get back to base. The boys from DARPA are going to want to know about it."

"Agree," Scotty answered. "I'm double-checking all the systems now."

I had started my turn and a few minutes later had us back on our original flight path crossing New Mexico and Arizona when Scotty said, "There it is again, according to my data, in exactly the same location over the Grand Canyon." There was a slight pause, and then, "Actually, about 4.5 miles from the East Rim of the canyon, and now everything is back to normal. That's weird as hell."

We were now getting low on fuel as I made my final turn toward California and Beal AFB. I had contacted the tower during our fly-around, and I have now confirmed our final approach to the tower.

"So, the readings changed on the array during our overfly of the Canyon."

"Changed, hell," Scotty said, "they started jumping all over the place, like nothing I've seen before. I mean, according to that, it's showing one hell of an energy field somewhere in the area, but according to all the data I have, there's nothing there. Just a couple of small towns and desert."

"Well, maybe the boys at DARPA can figure it out." I laughed, "That's going to add to our interesting flight report."

"I should say so," Scotty replied. "MIGs, SAMs, and an anomalous energy signature in the middle of nowhere. Like you said, just another day in the office," he quipped. A few minutes later, the big blackbird touched down, and I taxied toward its hangar.

CHAPTER 2

Present Day

You know how sometimes a phrase, jingle, or song gets stuck in your head, and you can't get it to leave, and it drives you crazy? I've been dealing with something like that for the last month. Not a phrase or song, something a little more complicated than that. I sat staring out my office window, my mind a whirling vortex, and wondering what the hell really happened to Cleopatra. My mental conundrum is a holdover from our last adventure, when we searched for golden statues that might have given us a clue to Cleopatra's final resting place. An Intriguing prospect, since to date her tomb has never been found. What my Risky Business crew and I had discovered in Egypt and subsequently at the archaeological site of Teotihuacan in central Mexico, thanks to my very special colleague, antiquities expert Dr. Tessa Worthington, had really presented us with an unimaginable mystery.

We discovered evidence, at least some clues, that led us to believe Cleopatra may not have died in 30 BCE, as the historical records indicate. In fact, she, along with a male whom we think might be her father, may have turned up in Mexico sometime after her reported demise. Cue the "Whiskey Tango Foxtrot" part of the brain. Earth-shattering, hell yes. Mind-boggling, absolutely. A possibility... remains to be seen. Hence my raging mental tempest.

While this was all spinning in my head, I had also been trying to help my colleague and attorney, Lawrence, work out the details of our current recovery operation of a French vessel from the 1600s off Amelia Island, Florida. The state was being a royal pain over our salvage and recovery rights. Our permits were all in order, and we were cooperating with the authorities for a change. Things were going well until we discovered that the vessel could be carrying a significant amount of treasure. Now the state wanted to take control of the operation and was questioning our salvage and recovery permit claims. My name is Colten X. Burnett, President and CEO of Risky Business, so these kinds of problems land squarely in my lap.

As I was grappling with these details of just another day in the bureaucratic jungles of treasure hunting, my door opened, and Doc came into the office. Doctor Ryan Greene was our resident researcher, linguist, and medic. Doc's nickname came from both his two Ph.D.s in Linguistics, specializing in ancient languages, and the medical training he had received in the Coast Guard as a rescue swimmer. His skills in both areas have been put to good use since he became one of the original members of Risky Business Ltd., my salvage and recovery company... yes, we were "real" treasure hunters.

"Hey, Colt, got a minute?" he jovially asked.

"Please, yes, anything to take my mind off this

state mess," I replied.

"Remember that box of stuff you got from River's sister that prompted one of our recent operations?"

"Of course, that stuff led us on the search for Aztec treasure in New Mexico," I answered.

"Yep, the same, well, I was going through it to catalog and store its contents, when I took a closer look at the newspaper clipping from 1909, which was in there." He handed me a yellowed piece of newsprint. It was from the *Arizona Gazette* dated 1909 and spoke of an archaeological discovery made in the Grand Canyon. I scanned it quickly and handed it back to him, saying, "Okay...."

"Did you read the part that stated they found Egyptian mummies in the cave?"

I immediately took the clipping back and began scanning it more closely, and said, "No, I missed that."

"The piece of paper kind of got lost in the shuffle when we found the map and those artifacts in the box. They captured our interest, and we didn't pay much attention to the old newspaper clipping."

"True," I said as I digested what was in the story. "It says here they found more out-of-place artifacts, a golden Buddha-style statue, and other objects that shouldn't have been there." I sat, mind swirling again as my eyes opened wider and said, "You don't think this could have something to do with Cleo, do you?"

Doc was grinning like a Cheshire cat. "It very well could," he replied.

"I would like to look into it further, since we don't have

any big projects that require my help going on right now."

"This could be interesting," I said. "So sure, go ahead," I answered.

"It may take some time, travel, and money," Doc added.

"As long as we don't need you here, it's fine with me."

Smiling, he left the office, and I considered the possibilities of this new discovery before I jumped back into my bureaucratic nightmare. I found it harder to concentrate as that question kept rolling around in my head: what DID happen to Cleo?

CHAPTER 3

It was the headline from the yellowed 1909 news article that had caught Doc's eye as he was sorting through the remnants in the box from our New Mexico adventure. "Explorations in the Grand Canyon: Mysteries of Immense Rich Cavern Being Brought to Light."

Doc had heard this story for years and had encountered both those who believed it and those who claimed it was a hoax. He remembered reading a couple of articles that thoroughly debunked the story, but this was different. The newspaper clipping had been folded into a piece of yellowed paper, and on it was written, "baa ha'a'h hasin," or that's what it looked like. On closer inspection of the newsprint, he found a circle with what appeared to be feathers drawn in pencil around the part that mentioned the cave opening.

It took him a while to understand what he was seeing. When he did, he immediately went to Colt and asked if he could pursue this story. The box was given to Risky Business by the daughter of an Apache medicine man. Inside, it had these clippings and a map with Aztec and Apache iconography depicted on it. It also had an Aztec artifact inside. Those things had consumed our attention, paying little notice to the rest of the papers inside.

Doc gingerly held the clipping and the paper it had been folded in as he made a call to Tony, our computer expert. Tony picked up on the second ring. Doc explained that he had a word that needed translating and asked if his translation program could help with a Native American text. "Sure, send it to me, and I'll get back to you as soon as I have something." Ten minutes later, Doc's phone rang.

"That was pretty cool," Tony said. "Turns out it was Navajo, and it means 'Sacred'."

"Thanks, buddy," that's what I needed," Doc replied. As Doc studied the clipping, he now believed the circle and feathers drawn over the newsprint was the Apache symbol for "Sacred Space."

What did a Navajo word for "sacred" on a piece of paper, a hand-drawn Apache design associated with "power or sacred place," and an old newspaper clipping, all in a box that belonged to an Apache medicine man, mean—if anything?

Now, with Colt's approval, Doc was officially interested....

He started at the beginning... who might be the actors in this mystery? He began an investigation into Kincaid, the explorer who apparently discovered the referenced cave, and S.A. Jordan, the Smithsonian scientist who supposedly visited the site and arranged for the removal of some of the artifacts. Of course, he investigated the newspaper and the article, written by an anonymous author, a major red flag to start with.

The Arizona newspaper archives yielded very

little, except for a copy of the article. No insights into the author or any efforts to corroborate the facts as presented, which were claims of proof of transoceanic contact. A concerning fact was that there was no follow-up to the initial article in the newspaper, not even a mention. With an assertion that could rewrite history books if true, the newspaper's silence led to questioning the validity and truth of the story.

Digging deeper, he found that a more recent debunking of the story stated there was no evidence that Kincaid or Jordan ever worked for the Smithsonian. No employment records could be found for either one. The lack of a named journalist for the article led to accusations of a pure hoax on the part of the *Gazette*. But why would an established newspaper print a story like this that seems so implausible?

Notoriety, increase sales? It's hard to say, but something wasn't right. This only spurred Doc's interest more. He got on the phone and called a scholar friend affiliated with the Smithsonian, asking about the best way to obtain access to their employment records. Brushing off questions, saying he was writing a paper on archaeological researchers and research in the 1900s, his friend gave him the name of the person responsible for the archives, and said that was the place to start. If he couldn't help him, he would know who could.

With the name in hand, Doc booked a flight to Washington, D.C. He had a starting point, and like any good researcher, that's all he needed.

Three days later, he sat in the office of Dr. William Benson, head of the Smithsonian archives. He presented his credentials and made his request for access. Dr. Benson acknowledged his papers and commented, "Dr. Greene, your reputation precedes you; I will be happy to help anyway I can." Benson had an associate take Doc to a room on a lower floor. A computer terminal and shelf after shelf of bound volumes filled the space. "This is our main archive; only a portion of our database is available to the general public online. However, you can access our entire database from this terminal and print out whatever you need. I believe you will find the information you are looking for here."

After three hours, he finally found Kincaid's name, not as an active member of the Smithsonian as had been indicated in the news article, but as a part-time associate in exploration from 1902 to 1908, a very low-level position at best. But there was no mention of him anywhere after 1908. So why did the article reference a 35-year affiliation with the Smithsonian in the 1909 article, rather than a past employee, if you will, but instead as a current and long-time member of the Smithsonian team?

Unless the article was indeed a hoax, as had been stated, Doc mused. Maybe this whole thing was a hoax, but that little germ of possibility had taken root. Four more hours curiously yielded nothing on J.A. Jordan, the purported Smithsonian scientist who had accompanied Kincaid to the cave and removed some of the relics within. Puzzling.

Doc realized this was going to take more sleuthing than anticipated, but he was determined to come to some definitive conclusion, hoax or not. So, he returned to his hotel and dug into the research he had brought with him—specifically, a copy of the 1909 article. Pouring himself a drink, he began re-reading the story, preparing to delve further into this mystery the next day.

As he read, the claims of an Egyptian connection were posited by Kincaid, asserting proof of transatlantic contact. Hieroglyphs and mummies led him to this claim. What caught Doc's eye was the reference to Jordan as a professor. He kicked that thought around for a while. If this Jordan were a teaching professor somewhere, he may not have been a full-time employee of the Smithsonian either —possibly a visiting or contracted academic hired just for this investigation. If so, he may have been picked for his expertise or belief in this purported Egyptian connection.

Doc now had a new avenue to explore and went to bed with a renewed sense of interest, looking forward to his return to the bowels of the Smithsonian the next day.

CHAPTER 4

Day two found Doc up early, continuing research at the Smithsonian. After three hours, he was still having no luck. He had reviewed numerous part-time employee records, dating back to just prior to 1909 and through 1911, and found nothing. After pondering his situation, he decided to take a different tack. If this Jordan were real and a professor somewhere, he would likely have some published papers. Doc decided to search for any documents presenting or supporting the idea of transatlantic contact between ancient civilizations, written between 1900 and 1909. His logic was that being a published academic on this topic could have come to the attention of the Smithsonian. It would be a good way for the museum to insulate itself from public or professional ridicule if the finding proved to be bogus. And if it turned out to be true, they could claim that Jordan was indeed affiliated with the museum and garner the publicity a discovery like this would bring.

The search yielded ten published documents related to the transatlantic topic. He scanned the authors quickly and stopped at number eight, "Transatlantic Contact of Ancient Civilizations," by Dr. S. Jordan, Professor of Anthropology, Georgetown University. There it was, proof Jordan was a real person.

He excitedly jumped up, thanked the people at the Smithsonian, and headed to Georgetown to meet with the dean of the Anthropology Department.

He was cordially received and presented the same request as he had at the Smithsonian: Looking into archaeological research and researchers of the 1900s for an upcoming paper. Once again, his academic credentials were recognized by the dean, and he was granted access to their archives and led into a room with four computer terminals.

His guide informed him that all the department's archives had been digitized and would be available to him. Doc thanked him as he left the room. Jumping right in, he found Jordan's name and his title of Visiting Professor, perhaps explaining why he had been challenging to find. Doc tried to dig further into his history at the university and hit a brick wall. Research was available to him, but not employee records. After a few futile attempts to gain access, he stopped. He was stuck and needed help. Pulling out his cellphone, he dialed Tony's number at the "Lair," the name Dimitri had given their headquarters building in Cocoa, Florida. Tony was the team's computer guru, and if anybody could help, it would be him.

Tony picked up on the third ring and cheerfully said, "Hey, Doc, what's going on?" After quickly exchanging pleasantries, Doc filled him in on the situation and what he needed to do. Tony told him to hang on as his fingers flew over his keyboard. "Hmm," he replied, "They have a pretty robust firewall, but I'm in. Send me the IP address of the computer you're on." Doc retrieved it and passed it along. After a few minutes, Tony finally said, "Okay, try to access the employee database now." Doc tried again and immediately had access.

"I'm in," he told Tony.

"Good, so when you leave, make sure you turn the power off to that computer; that will break the connection I've set up and make it impossible to trace any breach of the firewall.

"You should have plenty of time to do your snooping, but don't dilly dally. If their IT people are any good, they will spot the breach and be able to track it to that computer if it's still online. Once it's powered down, you're golden."

"How much time do I have?" Doc asked.

"I'd say fifteen to twenty minutes, but you need to be gone as soon as you can."

"Got it," Doc said and hung up. In minutes, he located Jordan's employment records, which spanned from 1907 to 1910. His teaching load and the courses he taught were all there, but as Doc was scrolling through the pages, he stopped. On the screen for 1909, it stated that Jordan had been granted an unpaid leave of absence, with no further employment records on file. He noticed an asterisk typed next to the word "Absence*." He scrolled down to the very bottom of the page and found an asterisk notation that read, "Smithsonian."

This obviously was an indication that Jordan had worked for the museum at the time of the reported discovery by Kincaid. He looked at his watch and saw that he had already burned up fifteen minutes and needed to get out of there. He saw the printer on an end table and, fingers crossed, clicked "Print Page" on his terminal. Seconds later, the printer came to life, and the page printed out. He immediately shut down his computer and traced the power cord to a wall plug; he reached down and jerked it out of the wall and headed for the exit.

Doc next stopped by the dean's office and left word with his secretary, thanking him for his cooperation and stating that he had obtained the information he needed. Then, he quickly headed for the exit. Outside, he flagged down a taxi, riding in silent contemplation back to his hotel. Once there, he promptly booked a flight back to Florida for the next morning. His work in DC was done, as the mystery continued to deepen.

Later, as Doc sat in his room, he ticked off the facts or information he had: The newspaper article that started it all.

The lack of any follow-up article to a supposed significant archaeological discovery.

The fact is that the article was written by an anonymous source, and the newspaper still published it.

And the Smithsonian disavowing any knowledge of the discovery or the employment by them of the two main actors involved.

Everything would seem to point to a hoax on the part of the paper, but why? Now the wrinkle, proof that both Kincaid and Jordan had, in fact, been in the employ of the Smithsonian at the time of the article. Why would the Smithsonian deny that? What would be their motivation to do so? That fact called into question the validity of their statement that they had not received any artifacts from anyone during that time, when the article explicitly states that some were removed and taken by them. Fact or fiction... another unanswered question.

Doc knew he wanted to delve further into this mystery and felt confident Colt would go along with it. He packed his bag as the story kept running through his head, and the myriad of questions surrounding the mystery kept growing. His flight back to Florida was uneventful, and one of Risky Business's security team was waiting to pick him up. Forty minutes later, they arrived, and as he walked through the doors, he knew he was about to face one of the biggest challenges in this project, or so he thought.

Settling into his office, Doc called Colt and had his administrative assistant set up a meeting for the next day. Then, sitting down at his terminal, he continued his research, digging into anything he could find concerning the story in the *Gazette*. When he arrived at Colt's office the next day, Joe and O'Reilly had just finished a meeting and were getting up to leave when Doc said, "Can you guys stick around?"

Joe looked at O'Reilly and said, "I don't have anywhere to be, so sure." O'Reilly nodded in the affirmative, and they both sat back down as Doc pulled up another chair, all three of them facing Colt, who was sitting behind his desk, leaning back in his chair, hands clasped behind his head. Smiling broadly, he cheerfully said, "So what's up, Doc?" No one missed the cartoon humor as they all chuckled.

"Well, you remember the request I made concerning the story about the Grand Canyon and the Egyptian artifacts that were supposedly found there?"

"Yeah, I do," Colt replied, "That was from information you found in the 1900-something newspaper article."

"That's the one," Doc answered as he handed out a sheet of paper to each of them. As they read, he continued, "This is something I think we really need to explore further. Not that there is any treasure involved, but the possible historical significance, if true, is huge." He had typed out an executive summary of what he hoped would be a new investigation/project for Risky Business. As they finished reading, Joe said, "I remember reading about this on the internet. It sounds interesting, but hasn't it been debunked... found to be a hoax?"

"That's just it, it is claimed to be a hoax by numerous sources, but what I've discovered calls that assessment into question."

"Intriguing," Colt said, "You actually think the newspaper article is real?"

"I don't know," Doc replied, "but I sure would like to find out, especially if it could have something to do with Cleo."

Joe and O'Reilly looked at Doc, rather wide-eyed as Joe whistled softly, looking at Colt and said, smiling broadly, "I'm in."

O'Reilly, also smiling, said, "Damn straight, count me in."

CHAPTER 5

Colt sat, thoughtfully reading the document, and finally said, "Well, it's a long shot, but if you think it's worth digging into, then I'll trust your judgment, but I can't see involving the whole team unless you find additional evidence that warrants it."

O'Reilly spoke up, "I think gathering intel and getting the lay of the land would be our first order of business, low-key, of course. I can check out the local helicopter canyon tours in the area, and we can play tourist for starters. I would like to see how things in the area look from the air."

"Agree," Doc replied. "This should be a basic information/fact-finding mission, for now."

"If there are any real facts," Joe retorted with a chuckle.

Colt smiled as he said, "Well, Doc, looks like you've got a team. I'm fine with it; just keep me posted on your findings."

"Roger that," Doc replied, wrinkling his eyebrow at Joe for his remark.

"I'll let Max know you'll be needing the jet soon." Max was our corporate pilot and was essentially on call 24/7.

"Great, thanks, Colt," Doc said as they got up. "We won't be leaving for a few days yet, but I'll keep you informed."

Re-reading Doc's executive summary, I wondered if this was a wild goose chase. It did sound interesting, and Doc's findings did add an element of intrigue. I sat there ruminating… what if there was a Cleo connection, I mean, after all, who doesn't like a good conspiracy theory?

Doc sat in the comfortable leather chair, deep in thought as the jet engines hummed. Joe had moved to the chair opposite him and said, "So you really think there is a Cleo aspect to this story?"

Looking up from his notes, Doc replied, "At this point, it's a possibility, nothing more."

Joe continued, "It's kind of a stretch, don't you think?"

Doc leaned back into the supple leather, picked up his drink, and, smiling, said, "Joe, of all people, after everything we've been through together, are you really asking that question?" he replied, chuckling.

Grinning, Joe said, "Well, when you put it that way, I guess anything could be possible."

"Exactly," Doc answered, "and that's precisely why we're going… to explore that possibility."

We landed at McCarran about four hours later, grabbed a rental car, and headed to the Excalibur Hotel and Casino. O'Reilly had called ahead and had gathered some pertinent info on the canyon tours. She had chosen what she thought was the best company flying and booked a helicopter tour for the next day.

The next morning, we arrived at the tour facility at the prescribed time. We were greeted by a very petite, good-looking young woman, dressed in casual dark blue slacks, a white blouse with captain's insignia, epaulets, and the name of the helicopter tour company embroidered on it. I was somewhat surprised when I saw her. I mean, she made Reggie look tall by comparison, and Reggie was about five feet nothing, but her presence was exceptional. An air of confidence and toughness surrounded her as she came forward to greet us.

There was no one else around, and she said to O'Reilly, "You must be my 9:00 tour group."

O'Reilly said, "If you're the captain, then yes, we are."

Captain Aurora "Rory" Naismith walked to the counter and said, "Come over here; we have some paperwork for you to fill out."

It was not the warm tourist reception I had been expecting. Not that she was rude, just all business. Paperwork, weigh-in completed, and payment taken care of, we headed out to the tarmac and the helicopter parked there. O'Reilly was walking next to the pilot and observed, "An A-Star 350, nice bird."

The pilot gave her a sideways look and said, "You know your helicopters."

"Yeah, I've spent a little time around them," O'Reilly answered and said nothing more.

The flight took about an hour, and Capt. Rory, as

our pilot had instructed us to call her, gave us her usual tourist spiel along the way. Interesting, but no revelations. We had opted for the canyon flying tour with no landing; we just wanted to get a visual of as much of the area as possible. I had been to the canyon before, but not on a flying tour. As we approached the rim, the majestic beauty of it spread out before us like some giant hands had tried to tear apart the earth, leaving it with a massive, breathtakingly ragged edge. The vibrancy of the colorful earth tones, combined with the drop to the canyon floor, took my breath away.

Everyone was silent as we crossed over the rim, and the abyss below opened like the maw of some enormous beast waiting to devour us. The crags and rocky spires surrounded us like teeth ready to rend us and our frail craft into nothingness at any minute. Yes, I was impressed to say the least—as were O'Reilly and Joe. We shared a glance, and the looks on our faces underscored the awe of the spectacle below us. That breathtaking moment was shattered like a fine crystal goblet being dropped on a tile floor when Rory began her tour guide monologue again.

She proficiently banked the chopper to give us views of the North Rim and the canyon terrain, which I suppose was her standard tour route. I asked her if she would take us by the East Rim and if she could get a little lower. "The East Rim, no, but lower, you bet," she said. The East Rim, Doc mused, was where Kincaid said he found the cave entrance.

When I asked why, our somewhat enigmatic captain was polite but firm. "The East Rim is not part of the tour." I told her I would be happy to pay extra if that was the issue, but Rory firmly said, "Sorry, no can do. Plus, there is a no-fly zone in that area." That really piqued my interest, and without hesitation, I rather brazenly asked her why.

"Just the government's rules. Something to do with disturbing the animals, disrespecting sacred lands, and endangering the natural environment—and this job doesn't pay me enough to risk a hefty fine or losing my license," Rory unapologetically explained.

I thought for a minute and said, "Then maybe we can drive there when we get back?"

"You can get to some of it, but there's a lot totally off-limits and some partially restricted areas also."

I tried to be nonchalant in my response when I asked, "Are there any other no-fly zones in the canyon?"

"Yes, there are a couple more, but they are in areas where there isn't much tourist interest," she replied.

She banked the chopper and dropped into the canyon. Its exceptional beauty engulfed us as she adeptly followed the canyon walls, twisting and turning the helicopter like a ballet dancer on stage. It was indeed breathtaking. Rising above the rim, she made a turn and dropped down for a low-level run. Luckily, I was used to O'Reilly's flying antics, so I relaxed and enjoyed the view, guessing most of her other tourist passengers would consider this the "white knuckle" portion of the tour. Not us! Returning to our starting point, she climbed above the rim and took us to around 5,000 feet, giving us the same route we had just flown, but this time with an aerial perspective at altitude.

I had been hopeful that our flight might reveal some clues, but under these circumstances, all we got was a somewhat generic view of the majestic wonder below. However, the idea of no-fly zones and restricted areas got me wondering. On the way back, I probed a little deeper on the subject of restricted areas.

Shedding some of her previous formality, Rory informed us that the National Park Service had made certain areas of the East Rim off-limits due to hazardous terrain and the danger it posed to hikers and sightseeing visitors. Then, almost as an afterthought, she mentioned that the government had a research facility nearby, and that area was also a restricted no-fly zone. It was a large, fenced area, a few square acres, she thought. I looked at my companions and saw their questioning expressions. I smiled and nodded slightly and continued to engage our pilot in general conversation.

We landed, and as we were walking to the office, I asked once again, "So the no-fly zones really keep you from flying tourists through a lot of the canyon?"

Rory laughed and said, "Yeah, you can't legally do it, and they do have Feds watching, but I have heard of some rogue pilots crossing the boundaries and getting away—but if they ever get caught, the park service and FAA will have them behind bars in no time. They must do it for the adrenaline rush that I'm sure comes along with breaking rules, or for a hell of a lot of money."

Acting like any appreciative tourist with vacation money to spare, we thanked her for an interesting tour, tipped her $300, and headed back to Vegas. Our Team discussion on the way back to the hotel was more a stream of questions rather than a discussion. However, as we pulled up to the hotel and turned the car over to the valet, it was decided that the next logical step in our quest would be to head to the East Rim the next day. After all, we did have to live up to our "Risky Business" name. We hit the buffet in the hotel and, after a meal and a couple of beverages, headed to our rooms, wondering what tomorrow might bring.

We left for the airport early the next morning and were lucky enough to get seats on a commuter flight from Vegas to Peal, Arizona. We rented a 4-wheel-drive Jeep Grand Cherokee, picked up some provisions, and headed south on Highway 89. We knew the highway ran parallel to the canyon and that our location put us close to its East Rim. The big question that remained was how we were ever going to find a starting point for our search, and how we would actually search the area.

CHAPTER 6

April 1909

It had been an arduous climb, and Kincaid could not believe the sight before him. Hidden behind the large rock outcropping was a set of carved stairs leading upward to the dark opening he had spotted earlier. This had to be an indication of human habitation at some point in the distant past. But who, how, he asked himself, his mind swirling as he slowly climbed the steps to the opening above.

Kincaid had been traveling down the mighty river below while searching for potential mineral deposits when he had spotted what looked like an opening in the sheer rock face high above him. As he approached this dark maw, his breathing quickened, and he fumbled with his carbide lamp, finally igniting it and carefully stepping inside the cave's entrance.

He paused to let his eyes adjust to the black void ahead. Holding his lamp high, he observed the natural rock formations of the cave's walls as he slowly began his entrance into stygian darkness. To his surprise, as he progressed, he noticed what appeared to be chisel marks on the wall, confirming a prior human presence. What he saw next sent shivers down his spine. His immediate thought: I have to notify the Smithsonian immediately.

Kincaid's initial memories came flooding back to him as he led the workers from the Smithsonian into the cave's crypt room. Dr. Jordan was working there with three other men, cataloging the wealth of artifacts they were recovering. They had already sent the museum one shipment, which included two of the mummies they had taken from the crypt room. The cave system was proving to be a gold mine of age-old artifacts and definitive evidence of trans-Atlantic contact of ancient cultures, much to Jordan's delight.

The museum's assigned specialists had been working there for three weeks, exploring the cave system and recording the strange hieroglyphs they had found on the walls. Kincaid's interview with the local paper had gone well. He was sure he had secured a place for himself and Jordan in the historical record with this discovery.

He had entered the crypt area and approached Jordan when a worker came running from deeper in the cave's bowels, breathlessly whispering to them, "Dr. Jordan, you have to come with me; you won't believe what I have found."

"What is it, man? Speak up," Jordan asked rather brusquely.

"You need to see it for yourself. Come quickly; it's another room." Turning on his heels, he hurriedly headed back into the darkness the way he had come. All the workers had noted the exchange, and as Jordan and I followed the worker further back into the cave, the others fell in behind us. Their additional lights added to the illumination of the large tunnel, and as we turned a corner, we found a young worker standing at a branching tunnel, our lights also revealing a huge staircase carved into a stone wall.

As the other workers arrived, the additional light more clearly lit the stairs and showed a giant statue staring down at us from the flat platform at the top, some twenty steps above. Even from this distance, we could tell the workmanship was incredible. The staircase was polished to a smooth, almost mirror-like surface. The room was huge and contained additional sculptures flanking the central figure on the platform. This was obviously a special place, more ornately decorated with wall carvings and more of the strange hieroglyphs than the space below.

The young worker turned to us and said, "See, Dr. Jordan, I told you and Mr. Kincaid that this was amazing," and began ascending the staircase before we could stop him. On the third step, he paused and turned to us, wide-eyed, mouth open, but no sound coming out. He stood for a few seconds, turning ghastly pale as his hand holding the lantern disintegrated and the light fell down the steps. We watched, horrified, frozen in place as the rest of his body turned to dust, leaving only a pile of empty clothing.

It happened so quickly that no one could react. Then, two of the workers on my left, who had moved a few feet in front of where Jordan and I were standing, began screaming as their bodies began disintegrating. I began feeling dizzy, and instinctively, I turned and started running through the gathered workers, who began dropping like stalks of wheat at harvest as I passed them. I didn't slow down to look back for Jordan. I knew without a doubt that he had suffered the same fate as the young man on the steps and the men around me.

Others had also started to run, but began to fall, their lights casting macabre shadows of bodies lying on the floor, turning to dust as their lights fell with them; some stayed lit, while others snuffed out. I had reached the back of the group as my breathing became labored, and my legs began to feel weak. As I slowly dropped to my knees, my last thoughts were that I hoped we would be remembered for the amazing discoveries we had made in this enigmatic cave system. As I fell forward, my face hitting the floor, and death's cold grip squeezed the last bit of life from my body, I feared that would not be the case.

Three days later, the four workers who had seen to the shipping of the artifacts by rail returned. Entering the cave, finding no one close to the entrance, they went deeper in until they came upon the piles of workers' clothing littering the cave's floor. One ran to the nearest pile and knelt to inspect it. As he looked back at his companions and tried to stand, the man fell over dead, his body turning to dust. The two other workers began running toward the cave's exit. They made it to the crypt room before one fell to the floor. Panicked, the third worker continued running for two more steps before dropping to his knees. Looking up, he saw the young man they had left to tie the mules and secure the wagons entering the far side some seventy-five feet away, and with his last dying breath, shouted, "Run!"

The young man did not hesitate and turned on his

heel, running to the entrance without stopping until he was outside. Fear gripped him, and his body began trembling uncontrollably. He dropped to the ground and began sobbing. What had happened? Where were the rest of the workers? Were they all dead? But how? He had no answers, and his terror-induced sobbing continued for what seemed like hours. When it finally subsided, the young man climbed back to the rim above, took one of the wagons, and headed back to town, some fifty miles away. Two days later, he showed up in Fremont, exhausted, terrified, and alone. No one in town knew about the project; it was kept secret to keep unsavory characters and sightseers away. He made his way to the small rail station where the station master recognized him and, seeing the level of distress, asked what had happened. The young man didn't answer but said he needed to send a telegram right away. The station master asked no more questions, sat the boy down, gave him some water, and sent a short message to the Smithsonian Museum in Washington, D.C., for the young man. "Emergency," stop, "Send help immediately," stop. It was the official message the museum designated for use only in the direst of situations.

On April 5th, Kincaid's first story was published in the Arizona Gazette. He knew he had somewhat embellished the story with details that were speculations on his part. Still, the reporter was enthralled by his tale and took copious notes, assuring him this was going to be a sensational story.

On April 8th, the Smithsonian team arrived in Fremont, found the young man at the local boarding house, and, with his guidance, immediately headed to the cave. He was questioned repeatedly along the way, but he provided little information. They realized that he really didn't know anything other than that he watched his two friends die from a distance in the cave in a most unbelievable way. He recounted his friend's last words, "Run," which he did—never looking back.

It was a six-man team that had arrived with four boxes of equipment and three canaries in a cage. All were armed. Since they had no idea what the emergency was, they had come prepared for all contingencies. Everything from a mining disaster to dealing with "various kinds of men of ill intent." That was according to Mr. Smith, the group's leader. He was a large, square-jawed man whose face was scarred and had turned into burnished leather by many years in the sun. His stoic countenance added to his stature, indicating that he was not a man to be trifled with. There was little to no conversation other than questions on the way to the cave. Mr. Smith continued to quiz the survivor for additional details about what had transpired. None were forthcoming.

Late in the afternoon of the second day, they arrived. The survivor led the men down the treacherous path to the cave's entrance. The area was littered with various bits of equipment. Ropes, picks, shovels, a wheelbarrow, and assorted detritus were left where all had been dropped. The men unloaded the boxes from the wagon and began unpacking a variety of items. The most notable were the military gas masks that came out. Mr. Smith and his second-in-command had gone to the entrance of the cave and were discussing a course of action.

The young man was summoned by a hand gesture from Smith. When he got to the two men looking into the pitch-black interior of the cave, Mr. Smith asked how far in the chamber it was, referring to it as "the crypt."

CHAPTER 7

Two of the men had been putting on protective outer gear. Donning the gas masks and picking up the cage with the canaries, they walked to where three others were standing at the mouth of the cave. On a signal from Mr. Smith, they lit their lanterns and, with the birdcage extended on a six-foot pole in front of them, began to enter the cave slowly. More lanterns were lit and held at the ready. The first two men walked some fifteen feet into the cave and stopped, checked the canaries, and continued forward. Two of the other men took lanterns and entered with Mr. Smith and the witness following. One man stayed at the entrance.

They proceeded without incident into the dimly lit cave of death. They all moved slowly and maintained a significant distance between them. They exited the tunnel entrance and stepped into the first room. The two men in front with Smith had stopped in the middle of the large room. One of them shouted back, "Nothing, sir, no problems."

Mr. Smith asked without looking at the witness, "How far to this crypt chamber?"

He answered, "Take the tunnel to the left for thirty feet, and it will lead to the crypt chamber."

Smith asked, "You said you entered the chamber... how far?"

He told him about ten or fifteen feet before he saw Jim. That was the name of the man who had shouted the warning.

In a loud, commanding voice, Smith relayed the information to the men out front, and they began to move forward. Fear had settled in, and the witness was beginning to tremble as he remembered the horrible sight. They exited the tunnel, and the lead men had stopped about ten feet into the chamber. Again, Smith asked, "Anything?"

"Nothing, sir," came the reply.

"All right, move on," Smith told the men.

Ten more feet, and their lantern light picked up the pile of clothes on the floor.

"Stop," came the command from Smith. "What's that on the floor?"

"Looks like a pile of old clothes," came the reply.

Smith looked at the witness; he was terrified and shakingly said, "That's Jim."

Smith's eyes narrowed, and his brow furrowed as his jaw clenched, and he said, "Are you sure?"

"I am," he answered.

"Move forward with caution; check out those clothes," Smith ordered. The two front men began moving slowly forward as the three others held back. We could see their lanterns lighting the scene before them as they slowly approached the pile of clothes.

"Any problem with the birds?" Smith asked.

"None, sir," came the reply.

They had reached Jim, or the pile of clothes, as they called it. One of them kicked it with his boot. Nothing happened.

"Just some dirt and old clothes, sir."

"All right, continue...." Smith hadn't finished his sentence when the man carrying the bird cage dropped it, screaming. The cage broke open as it hit the floor; the three birds flew out and disintegrated in mid-air, as the man's gear fell into a heap. An exclamation that no one could understand came from the second man as his clothes did the same thing. Their protective gear had dropped to the floor, empty, like skin that a snake had just shed. The outer layer was there, but nothing was inside.

Smith shouted the order "Out, now!" as the rest of them turned and ran for the tunnel. They didn't stop until they got to the mouth of the cave. The four of them seemed to have made it out safely. Panting and out of breath, the witness turned to Smith, who was staring at the cave entrance. He couldn't begin to describe the look on Smith's face. This man, commanding and fearless in his appearance and presence, stood, his whole body shaking. Without taking his eyes off the entrance, he mumbled, "God in heaven, what just happened?"

The rest of the men were equally shaken as the lone man who had stayed at the entrance tried to question the others to find out what had just transpired. "They disappeared... they just disappeared," one of the men was able to get out.

"What are you talking about?" he asked.

"It's like one minute their bodies were there, right in front of us, and the next minute, they were gone. Dissolved, disappeared, just gone," he shakily got out.

The questioner turned to Smith, still staring at the cave entrance, "What the…?" Smith stopped him in mid-sentence with a raised hand and, without taking his eyes off that deadly black opening, said, "Get the dynamite." His orders had been clear. If he deemed it appropriate, the project was to be terminated. There could be no trace of it or the people involved. The chaos within certain political circles in Washington that this discovery was creating had to stop. His job was to make it go away if needs be… whatever killed his men had just made his job easier. Whatever it was, it could not be allowed to leave the cave, at any cost.

The sun was lighting up the canyon walls when the charges were finally in place. All tools and supplies left outside by Jordan's party had been moved into the cave's entrance. They included much of what they had brought. Smith told them there would be no need to return with it. He had very carefully removed all traces of human activity at the site.

Smith walked the area one last time, stopping at the entrance to the cave, his face devoid of emotion. The sun cast its shadow into the cave opening, half of it blending with the blackness inside. In one quick move, he turned to the others and said in a voice that sent a chill down their spines, "No one is ever to speak of this, of what we saw or what we did. If you do, you know the consequences you will face. We were never here. His three remaining men all quickly responded, "Yes, sir." The witness got the feeling this was not the first time they had received this order and agreed to obey. He then turned to the witness, not saying a word, his eyes boring holes in his soul, and he knew he was about to die.

Smith paused for what seemed like an eternity, his stare never wavering, as the sweat ran in rivulets through the dust on the witness's face. All at once, his eyes softened a bit, and he said in his baritone voice, "Son, you have a decision to make, right here, right now." The witness was twenty-two years old but felt like a child about to suffer the ultimate parental punishment.

Smith took a step closer, now no more than two feet away. His six-foot-something frame loomed over him as he continued, "And so do I."

"I don't know you, or what kind of man you are, so I have to decide, do I have my men tie you up and add you to the trash in the cave that is about to be closed forever by tons of rock?" He reached into his coat pocket and removed a pouch, holding it in his hand, and said, "Or, do I trust that you will take this pouch, three hundred dollars in gold, and agree to the same thing my men just did? Never breathe a word of the work you did here, what you saw, or whom you met, including me. Can I trust you to do that?"

The witness slowly let out the breath he hadn't realized he'd been holding and quietly, but firmly said, "Yes, sir, you can."

"Good," Smith took his hand, placed the pouch in it, and closed his fingers around it. He stepped back and added, "If I ever do find out you've broken your promise to me, no matter where you go, I will find you, and you will not like what would happen next."

His last statement was like an icy spear piercing the witness's chest, as he knew Smith meant every word. The witness vowed then that it was a promise he would never break.

Smith turned his attention to his men, who had been standing a few feet away, and said, "All right, move out." Turning to his second-in-command, he said, "Light her up," and they all hurriedly headed back up the trail. The trail was nothing more than a single-person track that Kincaid had found that led to the canyon rim. On their way up, Smith had his men set additional, smaller charges that completely obliterated the track. It would never be used again.

At the rim, the ropes and pulleys that had been used to raise some of the artifacts that had been found earlier were gathered and loaded into one of the wagons. The timbers that had been used were pushed over the rim into the abyss below. Once again, all traces of the expedition had been eliminated.

They rid themselves of the mules and wagons once they arrived in town, made their way to the train station, purchased their tickets, and within two days, went their separate ways. The witness received one last warning from Smith as he boarded his train for California, never to see him again.

CHAPTER 8

Present Day

Joe had picked up a touristy map at the airport when we inquired about tours to the East Rim of the canyon as O'Reilly and I finished up with the car rental paperwork. We were informed that there were a couple of companies to choose from, but upon further investigation, I found that their tours covered sections that were not within the area I was interested in studying. My thought was to rent a vehicle, get a real road map, and head south. I wasn't sure what I was looking for, but I was hopeful I would know it when I saw it. Whatever "IT" might be.

"It" turned out to be a hand-painted sign on the side of the road pointing west. It said Fremont, AZ, ten miles. We had just passed through the town of Cedar Ridge, heading to the next small town, The Gap, when I saw the sign. I hit the brakes and immediately turned off the paved highway onto a single-lane dirt road, much to the surprise of my passengers.

Joe was riding "shotgun" while O'Reilly was consulting our maps from the back. Joe's surprise at the turn was evident when he turned to me and said, "What the hell?"

I laughed as we bumped along and replied, "At

least we're headed toward the canyon."

From the back seat, O'Reilly asked, "What did that sign say?"

"Fremont, AZ," I replied.

After a couple of minutes of silence, she said, "It's not showing up on any of our maps." Joe had checked the vehicle's navigation system and reported nothing there either.

"From the homemade sign back there, I didn't figure it would be, but I've got a gut feeling about this," I replied. Within a mile, a ten-foot chain link fence came into view about fifty yards away on the south side of the road. We passed another dirt road on our right as the chain-link fence continued, as far as the eye could see. I said to Joe, "Looks like somebody is serious about protecting their property and keeping people out."

"Yeah," he replied, "Wonder why a fence that tall out in the middle of nowhere would need to be topped with razor wire?"

"That does seem like a little overkill," I replied.

O'Reilly had been quiet in the back seat. I glanced in the mirror and saw her inspecting the fence with binoculars.

"See anything interesting?" I asked.

"I think so. There are several restricted area signs posted at intervals along the fence, and there was a larger one that read 'Private Property, Omega Research Center.' Guess that's the name of the group that owns all that property. Strange, as I thought this was all protected Native American land."

"I don't know, but I bet we'll find out when we get to Fremont." Soon, we spotted some buildings in the distance. As we approached, a hand-painted sign on the side of the road said, "Welcome to Fremont, AZ. Pop. 276. The dirt road led us over an old railroad crossing, right into the heart of town. I say town, but I'm not sure that's the right word. This place was a combination of wooden and adobe structures, maybe a total of twelve buildings lining the street.

However, Fremont struck me as being unique in its presentation. The dirt street was clean. There was no debris or dirt piles built up from use to be seen. The wooden buildings, constructed from weathered boards and planks, appeared well-placed and securely attached. Not the least bit ramshackle, as one might expect in a town so small and in the middle of the Arizona desert. Nonetheless, it did look like a town from the 1800s, with wooden boardwalks running in front of all the buildings and an overhanging roof protecting them from the elements. Well, at least from the sun, as I didn't expect they were much needed for rain. There were people, some brightly clad, walking busily about. The storefronts all bore neatly hand-painted signs alerting the visitors to what they would find inside.

The road or main street was wide enough for two-way traffic with room for diagonal parking along its length as well as several hitching posts. A few older pickup trucks and cars took up some of the spaces, but most were empty. There were spaces between groups of buildings, like side streets or an alleyway, and down them you could see smaller outbuildings in some places. All was neatly arranged and in good order, as we could see from the street as we drove slowly through the town. There was a hardware/mercantile store, a small traditional Southwest eating establishment with an outdoor adobe oven and seating, as well as a doctor's office/clinic, with a sign that read 'Nurse on Duty, Doctor on Call.' A drugstore/post office combo was located next door. A one-pump gas station, a feed store, and a well-used laundromat with a communal clothesline on the other side of the street added to the landscape. The largest and most prominent store was located in the center of town. The worn sign read "Zach's Trading Post" and indicated that it was a store specializing in rocks, minerals, crystals, and native arts and crafts. Its size was much larger than that of any other building, and on the wooden walk in front of it were several chairs for visitors or customers, currently occupied by two locals sitting there engaged in an animated discussion. I saw no sign of tourists anywhere. People were walking on the boardwalk and crossing the street, but all appeared to be of Navajo or other indigenous descent.

We continued driving through the little town, leaving the business area behind and passing through the residential area characterized by a mixture of small wooden homes interspersed with adobe ones. The facades were weathered, but all the houses appeared to be in good repair. Children played in small yards or in the street and waved at us as we drove by.

We continued until the town faded in the distance behind us. The low range of mountains on both sides grew taller as we drove. In a few minutes, a sign appeared that said "Rim Overlook, 5 miles" with an arrow pointing straight ahead. We continued until another fence came into view, on the south side of the road. The fence was on the same side as the one we had previously seen for Omega Research, only this one said, "Keep Out by order of the National Park Service, protected species area, trespassers will be prosecuted for violation of federal law."

"Damn," Joe said. "There sure are a lot of restricted areas around here."

"No kidding," O'Reilly replied.

As I looked down the road, I could see no end to the wire barricade, so I decided to turn around and head back to town, saying to my two passengers, "I think we need to look into this fenced-off area further and see what the locals have to say about it."

Our ride back to town was made in silence as we took in the desolate vista on both sides of the road. I pulled into a parking spot in front of the rock shop. "They should be able to shed some light on this restricted area stuff," I said as we exited the vehicle. Walking across the wooden walkway to the front door of the shop, I was once again struck by an unusual feeling. The two men were still talking in the chairs out front and only gave us a passing glance as we entered.

Something about this place triggered my "Spidey" sense as I entered. The place was very clean, neat, and larger on the inside than it looked from the street. As I scanned its spacious interior, the level of organization struck me again. I looked around and immediately got the sense that everything inside was where it was supposed to be. That was weird because I had no idea how a shop like this should be arranged, but it all felt right.

Just inside, in the middle of the room, was a low, round table with five chairs, and pamphlets and brochures were stacked neatly. A sign attached to the front of the counter by the cash register announced that adventure tours were available: Inquire here. I knew instinctively that we had come to the right place as I continued my scanning of the interior of the store.

There were wooden bins throughout the store, approximately ten to twelve inches square and eight inches deep, set on an angled base at waist height and tilted up at the back. They were laid out in a checkerboard pattern, and each was clearly labeled with its contents: rocks, minerals, geodes, crystals, and fossils, all neatly arranged and filled. Scattered around the store were also larger specimens of many of the smaller local artifacts. One geode, about two feet tall, had been split open, revealing an interior lining of beautiful purple crystals. Another flat piece of slate had the fossilized imprint of a giant ancient fern spread across its surface. Sitting on the floor in front of the counter was what looked like a massive gold nugget. The sign on it identified the piece as iron pyrite, also known as fool's gold.

The young man behind the counter, obviously a local, smiled as we approached and said, "Hi, folks, welcome to Zach's. Feel free to look around, and if you have any questions, my name is Joseph. I'll be happy to help you."

Extending my hand, I introduced myself only as "Ryan" as the three of us began to admire the local handiwork. We were the only customers in the shop, but there were others busily working at the far end of the building. Slowly making our way to them while perusing the variety of native American arts and crafts gave me a new appreciation for the time and effort put into all these pieces.

There were two adjoining work areas, easily accessible for close-up inspection of the work being created. The first housed a silversmith, an older gentleman, maybe in his late sixties, who was working on a bracelet inscribing intricate designs by hand. Nearby was a younger man, maybe in his late twenties, fashioning a silver necklace. As we approached, they both looked up and smiled. The older man said something to the younger one in his native language, and the young man said, "My grandfather says welcome; we are happy to have you watch as we work."

O'Reilly, feeling a little self-conscious, said, "Oh, we wouldn't want to distract you while you work."

The young man laughed as the older man chuckled. "It is no distraction at all; we enjoy having people see how our work is done. All by hand."

"It's beautiful work," she replied.

As they were talking, I looked at the back of the work area and saw a long bench against the rear wall that held a small electric smelter, some raw ore, and an area where molten metal was being worked. I asked the young man, "So, you smelt your silver from ore?"

"Yes," he replied, smiling as his grandfather kept working. "We mine all our metals from the surrounding mountains. Silver, gold, and copper mostly."

"That's very impressive," I replied.

His smile broadened as he said, "That's why we can say all our products are handmade locally." There was a sense of pride in his statement, and I acknowledged it.

"That is highly commendable and the sign of true craftsmen."

His smile got broader as he thanked me, and his grandfather glanced at me, smiling.

The building was filled with a variety of beautiful local creations and handiwork, from dreamcatchers and other hanging pieces featuring designs of threaded beads, feathers, crystals, leather, and silver components woven into them, to carved wooden objects in the form of a variety of animal and anthropomorphic figures. Everywhere we turned, our eyes were caught by the beauty of the artistic creations.

I was drawn to a wall that had several old maps framed and displayed, all hand-drawn, depicting what I assumed were different locations in the surrounding mountainous area and the Grand Canyon itself. One in particular that caught my eye was a detailed drawing of the length of the Grand Canyon. Many of its important features were identified by name or some other descriptor. There was a small taped red X on the glass covering the drawing with a "You are here" notation.

CHAPTER 9

We had moved back to the counter, and Joe pointed to the sign that mentioned the tours and asked, "What can you tell us about the tours you have available?"

Smiling, Joseph pointed at the table and chairs in the middle of the room and said, "Why don't you folks take a seat? I'll go over what we have available." He moved from behind the counter and joined us at the table. Picking up one of the brochures, he began explaining. "We offer day hiking trips and one or two overnight experiences. We furnish all food and equipment for those. They are led by experienced guides who have grown up in this area. They handle all food preparation and are trained EMTs, in case the need for medical attention arises. We also have access to aerial emergency evacuation if necessary."

"Very interesting," I said. "What about the cave tours that are mentioned here?" I asked, pointing to one of the pages in the brochure.

"I'm one of the guides for the day and overnight trips, but Zach does our cave tours."

"I'd like to find out more about those tours," I replied.

"Zach can give you all the details on those. Unfortunately, he's not here right now, but he should be available in the next day or so if you want to stop by then," Joseph said.

"We can do that," I said and added, "We were also interested in a flying tour of the canyon, but we haven't seen any indication that there are any available."

Joseph said, "We don't get a lot of requests for those, but yes, they are available. The major has a helicopter tour service a couple of miles from here. He's also the one who provides our emergency medical evacuation services if necessary."

"The major?" I asked quizzically.

"Yep, he owns Lone Wolf Aero Services. You may have seen a road off to your right on your way into town. Down that road, about a mile and a half, he has his operation set up. You'll see a sign and his hangar on the left side of the road."

"What are his hours of operation?" I queried.

Joseph laughed, "Well, that's hard to say. The best thing to do is to drive out and speak with him directly. He lives out there, so either he or his girlfriend, Sam, should be there. We contact him by radio if we need his services."

"Wow, that makes him a little difficult to get in touch with," O'Reilly said. "Probably not very good for business."

"That's not by accident," Joseph added. "The major is definitely a kind of lone wolf, and I'll warn you ahead of time, he is quite the character. But he's one hell of a pilot; that's why he earned the nickname 'Snake' while he was in the Army. He would fly anytime, anywhere, and under any conditions. It made no difference to him, and he's your only choice if you want a flying tour of the area."

"That we do," O'Reilly replied.

"Well, he'll be your man, but don't expect too much in the canyon. There's a pretty large section of the East Rim that he won't be able to take you to because of the no-fly zone."

"No-fly zone, what's that all about?" Joe asked.

"It's a lot of National Park Service and federal regulation BS, if you ask me," Joseph replied. "They've got a big chunk of parkland east of the rim designated as a habitat for some endangered species. So, it's a restricted area, with 'no trespassing' signs. Then there's the section of the rim area and into the canyon that's also off limits, but that's because they say it's too dangerous for hikers."

"Is that something recent?" I asked, probing a little further.

"No, it's been that way for as long as I can remember," Joseph answered.

"But Zach can answer any other questions you may have when he gets back. That should be in a day or two."

"So, Zach is the local area expert?" I asked.

"Pretty much, his family founded the town in the early 1800s. The Fremonts have kept this place alive for generations. They were responsible for drilling the first well that still supplies our water, setting up the town's power infrastructure, supporting local businesses and craftsmen, and helping us develop a tourist trade. We have five cabins or traditional 'Hogans' we built just to house visitors during tourist season."

"Then I'm guessing Zach's last name is Fremont?" I asked.

"It is," Joseph replied.

"Well, we certainly look forward to meeting him and learning more about the history of the area," I said.

"You folks vacationing? We don't get many tourists this time of year," Joseph said.

"No, I'm a historical researcher and am collecting information for a paper I'm writing on the early exploration and explorers of this area. My friends and I are hoping to talk to some of the older locals and gain some personal insights."

Joseph offered, "We have families that go back generations living here, so I'm sure they could be helpful."

"That would be helpful indeed," I replied.

"It sounds like you folks plan on being in the area for a while," Joseph stated.

"That was our plan," I answered.

"Where are you staying?" Joseph asked.

"We actually just got here, so we haven't really found a place yet. It looks like Cedar Ridge might be the nearest place with accommodations."

"That's true," Joseph replied, "But if you're up for

it, we could make arrangements for you in our cabins. We have five here in town that we rent out during tourist season. Since this is off-season, they've been closed up, and we would need a day to get them cleaned up and ready for guests, so if you could stay one night in Cedar Ridge, we could have them ready by tomorrow afternoon."

"That sounds perfect," I replied. "I'm sure we'll be availing ourselves of the tours you mentioned. In the meantime, we can look into the possibility of arranging an aerial tour of the area and canyon with the helicopter service you recommended, Lone Wolf Aero."

"Make sure you tell the major I sent you. Might get you a discount," Joseph said, laughing, "or not," he added jokingly.

We thanked Joseph, confirming we would be back tomorrow, and headed outside. A pickup rolled by as we got to our vehicle. Looking around again at the sleepy main street, O'Reilly said, "Not exactly a spa resort, but it seems like a nice, relaxing place for a vacation."

I laughed as I got in the SUV and said, "That it does… but looks can be deceiving." I started the vehicle and headed back toward the main highway. A mile and a half out of town, they came to the road Joseph had told them to look for.

The dirt road forked off to the left of the main road we were taking out of Fremont. We made the turn onto what was more of a track than a road. About a mile into our grueling washboard ride, we came to a sign. It was a large, wooden, professionally made sign, but it must have been made many years ago. The paint was faded and peeling, and it was tilting to one side, but it was still legible. The large black letters across the top read "Lone Wolf Aero." Underneath that, in red and slightly smaller lettering, it read, "Helicopter canyon tours $300/hr., 1 mile ahead. Open year-round."

As we were passing it, Joe said, "Check that out," pointing to the sign. In one corner was painted the unmistakable yellow and black emblem of the Army's Air Calvary unit, just like the ones we had seen numerous times at Fitz's place. "That's the same outfit that Fitzsimons flew with in Nam," Joe said.

"That could go a long way in explaining how this guy earned the nickname 'Snake.' If he's anything like Fitz, we could be in for one hell of an experience," O'Reilly added, laughing.

We spotted the large hangar looming in the distance to our left and soon came to the dirt road that led to it. As we turned onto it, we came to another sign, much like the first. At some point in the past, it had also been professionally done, but it was as weather-worn as the first one.

"Welcome to Lone Wolf Aero," it proclaimed, "Local area and Canyon tours available. Mathew MacDonald, Owner, Operator, Pilot. For tour details and group pricing, inquire at office. Discounts for veterans."

CHAPTER 10

Ahead, in a cleared oasis (so to speak) in the surrounding scrub and cactus, was an old Airstream house trailer, and fifty yards beyond it was a large hangar building. We pulled into a parking area next to an aging Ford F-250 and got out. There was a triangular Sun Sail shade strung from the side of the trailer out to an old pole sunk in the ground for its third mounting point. Under the shade was a large wooden cable spool, about five feet in diameter, serving as a table, with five of those cheap aluminum lawn chairs arranged around it. Prominently displayed off to one side was a hand-painted sign on a small post that said "Office."

Outside, next to the open trailer door, was an old refrigerator adorned with a variety of stickers. Beer advertisements, military unit insignias, humorous bumper stickers, all surrounding the largest one of all, "Helicopter pilots don't fly through the air... They beat it into submission." Next to the refrigerator, leaning against the trailer, was what appeared to be a piece of an aircraft door. The scratches, scrapes, and bullet holes were a testament to its prior life. Along the top edge, just below where a window used to be, was painted "Maj. Matt 'Snake' Madison," in precise lettering. There was music emanating from somewhere in the bowels of the trailer. I recognized "House of the Rising Sun" by the Animals. I glanced at my companions, who were surveying the scene, grinning slightly.

The aroma of meat cooking on an open fire filled the air. As we walked toward the spool table, the open pit fire with a grill on top covered in meat came into view.

"Not exactly what I expected," Joe said.

"No kidding," O'Reilly added. We were halfway to the table when a man came around the end of the trailer with a small bundle of wood under one arm. The moment became frozen in time as the man's hand flashed to the holster he wore low on his hip, drew the pistol, and fired a shot in our direction. We were rooted in place, eyes wide, trying to comprehend what had just happened. The man holstered the gun and continued walking toward us, a smile on his face. "Sorry, didn't hear you pull up," he said as he dropped the wood next to the fire, reached down to the ground behind the table, and pulled up the headless body of a five-foot rattlesnake.

"These things are bad this time of year," he said as he draped the body over the back of one of the chairs. "I was afraid you wouldn't see that fella lying there and walk up on him. That would have been *no bueno*."

The entire encounter took less than a minute. We still hadn't moved. He continued walking toward us, now with his hand outstretched, and said, "Hope I didn't scare you; you've got to be careful and quick around here. Matt Madison," he said, still smiling, "What can I do for you folks?"

The spell was broken as everyone took a breath, and I took his hand, now smiling myself and said, "Ryan Greene, Matt. These are my colleagues Shannon O'Reilly and Joe Sebastiani. We wanted to inquire about your helicopter tours."

The radio on his belt came to life, and a voice said, "I heard the gunshot, Major. Everything all right?"

He pulled it off his belt and keyed the mic, "Yep, everything is fine, just a little varmint eradication. Food will be ready in about fifteen minutes—oh, and we have guests."

"Copy that, I'll be there as soon as I finish up," and the conversation ended.

Hanging the radio back on his belt, the major stepped to one side and swung his arm in an arc toward the table and chairs, saying, "Please, come into my office and have a seat." As we sat down at the table, the major walked to the old refrigerator and asked, "Would you care for a cold beverage?" as he opened the door. Looking inside, he said, "I have water, soda, and beer," pulling a beer out for himself.

It was hot, and the beer was tempting, but we all opted for water. He grabbed three bottles of water and his beer and sat down at the table with us. The major was a striking figure, tall, around six one or two, maybe in his early fifties. His long salt and pepper hair was pulled back and woven in a braid that reached the middle of his back. He wore a silver earring and several colored beaded necklaces; one had a small leather pouch attached, and there was a longer, heavier silver one with some sort of medallion on it. His skin was the color of burnished leather, and it was clear that the wrinkles on his face had been earned the hard way. He was wearing an old Army T-shirt with the sleeves cut off, a pair of BDU (Battle Dress Uniform) six-pocket pants, and flip-flops. His web belt hung low with the holstered 9mm on one side, and on the other, I recognized the K-Bar fighting knife in its sheath. Joseph was right, the major was indeed turning out to be a character.

But when this imposing figure sat down and smiled, any preconceived notion we may have had about this man based on his appearance vanished. He immediately put us at ease, exuding a relaxed sense of friendliness, comfort, and confidence. Very similar to what one felt in Colt's presence, I thought.

"So, you folks interested in a flying tour of the canyon?" he asked as he took a long pull on his cold beer.

"Yes, we are," I answered, following up with the same research story on him that we had used on Joseph.

"Interesting," he said. "It's off-season, so we don't get many tourists this time of year, which pretty much leaves my schedule wide open. Weather and maintenance are about the only two things that keep me grounded now. Oh, hell," he exclaimed as he jumped from his chair. We all reflexively looked to the ground to see if he had spotted another reptile interloper, but that wasn't the case. He quickly went to the fire pit and, with a long barbecue fork, turned the steaks that had been grilling, adding a new piece of wood to the fire.

He was laughing as he returned to the table, "Damn, in all the excitement, I forgot what I was supposed to be doing. Taking another drink from his beer, he asked, "So when would you want to book your flight?"

I paused for a minute before I answered. "I'm thinking we are going to need more than a single flight. In fact, probably multiple flights over an extended period of time. We want to photograph and map the area thoroughly, and I'm pretty sure that may take us a while."

He rocked back in his chair, smiling, raised his beer, and said, "If you have the money, I have the time."

"We saw on your sign that tour flights were $300. How long a flight would that be?"

"That would be about an hour long," the major replied casually.

"That seems like a bargain, since you're the only game in town, as it were. You could probably get more than that," I said.

"Probably," he replied, "But I'm not trying to get rich. I just need to pay the bills and keep up with the cost of fuel. I do that, and I'm happy."

"Well, since our schedule may be a little erratic, which is yet to be determined, and we may need you on short notice for longer than one-hour flights, what if I give you a three-thousand-dollar retainer to start with? My main request would be to expect you to give us priority should you have any other flights come up. We would certainly endeavor to give you at least two hours pre-flight notice, of course."

The major was thoughtfully considering my proposal when his radio came to life. "Headed your way,

Boss." He had placed it on the table when we sat down.

He keyed the mic and said, "Copy, and don't make a lot of dust; we still have company, and I don't want sand on my steak."

A laughing voice responded, "I'll do my best."

The major laughed as he placed the radio back on the table and said, "Get ready to meet my partner," and took another drink of his beer.

We heard the ATV before we saw it, coming from the direction of the hangar. A couple of minutes later, the brightly colored multi-person four-wheeler pulled up at the end of the trailer, followed by only a small cloud of dust. As it cleared, the door opened, and a tall brunette stepped out. The major was looking in her direction and said loudly, "Not bad, Sam, I can hardly taste the dust over here," following it up with a fake cough.

We were all staring at the approaching woman. Tall, short brown hair, maybe late twenties, wearing a baseball cap, tank top, and cutoff jean shorts. But that's not what drew our attention; both her legs were prosthetic limbs wearing combat boots. She walked to the refrigerator, took out a beer, and joined us at the table. As she sat down, the major said, "Folks, this is Samantha Meadows, my crew chief and the other half of Lone Wolf Aero."

Over my initial surprise, I said, "Pleased to meet you, I'm Ryan Greene, and these are my colleagues, Shannon O'Reilly and Joe Sebastiani. They nodded in her direction as I introduced them. Sam's face was neutral as the introductions were made.

The major said, "These fine folks want to engage our services for an extended period of time."

"That so?" Sam said with the hint of a smile appearing.

"Yes, it is, here," the major said as he tossed a red shop towel to her and said, "You got a big spot of grease right here," motioning to his right cheek.

She caught the towel, wiped the grease off, and said, "One of the hazards of the job," now smiling and taking a drink of her beer. She looked at the major and said, "So, how long is an extended period of time?"

The major turned to me and said, "Dr. Greene?"

I took a sip of water and replied, "Well, that's hard to say. I think we can start with two weeks and go from there. If we need you for longer, hopefully we can make acceptable arrangements at that time."

"He's offered us a $3,000 retainer for those two weeks," the major added.

Now, Sam looked at me and said, "$3,000?"

"Yes, and that's whether we fly or not. You may also take any other flying jobs that may be necessary or take any business that may come your way, as long as it doesn't interfere with our flight schedule. Which, let me add, will be pretty flexible."

Sam finished her beer and got another from the fridge. Sitting back down, she looked at the major and said, "I've got about a day's worth of maintenance I still need to perform."

I chimed in and said, "That won't be a problem. In fact, I would be happy to have our agreement begin two days from tomorrow, if that gives you enough time."

"That should be plenty. I can have our bird ready by then," Sam replied.

I turned to the major and said, "Well?"

He smiled, stuck out his hand, and said, "I believe we have a deal."

I took his hand and said, "In that case, we will see you two days from tomorrow. I assume cash will be acceptable?"

"Very acceptable," he said.

"Then we will let you get to your meal and see you in a couple of days," I said as we got up from the table and turned toward our vehicle while Sam began removing their steaks from the grill.

Joe turned to the major as we left and said, "By the way, that was some nice shooting. A head shot from that distance... impressive."

Smiling, the major said, "Thanks, out here we do get a fair amount of practice."

Joe nodded and said, "I'll remember that."

As we headed to Cedar Ridge, our discussion was focused on timing and logistics. We needed to meet this Zach fellow and see what kind of arrangements could be made for a land-based appraisal of the area, and certainly, we needed to take advantage of the cave tours. The biggest question yet to be answered was whether we were in the right area. Is this the area where Kincaid's cave is located?

My research indicated we should be very close,

but how close? The aerial survey that Joe will conduct, using our ground-penetrating radar and digging device (we affectionately nicknamed "the mole"), which we obtained from our extraterrestrial friend Jeannie, should help us identify the cave's exact location, if it's in this area. Question two is how long can we keep our real reason for being here a secret from the locals, and is keeping it a secret even necessary? Currently, we have numerous questions with very few answers.

CHAPTER 11

The next few days flew by. We had provisioned up in Cedar Ridge and were set up in the cabins that Joseph had ready for us. Zach was due back any day, and we were looking forward to spending some time with him and learning more about the area and its history. I was anxious to see if the Kincaid expedition came up in our discussion, and figured out how I could weave it in if it didn't. Joe had prepared the GPR/digging device, the mole, to scan the area during our aerial survey flight into the canyon. We decided, however, that our first flight should be a reconnaissance one, sans device, to acquaint ourselves with how things looked from the air, the terrain we would be investigating, and what our flight limits might be.

Our drive out to "Snake's," or the major's place, was uneventful. We had called ahead and let him know we were coming to plan our flying schedule. I was amazed that our cell phones worked so well in this desolate area. Cell reception was excellent. When I mentioned it to Joseph before we left, he informed me that Zach had set up a private cell tower in the town that allowed for connectivity. Before that, he said they had no cell reception, and CB radios were used for communication.

I said I hadn't seen a cell tower on our way into

town or around town anywhere.

In a very offhanded manner, he said, "Oh, the tower was out back, behind the store, and only twelve feet tall, so it wasn't very noticeable. He built it close to the solar array that he had also built to provide power for the community."

That caused me to raise an eyebrow. A private cell tower providing five-bar service in the middle of nowhere... a solar array to power the whole town, and all constructed by this Zach person—highly unusual at the very least. My interest and anticipation were growing as I looked forward to our meeting.

I was mulling this information over when we pulled up to the major's trailer. As we got out, the sound of an incoming helicopter broke the desert silence. We saw the military green UH-1 Huey coming in for a landing at the helipad by the hangar. We walked around the end of the trailer to get a full view as the Huey lightly touched down on the pad. Sam was standing out there, waiting, with the radio in hand. From where we stood, we could see the faded paint on the helicopter had been touched up, and where more was needed. It had a very well-used look about it.

The Huey wasn't the only thing that captured our attention. At the end of the Airstream was a circular, natural rock-lined flower bed approximately twenty feet in diameter. I guess calling it a flower bed would be a misnomer, because there were no flowers in it, but a large, healthy-looking apple tree stood in its center. The soil was a rich, black-brown, and neatly tended, in contrast to the desert-tan, sandy land that surrounded it. Its bright green leaves and bright red apples were a standout in this harsh, desolate monochrome environment that surrounded us for miles. It was obvious that its healthy appearance was due to the care it received, the rich soil in the planter area, and some type of watering system keeping it moist.

The Huey had shut down; the major had gotten out and was talking to Sam. Finishing and seeing us, he threw up a hand in a wave and headed in our direction. We were standing by the spool table as the major went to the fridge, grabbed a beer, and joined us, saying, "Sit down, please," as he pulled up his chair under the sunshade.

"She sounds pretty good," O'Reilly said, nodding toward the Huey. "Getting her ready for our tour?"

"Oh, that old thing. Nah, I can do better than that for my paying customers. That's just one of my project birds," the major replied, chuckling.

"One of your project birds?" O'Reilly asked.

"Yep, that hangar out there is bigger than it looks," he quipped.

Sam had joined us, stopping by the fridge, pulling out a cold six-pack, and bringing it to the table. Sitting down, she said, "I'll bet he didn't even offer you a cold beverage," as she slid the beers in our direction. The major took the bait and said, "Well, I was going to…."

Sam scoffed and said, "Sure you were," as we each took a beer and thanked her. "We need to treat our paying customers in the manner a paying customer should be treated. Come on, Snake, where are your manners?" she said scoldingly.

The major threw up his hands and said, "I give, you're right. Being out here pretty much alone, one forgets the civility that should be afforded our customers. Apologies, folks," he said, raising his beer in mock salute.

We all laughed, and I said, "Apology accepted, and the cold beer is much appreciated," returning his raised can salute.

"Good, so let's get down to business. Just what kind of tour are you looking for?" he asked as he unfolded a large aerial map of the area on the tabletop.

Looking over the maps and photos he produced, we began our planning. The no-fly zones were clearly marked on the maps, so I asked the major about them.

"We've been told it has something to do with sensitive environmental considerations—endangered species living in that area. Never had much reason to question it, since there is plenty of canyon out there to see."

"How long have they been there?" I asked.

"Well, they were on the maps when we got into the area, and that was over ten years ago. I was kind of curious about it at first, but since it didn't really affect my business all that much, I lost interest and learned to live with it," the major answered. "Why, is that going to be a problem?" he asked, frowning slightly.

I paused for a bit, then said, "It might be. We wanted to do a thorough aerial survey of this area," I said, indicating a large circle on the map with my finger.

"Well then, that could be a problem. You see here

—the zone applies to the area from the canyon floor to above the rim for about three or four miles inland. All the way to the base of that small range of mountains that runs perpendicular to the canyon."

Pausing, I finally said with a sigh, "I'm afraid that is going to be a real problem for us then," frowning and peering intently at the area on the map.

The major was studying his potential employer, as he thought, "This guy is the real deal, a well-known and respected historical academic; I've found that out." The internet was a wonderful thing. But there was more than that. He was affiliated with a rather well-known treasure-hunting corporation down in Florida. That had gotten Matt wondering, could there be a connection between his research here and the company in Florida? He had been pondering that question ever since he looked up the background information on Dr. Greene. Unfortunately for him, he could come up with no logical connection.

"What say we put a pin in it for now, and how about joining us for dinner? I was about to stoke up the fire and throw some burgers and fresh corn on the grill. I've got my world-famous baked beans cooking in the crock pot inside, so there's plenty of grub for everyone."

Smiling, Sam said, "I'll put some more beer in the fridge. We've got enough in there now to last us until it gets cold."

"See, there you have it, how could you say no to a good old Arizona outdoor home-cooked meal?" the major added.

I looked at Joe and O'Reilly and got the head nod of

"Why not?"

"Since you put it that way, Major, we accept."

"Excellent," he jovially replied, "and it's Matt. I shelved that 'major' stuff when I got out; now, it's just to impress the tourists," he replied, leaning back in his chair and laughing.

Sam had procured three more six-packs from somewhere and placed them in the fridge, removing a cold one to put on the table as Matt went around the end of the trailer and returned with an armful of wood. He soon had a fire going in the pit and sat back down, saying we would need to wait until the flames died out and we had a nice bed of coals to cook the burgers on.

Our conversation centered on plans for our first flight, including timing and general decisions about the area we wanted to see. A touristy overview flight was scheduled for the next day, with more specific areas to be covered following its completion. I asked Matt about what he knew of the area's history and any knowledge he had of its early explorers. He happily broke into his tour guide spiel and regaled us with the general information I had requested. Nothing new came to light, nor was there any mention of Kincaid or his supposed cave discovery. I decided not to bring it up just yet and listened attentively to his remarks, asking general questions along the way.

The next day, we arrived at 7:30 for our first day's flight. To our surprise, the vintage Huey that had been sitting on the helipad had been replaced with a shiny Bell 407, 5-passenger, 2-crew bird—just like the one O'Reilly had rented for us on our last adventure chasing

Aztec gold in New Mexico. She smiled as we walked toward the helicopter and said, "Much better than that Huey," quickly following it up with, "not that there's anything wrong with the Huey as far as reliability and flyability go; it's just that its creature comforts suck."

"Hey, two different birds, two different applications," Joe quipped.

"I agree completely," O'Reilly added as we got to the pad. Sam and Matt were just finishing their preflight inspection, and Matt approached, smiling, when he saw our expressions.

"Told you I could do a little better than that Huey for our paying customers," he said.

"Nice bird," O'Reilly said, "love the way they handle."

Matt raised an eyebrow, "You fly?" he asked.

"Yeah, I've had my share of seat time," she replied.

"Great, then maybe you want to sit up front where the action is?" he asked, smiling broadly.

"Sure," she replied, "I always like to be where the action is," and with that, climbed aboard as the rest of us were ushered into the passenger seating.

Sam was on her headset, standing on the pad outside the helicopter, as she gave Matt the standby signal, and he brought the bird to life. After another quick walk around, she appeared out front, gave Matt a thumbs-up, and cleared him for takeoff. The turbine whine increased as we smoothly lifted off.

Joe and I had strapped in, put on our headsets, and had a great view as we rose into the air. We had specifically requested that the door remain open during the flight, so our field of vision was not impaired. It was noisier and windier, but the vista below us was breathtaking as we banked and headed to the canyon. For the next two hours, we got the extreme tourist experience as Matt gave us a running dialogue over the comms.

He provided the highlights of specific landmarks and our location in the canyon. He answered all our general questions, specifically notifying us when we approached some of the no-fly areas and altered course. Joe noted each on his GPS for future reference, and I busily snapped digital pictures of the terrain below. The time went by quickly, but we got what we wanted. Our subsequent flights would involve using the GPR unit we had obtained from Jeannie during our Ecuador adventure. We were hoping it would provide us with the subsurface detail or clues we were looking for to answer our questions about Kincaid and his underground discoveries.

CHAPTER 12

We flew every day for the next five days, covering miles of the canyon but primarily focusing on the eastern side of its wall from bottom to top. Joe was scanning continuously with the "mole," his nickname for our GPR device. Its abilities continued to amaze us. The depth penetration was impressive, and its ability to store scanned data for later retrieval, as well as the real-time visuals we got, made for a thorough 3D underground picture of the scanned area.

We had established somewhat of a daily routine. Fly in the morning for X number of hours. Come back, unload our gear, and sit around the table in the shade with a cold beer and do a flight debrief with Matt and Sam, then plan for the next day's flight. It was a laid-back and easy-going experience for all of us, as we discussed our data findings and began developing a personal connection with our flight crew.

On our fifth day of flying, things were progressing much as they had in the past few days, until we flew over a section adjacent to one of the no-fly zones. I was taking my digital photos when Joe grabbed me and pointed to the screen on the "mole." It plainly showed portions of a cave much like the ones we had been seeing the last few days, not surprising since the area had numerous caverns that were part of the natural geologic formations. I was used to seeing them on the screen; nothing really unique about any of them except that the one Joe was pointing to made a ninety-degree turn, proceeded for a distance, and then made another ninety-degree turn before continuing. Joe shut off his coms and said, "Mother Nature doesn't do perfect ninety-degree turns, especially not two in a row."

He was right; this might be significant. I checked the GPS coordinates on our map and found that the location was just inside the no-fly zone we had just passed while heading back to Matt's. I keyed my mic and said, "Matt, can you go back a couple of miles and fly the same route we just covered?"

"Can do," he replied as the bird made a gradual 180-degree turn. In a couple of minutes, we were back on our return heading. Joe and I had our eyes glued to the "mole's" screen. There it was again. We increased the magnification of the image, and the two ninety-degree turns became clearly visible, along with arrow straight tunnels continuing ahead. I looked out the door at the terrain we were passing and saw that the tunnels we were looking at ran under the foothills of the mountain range that was perpendicular to the canyon.

I keyed my mic again and said, "Can you make the same pass again, only this time get us closer to the canyon wall?"

"Sorry, Doc, no can do. That's one of the restricted no-fly zones. Runs for about four miles. This is the best I can do legally."

His last comment caught my attention, but I didn't press the subject and said, "Okay, then, I think we can call it a day and head home."

"Roger that, I was getting kind of thirsty," he replied with a chuckle. "ETA about twenty minutes."

I looked at Joe; we were both grinning. O'Reilly had turned in her seat in the cockpit to look questioningly at us. Still smiling, I gave her a thumbs-up, and she nodded slightly in acknowledgment, a smile forming as she returned her gaze to the vista out the cockpit windshield.

Our flying weather had been good, except for one day when the wind had kicked up and filled the sky with a thick brown dust cloud—a sand cyclone that kept us grounded. However, none of that mattered right now, because we may have just discovered the key to the next phase of our investigation. Our flight back was uneventful, but the breathtaking landscape made for an enjoyable ride.

Sam was standing by at the landing pad as we touched down and Matt went through the shutdown procedure. She chocked the wheels and did a walkaround inspection as the rotors slowed to a halt. Matt was out and walking toward his trailer as O'Reilly waited for Joe and me. Something was bugging Matt— a feeling in his gut. He remembered it from his combat days—the feeling he got when something wasn't quite right, when something was missing.

In those days, it was when he felt critical information was missing from an operational plan, or if the information seemed sketchy. He always trusted his gut. It had saved his ass and his men more than once. But this wasn't combat, and no one was in harm's way, so why was his gut telling him to watch out? He opened his beer and took his seat at the spool table as he usually did after each flight, sitting there with a furrowed brow as the others joined him, ready for the flight debrief and to begin planning for the next flight.

Matt noted that the chatter between his customers was a little more animated than usual, but became subdued as they joined him, beverages in hand. It had been hot and dry flying with the doors open on the chopper, so they all looked forward to this shaded respite. Sam had finished fueling up and putting the bird to bed and joined them. She was smiling as she saw the animated discussion between Doc, Joe, and O'Reilly. Her smile quickly faded when she saw the look on Matt's face... she had seen it before, in another place and time.

She sat next to him and quietly asked, "What's wrong, Boss?"

He paused, then replied, "Not sure, but I don't care for it." He was about to say more when I turned to them and said, "That was a good flight today, Matt," as the others looked on, seemingly pleased.

Matt paused before speaking, "Was it?" he asked. His tone and response took me by surprise.

"Well, yes, it was."

"And why was that?" Matt asked a little tersely.

I sat there in silence as the smiles faded from the others' faces.

Matt caught himself, realizing he was coming off

too sharply and there was no need for that. This was not combat, nor was it life or death, even though he knew something was being held back—some piece of information that, in his gut, he felt he needed. Immediately, his face softened, and he said, "Hey, Doc, I'm sorry. That was uncalled for. It's just that sometimes I get the feeling I'm being kept in the dark, and it sets me off. I've seen what having inaccurate or insufficient intel can do and how disastrous it can be. I didn't mean to come across harshly. But your special interest in the no-fly zones out there and that gizmo that Joe is using to scan the canyon isn't a normal piece of photographic hardware, so I...."

I held up my hand to stop Matt and said, "You're right, and I apologize for not being completely up front with you. You've checked us out, I'm sure, and know what our company, Risky Business, is about." Matt nodded in assent. "Well," I continued, "we're looking for Kincaid's lost cave. I'm sure you've heard of it."

Matt leaned forward, resting his arms on the table, and said, "So that's it...," chuckling slightly. "Yes, I have heard of it, and believe me, you are not the first to hire me to try and help find it. His body language changed, relaxing. Chasing myths and legends is not really my thing, but if the customer is willing to pay the bill, I'll fly," he replied, now smiling.

Everyone had taken their seats around the table. I looked at him and said, "I've got a news flash for you. It may be a legend, but I have uncovered evidence that says it's not a myth."

Matt laughed and said, "No offense, Doc, but I've heard that song before, many times, and the last verse is always the same, Nada. Everybody goes home empty-handed, except for me, of course. Like I said, customers pay, I fly." He raised his beer in mock salute to Doc.

Now, the team and I laughed out loud as I returned his mock salute with my bottle and said, "Well, I've got news for you, Matt, sticking with your musical metaphor, there's another verse to that song that no one has ever heard, and we have the lyrics. The 'camera' Joe has been using to scan the area we've flown over is actually a prototype GPR unit that we've developed," I lied, "and we've been scanning for underground anomalies, and yes, we think we've found some."

The look on my face resonated with Matt. He saw sincere determination, confidence, and resolve reminiscent of the faces of many of the men he had flown with in combat. Now, reflecting on his research into the Risky Business company and their exploits, and this revelation, he began to wonder if he had perhaps dismissed their quest too quickly.

"There's one more thing. You're aware of my interest in the no-fly zones. I may have to ask you to 'bend the rules' a bit, and there's the possibility of even breaking the law if you agree to get involved," I said. "I don't know if you would be willing to take that risk?"

Sam broke out into peals of laughter and, in a mock voice, said, "Oh, no, sir, please don't throw me into the briar patch," laughing until tears were running down her face. In between bouts of trying to catch her breath, she said, "You really don't know who you're talking to. Ask Snake to bend the rules or even break the law... how dare you?"

The fits of laughter continued as Matt's face turned bright red and he said, "Come on, Sam, that was a long time ago in another world."

Sam, getting her laughter under control a bit but still enjoying the moment, continued, "All that means, Snake, is you may be a little out of practice." The laughter continued, but it was more subdued.

"Please ignore her; good help is so hard to find nowadays," Matt said, now smiling.

Not wanting to let it go quite yet, she said, "Boy, have I got some stories for you guys." Matt started to protest again, but Sam threw up her hands in mock surrender and said, "That's all I'm saying for now," and took a healthy swallow from her beer, still smiling broadly. We had all been laughing along with her, but the moment of this inside joke had passed. Nonetheless, a telling bit of information had been exchanged... Now, the ball was in Matt's court, as we turned to him in a much more relaxed, yet anticipatory, atmosphere.

Matt was now seriously thinking, what if they did have information that could lead them to this cave? What if they could prove this legend was real and they found the damn thing? That would be monumental in the world of archaeology and definitely a new chapter in the history books. He took a long swallow of beer and thought, "I wouldn't mind being one of the ones to help write that chapter." The potential challenges that would be part of the story were tantalizing.

With that thought in mind, Matt looked at everyone seated around the table and, after a minute, raised his beer and said, "I'm in."

He had no idea, actually, none of them did, of what lay ahead.

No idea at all.

CHAPTER 13

Zach slid his sunglasses into place as he exited the gloom of the cave opening. The late afternoon Arizona sun still beat down relentlessly as he adjusted the old leather saddlebags across his right shoulder, preparing to start his mile-and-a-half trek through the snake-like winding path along the base of the mountain range looming to his left. The crags and crevasses provided momentary shade as he navigated his way through them, following a path that was all too familiar. Stepping confidently through the rough terrain, he chuckled to himself, thinking, "As many times as I've done this, I could make this trip with my eyes closed."

The weight of the bags didn't slow him down; fifty pounds of gold ingots in one and about the same in raw silver ore in the other made for a balanced load. Once again, something he had become used to over the many years he had made these trips. His mind wandered as he walked along, not even looking at the ground or thinking of his surroundings. His body knew exactly where to step as he rapidly headed toward the spot where he had left his old Ford Bronco five days ago.

His thoughts turned to the cryptic message he had received the previous week. "Help was coming," strange, but receiving it in a dream made it even more intriguing. He arrived at his destination, pulled the desert camouflage netting off the Bronco, and tossed the saddle bags behind the driver's seat. He wasn't tired or winded but took a drink from his canteen anyway as he settled into the driver's seat. He started the engine that purred like a kitten and pulled away, passing the large, wooden sign that read, "Welcome to Zach's Cave Tours. Danger, Proceed no further without a guide." He glanced in his rearview mirror and saw the black opening of the cave, like the maw of some primeval beast, ready to swallow anyone who dared to approach. His circuitous return to his vehicle probably hadn't been necessary, but it was a precaution he had been employing for some time, just in case.

It was off-season, so the cave tours didn't have much business, but that was okay with him; he had other things that demanded his attention. As he left the winding dirt road in the foothills and headed out on the flat desert stretch, Zach let his mind begin working through the problem at hand. The five-mile drive gave him time to think as his old Bronco kicked up a cloud of dust in the late afternoon sun.

He looked to the East and could make out, in the distance, the fence that surrounded the solar research center constructed over the last two years, with the field of solar panels clearly visible. He shook his head contemplatively. That center presented a problem in numerous ways to the geography he was committed to protecting, with no easy solution in sight. The fence around the center extended to within a mile of the road that led to the main highway to Fremont. He had tried to convince the Navajo elders that leasing the land to the company was not a good idea when he first learned of the project. Not that he was opposed to solar energy, but when he began investigating the multinational company that wanted to build it, some disturbing facts came to light. The most glaring aspect was that this company was a subsidiary of a large Chinese weapons manufacturing conglomerate. Things hadn't added up until later when he got his hands on information that confirmed all his warning instincts.

He had reached the main road, turned East, and drove into Fremont a half mile away. The town looked the same, neat, clean, and the residents he passed all waved in response to his presence. What was different was the new vehicle parked in front of the cabins they rented out during the tourist season. Guess we have visitors, he thought as he pulled up and parked in front of his trading post.

He got out, retrieved his saddlebags from behind the driver's seat, and headed inside. A couple of tourists watched the ladies weave traditional Navajo blankets, while another observed the two silversmiths working on their jewelry. In the main common area, where chairs and tables were set, Joseph and three others were present, whom he did not recognize.

Joseph smiled broadly and said, "Hey, Zach, welcome back. I've got some people who have been waiting to meet you. We had turned toward the man who had just entered. "Sure thing, just give me a minute to put my bags away," he said as he went through the door behind the counter into the back room.

I turned to Joseph and said jokingly, "At last, we get

to meet the elusive Zach."

Joseph laughed, "Yep, that's him. Glad this was one of his shorter trips."

"One of his shorter trips?" O'Reilly commented.

Joseph, still smiling his ear-to-ear grin, said, "Oh, yeah, sometimes he's gone for a couple of weeks. But he usually lets me know ahead of time so I can plan work schedules and such."

"Not much around here," Joe commented quizzically, trying not to sound too nosy.

"Oh, he likes to hike and explore the mountains," Joseph replied. He spoke very matter-of-factly, as if no further explanation or information was necessary, still smiling broadly. I thought, from his response, that this must be a regular part of Zach's routine. Interesting....

Zach was a rugged-looking character. About six-foot-three, maybe 225 pounds, well-tanned and muscled. His broad chest and narrow waist were emblematic of someone who was accustomed to hard work and spent time outdoors. A T-shirt with cut-off sleeves, dusty jeans, and worn boots rounded out the first impression he left as he headed to the back room.

Zach came out of the back room a few minutes later, walked over to the silversmith, and set a large leather pouch on the table. He said something to the elder in Navajo and returned to his guests. Obviously, he had washed the desert dust off his suntanned face and slipped on a clean T-shirt with an Indian motif printed on the front before coming out. He walked up to the group, stuck out his hand to me, and said, "Zach Fremont."

I accepted his firm grip and introduced myself and the rest of the team, saying, "Pleased to meet you, Zach. We've heard quite a bit about you from Joseph."

"Well, I hope he hasn't bored you with his stories," Zach replied.

"It's been an interesting history lesson on this area and your family's founding of this town."

Zach had pulled up a chair, turned it backwards so he could rest his arms on the back, and said, "Yeah, the Fremonts go back quite a ways around here."

"So, we gather," I replied. "Joseph has filled us in on some of the history."

Zach laughed, "He knows the history of the area as well as anyone." He had grabbed a cold bottle of water from the cooler before sitting down. "So, you folks here on vacation, or did you get lost?" he asked, laughing. "Since it's not tourist season, that would be a possibility," he continued amicably as everyone laughed at the joke.

Still smiling, I answered, "Actually, neither. We're part of a company called Risky Business, which started out as a treasure hunting company in Florida but has now grown into a more investigative, research, and recovery business, looking into a variety of geographic areas worldwide involving myths, legends, and historical mysteries that sometimes involve treasure or lost or stolen artifacts."

Joseph's eyes grew wide at this revelation as Zach said, "Really? So, what brings you to our particular area? There are plenty of stories of lost treasure in Arizona."

"True," I said, "but the one we're interested in is Kincaid's cave and the mystery surrounding it."

"That's a tall tale that has been floating around this area for years," Zach responded, eyes narrowing.

"True," I answered, "but we have reason to believe it's more than a tall tale and that there is much more to the story."

"Sounds like you may have some evidence that it's true," Zach said with a slight intensity in his voice that hadn't been there before. "There have been a lot of people who have come through here over the years chasing that same story. All of them with this lead or that lead, or some wild theory about it, and every one of them threw in the towel when they came up empty-handed."

"I'm pretty well aware of all that and have researched the numerous stories and all the articles debunking it as nothing more than a local myth," I replied. "And they're pretty convincing, but what I found is that the debunkers stopped short at the same point in the story, since there was never any evidence presented to the public to support this wild story of Egyptian sarcophagi, Buddha-like statues, and mummies."

"Exactly," Zach replied with a small laugh, "No proof, nothing."

I had noticed the looks Joseph and Zach had shared while I was making my comments. Without any facial expression, I said, "Well, that's all about to change, because I have proof that Kincaid's cave is real. No wild theories; it actually exists!"

CHAPTER 14

There was silence around the table. The looks flying around were like a fly trying to decide where to land. Joe and O'Reilly were surprised that I had dropped that bomb so soon after meeting Zach. They knew word would get out soon or be shared intentionally since Matt and Sam had been informed, but this was a sudden, unexpected development, and they watched Zach and Joseph's reactions closely.

Their faces gave no indication of the surprise or disbelief that had been evident just minutes before. It was as if their emotional response circuit had been turned off. Finally, Zach said, "Proof, huh?" paused and continued, "What kind of proof?"

Now, I pulled my cards back and said, "As a scientist and a businessman, I'd rather not get into that right now. Suffice it to say, it's enough to warrant further investigation by our team. That's why we're here. To investigate further and follow up on it.

"Since your town will likely be our base of operations, I felt it only fair to inform you, and apologize to you, Joseph, for the bogus story we gave you when we first got here, but we wanted to keep our operation low-key."

A moment later, it was as if someone had opened a

door, and a gust of fresh air blew in as Zach said, "Well, it won't be the first time we've had people staying here who were on the same hunt as you. However, I can say that no one with your credentials has presented a more convincing argument for having proof than you, Dr. Greene, whatever it might be. I don't see a problem with it as long as you respect the land and don't cause any trouble for the town or the folks living here."

I replied, "It's Doc or Ryan, Zach, and I can assure you that we would not intentionally cause you any trouble, but I do have to warn you that unintentional consequences do often occur on some of our expeditions."

Joe cleared his throat and said, "Not to quibble, but actually they usually occur on all our expeditions."

O'Reilly choked on the laugh she was holding back, and Zach smiled.

"Well, I guess that's a bridge we'll cross when we come to it."

The tension in the room evaporated, and I said, "Zach, we would like to engage your services as a local historian and expert on the local surroundings. Plus, we definitely want to go on your cave tours. I still have a lot of information to collect and questions to have answered. I would also like to rent the remainder of your cabins. I plan on having the rest of our team join us shortly."

Zach looked at Joseph, who had been quiet during our discussion, and said, "I believe we can handle that."

Joseph nodded and said, "I'll take care of it, Zach."

"Well, it's closing time, and we have a lot to think about, so let's continue this discussion tomorrow, Doc. I'm very interested in hearing what more you have to say on this subject," Zach said.

"Agree," I replied. "We've all had a long day, with our flying excursion and all. We look forward to moving forward with our investigation and gathering more information about the area and its history. I'll contact the rest of our team and let them know to pack their bags. So, until tomorrow." I stood and extended my hand to Zach.

A firm handshake later, and the team was walking down the boarded sidewalk that fronted all the buildings in town back to their cabins. The desert twilight cast an eerie orange glow on the horizon as the weathered boards creaked under their feet, as if they were trying to reveal the secrets of those who had trodden them in the distant past. Their muffled, rasping voices only added to the strangeness of the moment.

Moments later, O'Reilly said, somewhat irritated, "What in the world caused you to let this guy know what our intentions were so soon before we had a chance to check him out?"

Joe chimed in, "Yeah, I thought we were going to be a little lower key with this investigation."

I paused before answering, and in the silence, the antique boards continued their story as everyone slowed their pace. "Did you notice Zach's jewelry?" I finally asked, surprising my colleagues.

There was a pause, then O'Reilly said, "Well, yeah, he had some nice silver jewelry, I would imagine made by the workers in the trading post."

"Probably, but did you notice his silver bracelets?"

Another strange question, "Yes, they were very nice on both his wrists," O'Reilly responded.

We had reached our cabins; I opened my door and motioned for the others to come inside. The accommodation provided was quite comfortable in a rustic southwest kind of way. They both took seats, eyes on me as I sat down. "What the heck are you getting at, Doc?" Joe asked, sounding somewhat bewildered.

"His silver bracelet, the wider one on his left wrist," I said.

"Yes, the one with the stone and engravings was beautiful, and from what little I saw, it was excellent craftsmanship," O'Reilly noted.

I sat there with my Cheshire cat smile, not saying a word, letting her comment sink in. With my companions still looking bewildered, I finally asked, "Did it look the least bit familiar?"

Joe and O'Reilly sat there, still looking bewildered, the silence palpable. Then, suddenly, they both sat straight up in their chairs in unison, eyes wide. O'Reilly spoke almost in a whisper, "Colt's portal bracelet."

Joe said, "Are you kidding me? No way."

Now, with both of them looking dumbfounded, O'Reilly said, "It couldn't be… could it?"

Now smiling broadly, I said, "I don't know, but there's one way to find out without just asking him and sounding like nut jobs if I'm wrong." He picked up the

SAT phone and hit speed dial with Colt's number.

The phone was on speaker, and they recognized Colt's deep voice when he answered. "Hey, Doc, I was just wondering how things were going out there. I haven't heard from you in a while."

"It's going… interestingly well," I replied.

There was a pause, then Colt responded, his voice questioning, "Okay, you've got my attention."

"How soon can you and the rest of the team get out here?" I questioned.

Another pause, "Trouble?" Colt asked, sounding tense.

"No, not really trouble, but I think we may have uncovered something quite significant, and we're going to need all hands on deck for this one, I think."

"Any details?" Colt asked.

"Not over the phone," was the response.

"Special gear?" was Colt's next question.

"Climbing and rugged terrain, oh, and come prepared."

Colt knew precisely what that meant, armed and ready for the unexpected.

"Roger that," Colt replied, now with a sense of resolve in his voice.

"Oh, and one other thing, you know that trinket you picked up down south and always travel with? Bring it!"

Colt's brow furrowed. Doc could only mean the

portal bracelet he had gotten from Jeannie. His mind was racing, but no other comments were necessary. He gave a curt, "See you in thirty-six hours," then the line went dead.

I looked at my two friends sitting there and said, "Well, as the saying goes, the game is afoot."

Zach and Joseph closed and locked the doors to the trading post. They turned off all the lights except for the one that cast a golden glow over the post's interior, as the two retired to the back room. Turning on the lights as Joseph took a seat, Zach picked up his phone and dialed. Two rings later, a female voice on the other end said, "Hello, Zach."

Zach responded, his tone pure business, "Courier pick up."

The female voice responded, "Weight?"

"Fifty pounds," Zach replied.

"Cash required?" the female voice queried.

"One hundred thousand," Zach said.

"The rest disbursed in the normal fashion?" the female asked.

"Yes, time frame?" he asked.

"Pick-up in forty-eight hours," came the reply.

"Fine, I'll be ready."

He hung up and looked at Joseph, who asked, "Think we have a problem with our visitors?"

Zach was quiet for a minute as he pondered the question. He had a lot on his mind and was trying to sort everything out mentally.

"I'm not sure, but we'll know more after we meet tomorrow."

"We still have the solar energy group that we have to deal with," Joseph said.

"I know, this throws an added wrinkle into the works that will have to be dealt with. I'm going to need you to work with me closely on this, so you will have to arrange for the post to be covered in our absences."

"Not a problem, we have plenty of help waiting to be called on," Joseph replied.

Zach fell into the overstuffed chair across from Joseph. His phone call had taken care of the almost $2.5 million in gold he had brought back from his visit to the mountains. It provided him with more than enough cash to maintain in-town operations, with the rest being distributed among his accounts set up through the secure financial network he had established many years ago. His accounts and investments around the world kept his wealth concealed but always available with just a phone call.

Okay, that was one job he could scratch off the list. "Let's call it a night, Joseph," Zach said. "I'll see you in the morning, and then we'll see what more our guests have to say."

"Sounds good to me," he replied, "see you in the morning." Joseph left through the back door, and Zach settled deeper into his overstuffed chair, leaning his head back and closing his eyes in the dimly lit room.

His mind was swirling with the situation unfolding at the supposed solar research center, and now these Risky Business people. How was he going to handle all of that? He saw no easy answers to either as he tried to clear his mind. He wasn't sure how long he had been sitting there when he heard a tinkling sound like wind blowing through a crystal chandelier. His eyes were closed, but he wasn't asleep when he heard the same voice he had heard in other dreams. It was familiar and soothing, almost melodic as it said, "Don't worry, Zach, help is on the way. Trust them."

He slowly opened his eyes to an empty room and said out loud, "How will I know them?"

The voice replied laughingly, "You already do, but you must trust that they are your answer." Then silence.

It slowly dawned on him that he knew that voice. A memory from his distant past and the hint of a smile appeared as a feeling of well-being gently swept over him, and he fell into a restful sleep in his chair, not waking until morning.

CHAPTER 15

Matt sat watching glowing embers casting their glow in the darkness of the cool Arizona night. What was left of the evening cook fire kept him company as he sat in the darkness, admiring the night sky with the Milky Way clearly visible in all its majesty overhead. Sam had turned in for the night, so he had this moment all to himself.

As he relaxed, he let his mind wander and recalled the humorous conversation earlier with the whole crew and Sam's pleasure in sharing it with everyone. Her comments were not out of place, as he smiled and thought of the situation that had prompted them long ago.

They stemmed from an incident during his second tour in Afghanistan. After completing helicopter training at Fort Rucker as a second lieutenant, he applied for and secured a position as a Cobra gunship pilot and was subsequently sent to Iraq during the first Gulf War. He fell in love with the Cobra; its nimbleness and firepower made it a formidable and effective weapon.

That's where he met Warrant Officer Bill Jefferson when he was assigned as his gunner. Bill was a good old son of Texas, with a drawl and all, and one helluva shooter. He had enlisted shortly after graduating from high school, leaving behind a budding career in the rodeo circuit as a bronc rider, having even won a big silver championship buckle before enlisting. His natural talent in helicopters, however, did not go unnoticed, and he worked his way up to Warrant Officer.

He and Bill became fast friends and a force to be reckoned with in the air. They stayed together as a team through two Iraq tours and soon transitioned to the new Apache gunships. Faster, better avionics, and more firepower, but Matt missed the nimbleness of the Cobra. The Apache was a bit larger and offered more bells and whistles in the countermeasures department, but it presented a larger target for the bad guys. Thanks to skill and luck, he and Bill were able to stay together as a team and rotated back to the States with their unit when their tour was over.

A year later, their unit was deployed to Afghanistan. Upon arrival, one of their personal rituals was to stop by the maintenance area and meet the team that kept their birds in the air. On this visit, after meeting the guys that were available, Matt noticed, over in the back corner, parked with no rotors, a Cobra gunship. Intrigued, he approached the Senior Master Sergeant, head of maintenance in the hangar, and asked what was up with the Cobra among all the Apaches being worked on.

"That's an interesting story, Sir."

By now, Matt had achieved the rank of major and said, "Go on."

"Well, that's actually a Super Cobra prototype, which wasn't even supposed to leave testing back in the States. She showed up here about eight months ago with ten other Cobras being decommissioned to be packed up and sent home."

"We got them ready and got the paperwork to ship them out, only there was nothing on that one, only the other ten. So, we sent the others out, and I inquired about this one. There was no other paperwork here, and stateside said they would look into it and just hang on to it for now. I followed up two months ago and got the same response. So, there she sits."

"What's her maintenance flight status?" Matt asked.

"Oh, with a little work, she'd be good to go," the sergeant replied.

"Mind if I take a look?" Matt asked.

"Not at all, Sir, go right ahead."

Matt turned to Bill, who was grinning, and with a slight tilt of his head, they headed to the Cobra. The next four months are the stuff legends are made of, they would say. With a little wink and nod with the maintenance squadron and a "We don't know anything about it, so who cares what happens to it," from the base higher-ups, the transformation began.

Matt and Bill flew almost daily in their assigned Apache. There was enough going on to keep them busy, but they found time to visit the maintenance hangar regularly, usually at night and with at least one case of beer on each trip, to check on the progress of the Cobra.

Parts were being scavenged and modified from Apaches that, for one reason or another, were deemed not flightworthy or repairable, so they were relegated to the boneyard behind the maintenance hangar. The Cobra's avionics were upgraded, and its armor plating was modified and replaced with the lighter and stronger material used on the Apache. Additionally, newer ballistic windshields were added.

Two new 20mm Gatling guns were hung on the stubby hardpoint wings along with the one in the turret. The addition of 70mm Hydra 70 rockets, 5in Zuni rockets, 8 Hellfire missiles, and two sidewinder missiles rounded out the Cobra's deadly bite. The two General Electric T700-401 turboshaft engines were in top-notch shape and had even been tweaked a bit by the maintenance team to give her a little added punch in the speed department.

That's what happens when you get a bunch of guys who were hot rod gearheads before the army working on a special, although unauthorized project like this.

Matt's Apache was out of commission for scheduled maintenance when they got the call for convoy escort. Rather than hand it off to another pilot, he decided this would be the perfect opportunity to bring out the Cobra. The NCOIC of maintenance assured him that, in his opinion, she was ready to go. That was good enough for Matt. So, the bird was wheeled out of the hangar onto the tarmac.

Matt and Bill saddled up and started their preflight when their radio squawked. The tower recognized the Cobra as an unauthorized aircraft until Matt identified himself and provided the tail number of his Apache, which was in maintenance. The tower questioned whether the use of this aircraft had been approved through the appropriate channels. By now, the Apache that had also been assigned to provide convoy cover was taking off. Matt followed suit and lifted off, following the other aircraft. The radio squawked again with questions, which Matt cut off in mid-transmission, "If you want convoy air support, then I'm approved, because right now, I'm all you got."

As both aircraft lifted off and headed to the main gate to pick up the convoy leaving the base, the lead Apache contacted Matt's bird, "Madison, is that you flying that beat-up antique?"

"Roger that, 'Buckeye,'" that was Jim Franklin's nickname—his friend and fellow Apache pilot from Ohio.

He jokingly replied, "Didn't know we had a used car lot on base. Hope it doesn't fall apart, and you can keep up."

Matt laughed and said, "I'll do my best; I got your six, lead the way."

Both choppers cleared the base and picked up the five-vehicle convoy as it hit the dusty road heading to a small village some twenty klicks away. The road wound through the hilly terrain known for IEDs and Taliban attacks. They were fifteen miles into their journey when the mortar rounds began dropping on the convoy, and the helicopters started taking small arms and machine gunfire from both sides of the road.

The radio squawked as Buckeye said, "Time to go to work, Madison," and he broke left as Matt broke right, identifying the location of the bad guys and engaging.

Matt said, "Okay, Bronco, let's see if we remember how to make this Snake bite and see if this baby is still up to the challenge."

Bronco replied from the gunner's seat in back and said, "You get us in there, Snake, and I'll light 'em up." And light them up, they did as Matt, aka "Snake," dropped the bird in and Bronco opened up with the 20mm mini guns, ripping through the hillside with a barrage of lead, leaving destruction and dead Taliban fighters in its wake. All systems performed flawlessly, and flying it was effortless, Matt thought. Just like riding a bicycle—once you learn, you never forget. He easily kept Bronco on target, and within minutes, the fight was over. All enemy fire was neutralized, and the convoy continued without any further contact.

When they returned to base later that day, Jim Franklin met up with Matt and Bill, who were walking toward the office. "Hey, Matt, that old bird did pretty damn good out there today, and you were dancing her around like a ballerina on stage."

"Yeah, she did good, still got a lot of fight left in her," Matt replied, "and some damn nice shooting, Jimbo."

Franklin responded, "Did I hear him calling you Bronco? And you called him Snake?"

They both laughed as Jim said, "Yeah, those were nicknames we picked up back when we were flying these things in Iraq."

Franklin slapped Matt on the back and, laughing, said, "Well, I think they're damn appropriate."

The mission debrief was somewhat contentious due to Matt's use of the Cobra without prior approval. Still, the mission's success and Franklin's glowing comments on its performance ultimately smoothed things over. In fact, so much so that when Matt requested to keep it flying, he and Bill were assigned as permanent crew members since they were the only ones in the squadron with extensive experience in the Cobra.

They flew sorties for the next four months with the Cobra performing beautifully. Then came the day of the "milk run." Two congressional types arrived at the base on an "official" fact-finding mission, which is political speak for photo ops to help their re-election campaigns. They wanted to be photographed meeting with locals in-country. Snake and Buckeye got called for babysitting duty, escorting their aircraft some seventy miles from base to meet with locals in a small village, in a very safe location, far from any Taliban contact.

It was one of those, no-questions-asked, just fly-escort-there-and-back, per the orders that came from way up the food chain. They grumbled amongst themselves but did as they were ordered, flanking the Blackhawk with the VIPs all the way to the village, orbiting for maybe ten minutes as the Blackhawk landed, let the VIPs and their entourage of assistants, photographers, and other press types get out, shake hands with some local goatherders, and get photographed pointing to the surrounding mountains at nothing. It was a good pose, after which, they loaded up and headed back to base. Snake and Buckeye were grumbling to each other about the waste of time and resources when a call came over the emergency frequency.

"This is Sierra Foxtrot 29 Bravo. Request immediate QRF and Evac. Current location, sending coordinates now. Pinned down, taking heavy fire, two men down, approximately twenty tangos to our east and thirty more on hillside west of our location, over."

Another voice responded, "Copy 29 Bravo, QRF ten Mikes out, over."

The desperate voice of 29 Bravo replied, "Ten Mikes, Hell, we'll all be dead in five, Over."

Buckeye squawked Matt, "That's a special forces unit, Matt. Their location is two valleys over, about three klicks from here."

Matt heard from Bronco, "I've got their location in the Nav system; we can be there in less than five."

"Got it," he said. Keying his mic, he said, "Control, this is Charlie Sierra 1 breaking escort formation heading to 29 Bravos location."

Control came back, "Negative, stay with your assignment, do not, I repeat, do not break formation."

Matt had already started his steep turn heading toward the special forces location. "Negative control, breaking formation now."

"This is a direct order; do not break escort formation."

Matt keyed his mic, "Screw you, I'm not letting our men die for these political assholes." He pushed the throttles on the two turbine engines to their stop and cleared the first ridge.

Matt's radio squawked. "I've got this," came Buckeye's voice, "Go get 'em, Snake."

Over the comm in the Cobra, Matt said, "Bronco, get me SF 29 Bravo on the horn."

Ten seconds later, Matt heard Bronco on the radio, "29 Bravo, this is Snake 1, sit rep."

The same desperate voice responded, "Small farm, five buildings approximately 20 tangos inside, and 30 more on the hillside on our six. We are in a small ravine in between, about 20 yards from farmhouses. Say again your identification?"

"We're the freaking cavalry," Bronco replied as Matt cleared the second ridge. One more to go. Matt keyed his mic, "29 Bravo, Snake 1, be there in three mikes; stay alive."

"Roger that, will do our best, over."

Matt cleared the third ridge and dropped into the valley. He saw the farmhouses ahead and quickly assessed the situation. "Bronco, crabbing in, facing the farmhouses; we need to take those out first and then turn our attention to the hillside."

"Copy that," Bronco replied, "point me in the right direction, and I'll bring the rain."

Matt dropped down to ten feet off the deck and keyed his mic, "29 Bravo, cease all fire on the farmhouses and concentrate your fire on the hillside. I'll take care of the buildings. We're about to rain seven kinds of Hell down on them. Snake 1 out."

"Copy that, Snake 1, we have a visual on you; they're all yours."

Crabbing sideways, nose pointed toward the buildings, they approached the first one, and Matt said, "Okay, Bronco, bring the rain." Matt slowed to almost a hover, moving slowly sideways, and Bronco opened up with the two 20mm Gatling guns and the 70mm rockets. The main house and the last building got two of the 70mm rockets and a burst from the nose Gatling gun. As Matt pulled up into a steep climb at a thousand feet, he banked hard to the left and dropped the nose in the direction of the hillside. Bronco saw the Taliban fighter stand and take aim at them with his RPG, and didn't hesitate as he hit the hillside with two Hellfire missiles, effectively neutralizing the Taliban forces there.

"You were about two seconds too late with that RPG," Bronco thought, grinning. Matt pulled another steep climb to around fifteen hundred feet and flew back over the smoldering scene below.

The radio squawked, "29 Bravo, QRF is three mikes out."

"Copy that, I have two men down, and we're mopping up here."

"29 Bravo, looks like our work here is done. Snake 1 returning to escort."

"You guys be safe down there," Matt said as he took the Cobra to two thousand feet and headed back to Buckeye and the escort that wasn't that far ahead. The fight had taken about seven minutes.

"Snake 1, 29 Bravo, don't know who you guys are, but if we ever meet up again, drinks are on me. Thanks for your help. I have to say that old snake of yours still packs one helluva bite."

"Not old, just vintage, and I'll take you up on those drinks," Matt replied as he hauled ass to catch up with the escort.

He clicked the intercom, "You know, Bronco, there's going to be hell to pay when we get back. Disobeying a direct order is some pretty serious shit."

"You know, I really don't give a damn. Saving those guys took precedence over everything else in my book."

"Copy that." Less than ten minutes later, they caught the escort just outside the base airspace. They watched the VIP Blackhawk set down close to OPs as they headed to their parking apron. They landed and just finished shutdown procedures when they got the call to report to flight operations ASAP. As they exited the bird, Matt turned to Bronco and said, "Well, here it comes."

Bronco, smiling broadly, slapped him on the back and said, "Well, Snake, this should be fun," as they walked toward the operations building. They saw Buckeye and his gunner heading in the same direction. They met up just before entering the building.

Buckeye looked at Matt and said, "Don't think we're being invited for lunch, Snake," a half-smile breaking his dour countenance.

"Very doubtful," he replied, then, with a devil-may-care laugh, said, "Maybe just drinks." A moment of silence, and then they all broke out laughing as they entered the building. Of course, it turned out neither was even close to the truth.

CHAPTER 16

This incident, which earned its place in the flight lore of his unit, was the reason for Sam's outburst of hilarity. Doc, being worried about Matt's willingness to bend or break rules, was indeed funny. But there's more to the story. The senators were livid about supposedly being placed in harm's way by Matt's actions, according to their account of the incident.

The more serious matter was his disobeying a direct order from the squadron commander, a lieutenant colonel with political aspirations upon retirement. Both crews were removed from flight status and confined to quarters until the official inquiry, which was scheduled to be held two days later.

The senators, who were up for re-election, were the ones pushing for this hearing, and on the day of reckoning, they were present, along with other presiding officers, when both crews entered the hearing. The squadron commander presiding was standing at attention while the crews were read the numerous charges being brought against them—Buckeye's lighter than Matt's. Things were not going well as statements were given by the senators, even when the pilots of the Blackhawk testified that no enemy threats were reported or identified in their flight path to and from the "civilian" meeting with the locals.

Matt had just been called to address the charge of disobeying a direct order from a superior officer when the doors to the meeting room brusquely burst open, and in strode an imposing six-foot, five-inch figure wearing the rank of full bird colonel on his uniform with his Ranger and Special Forces tabs visible on his sleeve, his green beret in his hand. His salt and pepper hair was cut short, and his steely grey eyes and air of confidence immediately put him in command of the room. An individual in civilian clothes followed him in, who also exuded a similar air of authority.

The captain, who had been reading the charges, fell silent as the bird colonel, in a deep baritone voice, said, "I'm looking for Snake. I understand he's here."

The squadron commander said, "Sir, these are official proceedings."

He was stopped in mid-sentence when the bird colonel said, "I don't give a damn about photo-op proceedings. My statement was an order, not a request, Lieutenant Colonel."

Matt spoke up, "That would be me, Sir, Major Matt Madison." Matt had been standing as charges were being read.

The full bird colonel strode across the room and stuck out his hand, "I wanted to meet and personally thank you for saving my men. The two who were wounded got medical attention in time to save both their lives due to your quick and decisive action. One of the wounded men was one of Mr. Smith's operatives here, referring to the man who had entered with him, obviously a CIA honcho. This was a joint CIA, Special Forces operation to buy intel from a Taliban informant. Turns out it was a damn ambush from the get-go.

"Thanks to your intervention, not only did you save my men, but we also recovered a trove of intelligence material and got the government's significant amount of cash back we were going to pay for information. You turned a shit storm into a pretty good day, I would say." Now, the room was completely silent, and several mouths were slightly agape as the two senators sat there sheepishly turning red-faced.

"Oh, and I have recommended you and your gunner for the Army Commendation Medal as well as the Bronze Star with Valor. Congratulations, Major," he shook his hand again and smartly saluted, which Matt returned.

"I'll let you get back to your official proceeding now, which I'm sure was a formal recognition of these gentlemen's meritorious service and valor."

As he turned, he gave Matt a slight wink and headed for the door. As he got there, he turned back and said to Matt, "Keep our men safe out there, Snake," and he and Mr. Smith left the room.

The room was flooded in silence. Everyone was looking at one another in disbelief, not sure what had just happened. The captain who had been reading the charges against Matt finally cleared his throat, about to start again, when the squadron commander said, "That won't be necessary." He paused and then said, "Madison, Franklin, you are to return to flight status immediately. Senators, I hope you have a good flight back to Washington. These proceedings are concluded." It looked as if the upset politicians were about to say something in protest when the squadron commander stood and said loudly, "The proceedings are concluded."

He took the papers from the captain's hands, picked up the small stack he had on the table in front of him, tore them in half, and dropped them in the trash can. "Gentlemen, you are dismissed," and he abruptly left the room, followed by his small entourage. The senators, remarkably silent, followed.

The flight crews stood there smiling, as Buckeye finally said, "Do you think that colonel knew what was going on here?"

Matt looked at him with an are you kidding me look and said, "He's the top Special Forces dude, and he had the head of the entire CIA operations unit here with him. Of course, he knew."

"He saved our asses," Buckeye added, "and made one hell of a point."

"I have no doubt that was payback for what we did, his way of returning the favor by saving our butts," Matt said.

Matt chuckled as he relived that whole scenario sitting under the Arizona night sky. From that time on, until his tour ended, the nickname Snake was reborn. His call sign, Snake 1, stuck with him as did his Cobra, and the legend of Snake grew, as well as his penchant for bending the rules or breaking them on occasion.

Sam was well aware of the whole situation, so that's why she had the laughing spasm when Doc asked if he would be okay with bending the rules. She knew if the right situation arose, Matt would have no problem bending or breaking any rules or laws that stood in his way. Matt finished his last swallow of beer and tossed the bottle into the recycle bin as he headed for his trailer. Damn, that girl knew him too well, he thought.

Zach had coffee on and the doors unlocked when Joseph arrived at the trading post. Zach was sitting at the round table in the gathering area in front of the counter as Little Feather and his father, the silversmiths, arrived and went to their work area, followed by the craft ladies. Soon, the place was buzzing with conversations and the sounds of workers plying their trades, tapping and hammering, as well as the sound of the loom in operation.

Joseph had gotten his coffee and joined Zach at the table.

"So, what do you think today will bring?" he asked.

"Don't know," Zach replied, but it should be interesting to see if they really have something solid, or, like all the others, just theories and wild ideas. Although," he laughed, "some of them have been closer to the truth than they ever imagined."

Joe, O'Reilly, and I arrived thirty minutes later. Zach pointed us to the coffee pot, and we all settled into the chairs around the table with the normal working sounds of the craftsmen and women in the background.

Zach let us sip our coffee before asking, "Okay, Doc, what's your story?"

"Let me start with the debunkers of the story. They base their position on the fact that the

Smithsonian has stated they have no knowledge of the Kincaid cave, the artifacts, or any other information related to it. They also state they have no record of a Dr. Jordan or Kincaid ever working for them. Then there's the fact that the newspaper article was written by an anonymous source and no subsequent articles appeared, which seems surprising for a discovery of that magnitude."

"All rather plausible explanations for a hoax," Zach commented.

"Very true," I agreed, "enough for the general public to write it off as such. But in my opinion, this is a very superficial explanation."

"How so?" Zach asked.

"It doesn't seem that anyone has really dug into the story. Asking the next questions and digging would require time and access to material that most people didn't or don't have."

"And you do?" Zach inquired over the rim of his coffee cup.

"Yes, I do," I replied, "and I have found some interesting facts."

Over the next thirty minutes, I filled Zach in on my research at the Smithsonian and Georgetown University, which revealed that Jordan had taught there, and he and Kincaid had both worked for the Smithsonian during that time period. Also, Jordan had been assigned to a special project as a contract employee by the Smithsonian.

"And what was this special project?" Zach asked.

"That's where I hit a dead end, no record of it appears in the Smithsonian archives, nor of the receipt of any unusual artifacts from Arizona."

"So, what do you really have if there are no records?" Zach asked, seeming a little more interested than before.

"I have a very large smoking gun," I replied. "Enough for our team to decide to conduct a thorough investigation," purposely leaving off the information about their recent GPR scan discoveries. He wanted to wait and see how this information was received and what Zach's response would be later.

There was a pause in the discussion as coffee mugs were refilled and some Navajo bread was placed on the table, courtesy of one of the weavers. Contemplation continued as the coffee and fresh bread were shared.

Finally, Zach said, sounding skeptical, "Well, Doc, you do seem to have more information than any previous investigators have had, I'll give you that, but there is still a lack of definitive proof."

"True, that's why the rest of our team will be joining us in less than twelve hours to continue our research in the area," I continued. "In our previous expeditions, we have found that most legends or myths all contain a grain of truth, which, once discovered, unlocks even greater truths that were once unthinkable. Check us out on the internet, and I think you will find we are a rather tenacious lot," I finished, laughing.

"I'll do that," Zach answered, not revealing the depth of research he had already done on Risky Business and having come to the same conclusion.

"We're hoping you'll be willing to help us," I said.

Zach just smiled and said, "I'll be glad to help if I can."

Later that evening, the big red Ford Expedition arrived.

CHAPTER 17

The team had taken their corporate jet to Arizona, loaded with their usual expedition equipment. Colt liked to have Risky Business prepared for any contingency. Past expeditions had helped them fine-tune their potential equipment needs, so packing and loading were routine tasks; the only wild card was Dimitri and his penchant for new methods of employing mayhem.

Colt didn't mind, since his little surprises had gotten them out of some pretty hairy situations in the past. As such, Dimitri had pretty much free rein over his supplies, which always consisted of the team's armaments and a variety of items that went boom!

After landing, true to form, they found a used car lot near the airport and purchased a vehicle that suited their needs rather than renting one. Since their vehicles always seemed to take a beating, if not being completely destroyed, this time they found a nice four-year-old four-wheel-drive Ford Expedition. Plenty of room for the whole team and their gear, with a big V8 for those times when power was the answer, not fuel economy, and Colt did kind of like the red color.

They returned to the airport and loaded all their equipment. Colt then directed Mac, their pilot, to head back to the home base in Florida, as they were preparing for at least a two-week stay in the small town of Fremont, Arizona, and a rendezvous with the rest of the team.

They rolled into Fremont just after dark and called Doc. He directed them to the cabins at the end of Main Street and was standing out front when they came into view. They pulled up next to the rented Jeep and got out as Joe and O'Reilly also came out to meet them. After greetings, hugs, and glad you're here exchanges, Doc led them inside his cabin, and they all found a place to settle in and sit.

"Glad you guys are here. How was the trip?" Doc asked.

"Good and pleasantly uneventful," Colt replied, "glad to be here and looking forward to finding out what you guys have been up to."

The next half hour was spent with Doc filling them in on their exploits and what they had learned so far, including their connection with Snake and his helicopter service, their reconnaissance in the canyon, and the discovery of the tunnels with ninety-degree turns, as well as their meeting with the mysterious Zach. Then Doc dropped the bombshell, "Colt, I think this guy Zach is wearing a portal bracelet similar to yours."

I was surprised, but not overly so, when Doc made that announcement, unlike Dimitri and Reggie, who both looked startled.

"You don't seem too surprised, Boss," Doc said.

"Oh, I'm surprised, but this could answer a

question I've had for the last three days. I swear I've heard Jeannie's voice during the night on two occasions. I thought I was dreaming, but she clearly said, 'Help him,' nothing more. I had no idea if I had actually heard her or what that could mean, until now."

"So, Zach is one of them?" O'Reilly quietly asked.

"We don't know that for sure," Doc quickly added, "but that's why I wanted you to bring your bracelet, Colt. If you wear it, he will recognize it for what it is, and that will open a whole new dimension to our investigation."

"But help with what?" Joe asked.

"That remains to be seen," I said. "First things first, does he actually have a portal bracelet, or is it just a piece of locally made silver jewelry which is prevalent in this area?"

"That's true, he even has two silversmiths working in his trading post," O'Reilly added.

Dimitri weighed in somewhat skeptically, "Well, I guess we'll find out for sure when we meet the dude."

"That we will," Colt added.

After another hour of catching up, Doc showed us to our cabins next door and let us get settled in. It was agreed that we would all meet at 8:30 the next morning and walk down to the trading post for our initial meeting with Zach and Joseph.

The quarters were comfortable, but I had a hard time falling asleep as I ran through the information Doc had shared with us, especially the part about Zach potentially being one of Jeannie's people. Guess I'll find out for sure tomorrow, I thought as I dozed off. As it turned out, I didn't have to wait that long, as the sound of the tinkling crystal chandelier in the darkness brought me wide awake, and the all-too-familiar voice of Jeannie spoke out of the darkness, "You are where you should be; help him."

Nothing more was said, and I knew better than to try to ask a question, knowing there would be no answer. Jeannie was cryptic that way, giving a few pieces of a puzzle and expecting me to figure it out. No explanations, no discussion, most times just enough information was shared to set me on the right path, whatever that might be. Well, that pretty much confirmed Zach's identity as one of hers, so that was a starting point. I tucked it away as I rolled over and pulled up my covers.

The one good thing about my enigmatic friend's nighttime visits was that, when they were over, they left me relaxed and able to fall into a deep, restful sleep. That was much better than tossing and turning all night trying to figure out just what the hell was going on, and for that, I was grateful.

The next morning, we met outside our cabins at 8:15, all looking refreshed and ready to go. I wondered if Jeannie had something to do with that, as we all commented on the good night's sleep we had gotten. I wouldn't be surprised, I thought. Get everybody up to 100% and ready for the day's adventure.

We entered the trading post to find Zach and Joseph sitting at the table with their coffee and fresh Navajo bread. They both stood as we entered, and Doc greeted them both, immediately launching into introductions of the new arrivals.

"Zach, this is Dr. Colten Burnett, our leader and CEO of Risky Business." I extended my hand and matched Zach's firm handshake.

In Navajo, I said, "It is an honor to meet you," a Navajo greeting of respect.

Zach smiled and responded in kind, and as our eye contact broke, he looked at the bracelet on my wrist. His surprise was barely discernible but not lost on me; I was expecting some kind of response. After greeting the rest of the team, Zach motioned them to the seats around the table. One of the women at the trading post brought over the steaming coffee pot, along with additional cups, for everyone.

Once everyone had their drinks and were sharing the homemade bread, Zach looked at me and said, "From what Doc has told me, I think we have a lot to discuss."

"Even more than we had initially expected," I said, "let me start," as I held up my wrist with the portal bracelet. "My entire team is intimately aware of the significance of the unique jewelry that you and I share, as well as its use. In fact, it has saved our lives on many occasions. Everyone here has met the individual who gave it to me on our expedition to Ecuador."

Zach nodded and said, "Then you have all met the Protector," a statement that was also a question.

All the heads around the table nodded in assent, and Dimitri said, smiling, "Yeah, we call her Jeannie."

Zach's furrowed brow indicated he didn't quite

understand. Dimitri continued, "You know, like the TV series, *I Dream of Jeannie*, where the astronaut finds a bottle on the beach and it has a genie inside. We helped her with some power issues she had in her city, and we became close friends. Oh, and she saved my life when I got shot, so we are definitely BFFs."

Now, Zach broke into a wide grin, nodding in understanding, "I see and understand the analogy now and will have to admit it does seem rather appropriate and less pretentious than the title of Protector."

I said, "So, now that we've come clean about our position, I'm intensely curious regarding your role in all this."

"Since you know of our presence and our history, I'll share that I am what we call a Guardian, and Joseph is my Watcher. I'm sure you're familiar with that title."

"Yes, we are. We met two of Jeannie's watchers during our original encounter. In fact, one of our team, a young Ecuadorian lad, Eduardo, was selected by Jeannie to become, I guess you would call it, a watcher in training."

"Ah, yes," Zach replied, that is part of what has become our standard procedure. Joseph's father was one of my watchers, as was his father and grandfather before him. The line of succession can be very long."

Doc looked at Zach and said, "So, I guess that means you've been around here for a while?"

Now, Zach laughed heartily and said, "Yes, Doc, you could say that."

Now that the ice was broken, to use an old phrase,

coffee was sipped, and bread was shared in a much more relaxed environment. Various discussions began among the team and Joseph, sharing information and recounting events in a very collegial fashion. I let it continue for some time, knowing the importance of team bonding as Zach and I watched in silence, smiling.

At last, I said, "So, Zach, you say you are a Guardian. Guardian of what, exactly?"

Zach, sipping his coffee, very casually said, "This planet."

Those two words brought all conversations to a halt as all eyes turned, somewhat in awe, to Zach.

Doc was the first to speak, "Guarding this planet... from what?"

From over the rim of his coffee cup, Zach said, "Everything."

The team sat wide-eyed, staring; even I had been caught off guard and sat staring with the others.

Zach, seeing their expressions, said, "I can see this is going to take some explanation, which I will be happy to provide, but right now, we have a particular threat that is going to require our immediate attention. Colt, I assume you received a communication from—to make it easier for all, I'll start calling her Jeannie—that I needed help."

"Yes, I actually did," I replied, now absorbing the magnitude of the discussion, "And you?" I asked.

"Yes, I received a communication too," Zach replied, "And I hope you can provide the help she seems to think you can."

"As do I," I solemnly replied.

"This is going to require a discussion which I prefer not to have here, in the trading post, even though this is a safe place. How about we meet at seven this evening out in the back of the post? I have a fire pit there and have secured the area from eavesdropping. In the meantime, Doc can give you a tour of the area and help you become acquainted with the surroundings, which will also provide an opportunity to discuss and assimilate this new information. All of this will play a part in what is in store for us."

"Sounds good, Zach, we'll meet you back here at seven," I replied. With that, the morning meeting/coffee break adjourned, and the team left silently, absorbing what they had learned so recently.

Zach and Joseph sat there a little longer, with Joseph finally asking, "Well, what do you think?"

Zach paused, and then stood up and said, "I think we're going to be just fine."

CHAPTER 18

We all loaded up in the Expedition, and Doc, O'Reilly, and Joe gave the rest of the team and me the nickel tour of the town. Next, we went out to the rim of the canyon, and Doc pointed out the fencing for the restricted park area and the no-fly zone, as well as a closer daytime view of the fenced-in solar energy facility.

We had burned up most of the day, so we went back to our cabins, freshened up, and met at the little restaurant in town for a quick meal before meeting with Zach. It was twilight when we got to the trading post, and the cool desert evening was settling in. The post was closed, but the aroma and smoke of burning wood rose from behind the building. We took the little side street around to the back and found Zach and Joseph stoking the fire in the pit that already had chairs set up around it.

Zach saw us and, smiling, said, "Welcome, pull up a chair and help yourselves to a beverage in the cooler. We settled in, and Zach jumped right into the discussion. "First, let me say I'm glad you are here because I find myself in an unusual situation. I know you are going to have a thousand questions, and I will try to answer them, but we need to discuss the immediate situation, which will require a brief history lesson. As we proceed, you will hear some truly unbelievable stories, but I assure you, they are all true. So let me address that first, Doc... Kincaid's cave is real. I know because I oversaw its construction approximately forty thousand years ago."

"And you personally... oversaw its construction?" Doc asked in amazement.

"Yes, I did. I told you I had been around here for a while," Zach replied, laughing. "As we talk, remember what I said about unbelievable stuff, which I'm sure, by this time, through your association with Jeannie, you are somewhat familiar with hearing."

"We are, please continue," I said.

"Kincaid, Jordan, and all their crew were killed in the cave. It was my fault. I should have stopped Kincaid when he first stumbled onto the cave, but for a host of regrettable reasons, I didn't. Their exploration into the caverns set off one of our intrusion security devices that was active and led to their deaths. By the time I took steps to cover up what had happened, the second group from back east had also entered the picture, with unfortunate losses of their own.

"In those days, the intellectual community was already denying the thought of ancient intercontinental contact, so it only took a little pressure from the right individuals and significant sums of money to put a lid on the whole situation. Washington and the academic community at the time were easily swayed by persuasive individuals pushing certain ideas and money flowing into the right places. We were able to resolve the entire situation, even after the article appeared in the newspaper. In fact, we purchased the paper and turned its attention elsewhere, ignoring any follow-up inquiries."

"What about the Smithsonian connection?" Doc asked.

"That one was easy; all it took was money, and we made sure there was plenty of that."

"You keep saying 'We,'" I said, questioning the statement.

Zach laughed again, "You don't think Jeannie and I are the only active ones on this planet?" he asked. "Our ships carried around two hundred and fifty thousand from our world. We orbited your planet, observing its entire surface, and allowed our people to pick the place they wanted to settle. Staying away from areas where natural humanoid development was occurring, at least in the beginning. You are going to have to accept one huge fact: you are us, and we are you.

"We have had a hand in guiding human development on Earth for millennia, and still do today, but I digress. I am sure the Protector never went into much of our historical detail."

"No, she didn't—only vague comments and hints. Those alone blew our minds as we tried to comprehend everything we saw, heard, and experienced. It was a very much a living-in-the-moment situation, and trying not to be overwhelmed by it," I said.

"Which was difficult at best," Joe added to nods of assent from the others around the fire.

Zach said, "Well, I have to tell you, you are in store for much more. As I mentioned, I will try to answer your questions as we proceed, but for now, I would like to address the issue at hand. Seventy thousand years ago, our scientists discovered a massive solar buildup on your, our sun. It became clear to us that a significant solar event was inevitable, and we communicated this information to all our people. Our scientists had begun developing a shield or force field, if you will, to surround Earth, and we also increased the planet's natural magnetosphere to help protect it from solar radiation. Not knowing the magnitude of the solar event or the effectiveness of our shields in protecting the planet, we encouraged various developing civilizations around the planet to begin building underground facilities that we hoped would help safeguard them, should our technological efforts prove unsuccessful.

"As it turned out, when the time came, there was more than one massive burst of solar energy. We knew that, due to the planet's rotation, some sections would be exposed more directly than others. Beautiful forests and grasslands once covered the entire southwest U.S. They got hit by only a small portion of one of the solar blasts. The trans-oceanic Middle East took a major hit. Our shield was able to mitigate some of the effects, but not all of them. Major civilizations that we had created around the world were destroyed, and thousands of people were killed. Massive cities and advanced cultures practically vaporized. What had once been a thriving technological world, over the course of a few days, was set back thousands of years."

"What about the underground cities?" Dimitri asked.

"Many survived," Zach answered, "and many did not, either not going deep enough or being ineffective due to direct hits by the strongest of the solar storms. Much of the world's population was lost, along with the brilliant history they had created, only to be relegated by later cultures to the realm of myths and legends.

"Not every culture or civilization on Earth had the benefit of our advanced technology. In fact, not all the inhabitants of our home planet came with the same level of technology. We did not impose our will on any of them, but instead let them develop on their own, just as we had when we initially arrived on Earth. We kept nothing from those who wanted it, but it was their choice. Our diverse planetary population is spread around the world, and a variety of civilizations have been created. Our sun's supernova and the destruction of our planet became just a part of our history.

"But let's get back to our immediate problem, going back to our underground world here. Some of us did have access to our best technology and used it to create the world that Kincaid discovered, although what he found was only a tiny portion of what we had created. We notably had access to our digging technology and created thousands of miles of underground passages and chambers that were deep, very, very deep.

"We required an enormous amount of power, which, as Guardian, I had access to on our ship."

"Wait a minute, after all these years and while all

this was going on, your ship was still in orbit around Earth?" Joe asked in disbelief.

"Yes, and I moved one of our power cells to our network of underground cities. I believe Jeannie gave you basic information on our power systems and their capabilities."

"She did," I replied. "In fact, we helped her repair her system so the Citadel in Ecuador could be brought back up to full power."

"Then, I'm sure she gave you some idea of the immense capabilities of our power sources."

"Yes, she did, and how dangerous it could be if handled improperly or used for the wrong things, like weaponizing," I answered.

Zach, looking very serious in the firelight, said, "You have no idea, Colt. Which brings us back to the problem at hand. Our underground power source is shielded to keep it safe and any energy signature contained. It seems that back in 1971, one of your SR-71s, equipped with a new prototype sensor array, detected the force field's signature during a flyover. Up until that time, you had nothing that would detect the force field protecting the energy source. Our energy remains completely undetectable by any of your scientists' instruments. The energy from the force field is a different story. Luckily, my equipment picked up the intrusion, and I was able to correct the problem with the field. I was also able to discover that the readings they had picked up had been written off as a glitch in their system by your scientists, and I figured that was the end of the problem.

"Until four years ago, that is. My technology continuously monitors all digital, radio, telephone, and video traffic wherever I want. Much like your NSA and CIA systems, it looks for keywords or phrases—only about ten thousand times better and faster.

"A couple of years ago, I received an alert to an encrypted phone call concerning a strange energy reading from a physicist to an international number, saying he might be interested in selling the information for the right price. Stating It could have vast military potential. Upon investigation, I discovered that the physicist was one of the developers of the new sensor systems that had been on the SR-71, and the number he called belonged to an energy research company in China.

"I locked into every one of their communications for the next year. This guy now works for that solar energy company you passed coming into Fremont."

Leaning forward in my chair, I said, "The one with the big fence around it?"

"The same," Zach soberly replied. "It's only a front for what they are actually doing, which is searching for the energy source recorded in 1971. They must be stopped, but I can't afford to draw any attention to my intervention; that's why I need your help... and obviously Jeannie agrees."

CHAPTER 19

Joseph added a couple more logs to the fire. The sparks rose like fireflies into the desert night sky. The stars shone brightly, and with no ambient light to interfere, their celestial patterns glittered and were truly breathtaking, something urban dwellers could never appreciate, I thought. After a few more pensive moments, I said, "So, do you have a plan on how to stop them, Zach?"

Zach laughed, "The easiest way would be to push a button and vaporize the whole site."

"You could do that?" Dimitri asked, intrigued.

"Easily," Zach replied. "I have a rather formidable arsenal at my disposal and almost unlimited power, as you know... but doing it that way is not an option. As I said, I have to stop them quietly.

"They started a drilling operation three weeks ago in the direction of the recorded location of the energy reading they got back in '71, taking and analyzing rock samples as they progress. It's not terribly accurate, but it could put them into one part of our tunnel system. They have about 700 feet of rock to go through to get there. Not easy drilling, but they have the latest high-tech equipment. When I discovered what they were doing, I began placing technical roadblocks in their path to slow them down—equipment failures, drill bits breaking—small issues that would not suggest outside interference but would be attributed to problems that could occur in any drilling operation such as theirs. I've been hesitant to escalate my actions, fearing that I might arouse suspicions of outside interference. I've been trying to buy myself some time to come up with a permanent solution."

"Then what you're asking for is our help in finding a way to drive these guys out permanently in such a manner that they won't come back, not letting them know there was an outside force working against them... without unnecessarily killing anybody?" I asked.

"Mostly, but there may be a caveat to the last part of your question," Zach replied. "We're not looking for violence, but the stakes are high."

"Now, that's what I like to hear... options. You know how I am when I get around bad guys, Colt," Dimitri said, smiling, and it wasn't a happy smile. It was one of those "Here, hold my beer, watch this," smiles.

"Rein it in, big guy, we have no idea what we might be up against, so don't assume the worst," I responded in an admonishing tone.

"Just thinking ahead," Dimitri said, still smiling.

Reggie spoke for the first time, "You're a train wreck, Dimitri; you know that?" At five feet nothing tall and maybe one hundred and ten pounds, she was one of the few people who could stand toe to toe with him, even if she did have to look up. It may have something to do with her upbringing and Hispanic genes. Her mother was from Barcelona, Spain, and her father was an Army colonel. That probably was one heck of an environment to be raised in.

"Yeah, but I'm a pretty effective train wreck," Dimitri replied jovially, knowing it was true.

Zach continued. "I've been monitoring the excavators' activities closely. Their operation is housed in a four-building complex. One is the front for the supposedly legitimate business and administration; one of the larger ones is for equipment storage and a workshop; and the third large one houses the drilling operation. The fourth is a kind of living quarters or barracks for the workers. I've counted about thirty men in the operation so far."

"Anything else you can tell us about it?" I asked.

"They do have a helipad and have helicopter traffic regularly, which appears to be for supplies, equipment, and people. They have two different kinds of birds. One is a people mover, and the other is heavier lift, equipment, and supply deliveries."

"So, they have pretty much a well-funded, self-contained operation, with limited outside contact?" Doc queried.

"Yep, we keep a closer eye on them now, and I monitor all radio communications. They keep messages generic, but I have found an encrypted communication system in operation using a satellite uplink system," Zach informed them. "It's very high tech, but it was no problem for me to get into."

"Sounds to me like you have this place pretty well wired," I said.

"Information-wise, yes, I do. However, figuring out how to use the information to get rid of these guys covertly has been my problem. I guess that's where Jeannie thinks you guys come in," Zach said as the fire was dying down.

"Well, you've given us a lot to chew on," I said. "We're going to need some time to digest it all."

"I understand," Zach agreed, "Let's call it a night. I have some routine tasks to attend to tomorrow, so I will be occupied for most of the day. I'll be in touch, and we can set up another meeting in the next day or so."

"Sounds good," I said, and the team rose, said their good-byes, and headed back to their cabins. As they were walking, Reggie said, "That was one hell of an ask, from my perspective."

"No kidding," O'Reilly said. "This isn't going to be a walk in the park, that's for sure. We have no idea exactly who we're going to be dealing with, other than what Zach said. Are they scientists and construction-type workers with special expertise? What have they got for security? Not to mention that big ass fence too. This is going to require some serious recon and planning."

Doc said, "If they are as sophisticated as Zach says, you can bet they have everything under electronic surveillance at the very least."

"They're bound to have some kind of physical security as well," Dimitri added.

"These are all things we are going to have to find out before we can come up with any kind of an action plan," I added as we reached our cabins.

Joe said, "You were right, Colt, we've got a lot to chew on."

"Well, everybody, try and get a good night's sleep. I have a feeling once things start rolling, that may not be a luxury we have anymore," I said, bidding them "sweet dreams" with a low chuckle, as they went to their cabins.

The next morning, they found themselves at the little restaurant in town, savoring coffee and enjoying some truly delicious local Navajo pastry, still mulling over the quandary that Zach had presented to them the day before.

"This is going to be tough," Dimitri said. "Doing something like this is not our normal operating procedure. We normally go in guns blazing and solve the problem."

Reggie remarked, laughing, "As I said yesterday, Dimitri, you're a train wreck, and that's not entirely true," as she took another sip of her coffee.

"Watch it, little lady, that kind of talk can get you in serious trouble," Dimitri said, trying to keep a straight face, feigning anger.

"Oh, I'm shaking in my boots," Reggie tauntingly replied.

Doc broke up the witty repartee when he said, "Reggie's right; that's not really true, Dimitri. Remember in Syria when we stormed into DuBois' compound? Yes, there was a certain amount of conflict, but we got in and out, and nobody knew Risky Business was involved; and then what about boarding and taking control of Jorgensen's Super Yacht? Forcing it back inside the 12-mile limit so federal authorities could take him into custody? Nobody knew Risky Business was there except Fitz. So, we can be stealthy when we have to be."

"Doc's correct, but everyone remember, those events took place outside the U.S.—International stuff, this is different. If it goes south, we could be subject to U.S. laws and on a Navajo reservation to boot. Not only do we have to keep our involvement secret, but what we are being asked to do is stop these guys, and our actions have to be downright invisible," I added.

They all sat silent for a while, until O'Reilly said, "We are going to have to rely on Zach to come through on his end. So, it's not just us; we do have some pretty powerful help available. A big challenge is to figure out how to use it."

Silence again.

Zach was waiting at the trading post when the courier arrived. A white unmarked van pulled up out front, and a middle-aged man got out with a silver metal briefcase in hand. He entered the post and walked to Zach, who was standing behind the counter. They nodded in acknowledgement as Zach turned and led him into the back room.

There, the man laid the briefcase on the table and turned it so Zach could open it. Doing so deftly, Zach lifted out the bundles of shrink-wrapped bills and set them on the table. The man handed over an envelope that held a folded piece of paper. Zach read it and nodded, picked up his old leather saddle bags from the floor, and set them on the table.

The man opened them and removed the small gold bars, placing them into the now-empty briefcase. He secured them with the straps, closed the case, and, picking it up, extended his hand, and Zach shook it. With a final nod, he left. Not a word had been spoken.

Zach went to the big bookcase in his back room, pressed a hidden button, and a well-concealed door swung open from the wall. Behind it were two safes. One was about six feet tall, while the other was about five feet tall. He opened the smaller one, revealing shelves of bundled bills and a half-dozen gold bars. He unsealed the money that had just been delivered and added the banded bundles of bills to the stacks in the safe, not bothering to count it. He knew it would be exactly as he requested.

He closed the safe and listened to the lock as it reset. He then turned his attention to the big safe and opened it, hoping upcoming events would not make its contents necessary. As the door swung open, rows and shelves of weapons and ammunition stood before him. He quickly surveyed them and, satisfied, he closed the safe's door. Stepping back, he easily moved the bookshelf into its place, leaving no trace of what lay behind it.

As he dropped into the overstuffed chair, he wondered if his new friends would really be able to help. He pondered the question as he thought about Jeannie's voice and assurance that help was coming. He thought, "Well, if she thinks so, then I guess we'll find out soon enough."

CHAPTER 20

As they were finishing breakfast, Doc said, "You guys feel like a little road trip? We've got some people you need to meet."

"Sure," I replied. They left the little restaurant and loaded into the Expedition. Doc gave directions, saying, "Just head out of town and watch for a dirt road on your left," as he made a phone call. After a quick conversation, he hung up and said, "Just had to make sure they were there. We're going to meet Matt Madison, the helicopter pilot."

"Good," I said a little dubiously, "I'm looking forward to meeting this hotshot in the desert."

"You've got a treat in store for you," O'Reilly said, laughing, "He's not what you would expect in your normal tour pilot."

To which Reggie added sarcastically, "That coming from you is not the least bit scary."

O'Reilly just smiled and said, "You'll see."

I turned onto the dirt road, and we soon passed the old sign that said, "Lone Wolf Aero." A couple of miles later, we spotted the old Airstream trailer and Matt's pickup truck. I parked next to it, and as we were exiting the vehicle, Matt came out of the trailer's door. He wore cutoff cargo pants, a sleeveless T-shirt, and a gun belt, and had his salt-and-pepper hair pulled back and woven into an Indian-style braid down his back. Smiling as he walked toward them, he said, "Hey, Doc, good to see you guys," and stuck out his hand. Doc returned the handshake as Matt acknowledged Joe and O'Reilly.

Doc said, "Matt Madison, this is Colten Burnett, president of Risky Business, Dimitri Sokalov, and Reggie Simpson, the rest of our team."

I had stepped forward, hand extended, saying, "Pleasure to meet you, Matt, and it's Colt."

There were handshakes all around, and Matt said, "Please, have a seat." Additional chairs had been added to the ones around the cable-spool table, and we all settled in. Matt picked up the radio lying on the table, keyed the mic, and said, "Sam, come to the office, our guests have arrived."

The female voice responded, "Roger that, on my way." A few minutes later, they heard the sound of the ATV approaching. Sam got out in jean shorts, a tank top, and a red bandana around her head, pulling the red shop towel from her hip pocket as she approached, smiling and wiping her hands.

"Folks, this is Samantha Meadows, my crew chief, head mechanic, and the other half of Lone Wolf Aero."

"The half that keeps him in the air," she said, laughing, as she shook hands and introductions were made as she joined us around the table under the sunshade.

Matt said, "It's a pleasure to meet a real treasure hunter, Colt. I've met a few folks who claimed to be, but none who have really found anything of value like your team has."

"Thanks, Matt, it's certainly not as easy as some would like you to believe. We're some of the lucky ones."

"I'm sure there's a lot more than luck involved, but from what I read on the internet, you've been quite successful."

I smiled and said, "We've done all right for ourselves," nodding toward the others seated at the table. "Definitely a team effort."

"So, Doc tells me you're looking for Kincaid's cave," Matt said.

"Right, his research seems to point to the fact that it is indeed real and located somewhere in this vicinity," I said.

"Well, I've heard all the stories, and you aren't the first ones I've flown around who've been looking for it. Over the years, we've had our share of those with a casual interest and those who were more serious about their search. But like I told Doc, they've all come up empty-handed. Some just give up, some are run off by the park rangers for trespassing on posted land."

"The restricted areas," Doc added.

I knew the location of the cave all too well. Zach had described it in detail, but I had to keep that confidential information to myself, at least for the time being.

"So, the no-fly zones apply to some of the land area as well as down in the canyon?" I asked.

"Yes, they are adjacent to the areas in the canyon.

According to Park Service and FAA regulations, I can only fly over them at altitude. Nothing low-level."

"Doc did mention you might be amenable to disregarding those constraints and helping us survey the area more closely. Bending the rules a bit," I said, smiling.

Sam broke out into a loud chuckle, which Matt quickly cut off. "Don't start that again, Sam," he said half-heartedly, smiling slightly.

"Not saying a word here, Boss," she retorted, choking off the chuckle, but still smiling.

After a pause, Matt answered, "Well, there's always that possibility, depending on how bad my engine problem is. You know if a helicopter has engine problems, the first thing they do is lose altitude, so like I said, depending on how bad the situation is, it might require some low-level flying for a bit." Another pause and a smile, "At least until I can get the problem sorted out," he finished.

O'Reilly jumped in, "Got to be very careful when you have those kinds of issues. A low-level, slow emergency landing would be preferable to a sudden, uncontrolled descent from altitude. The explosion on impact would be devastating to the surrounding area and any endangered flora or fauna that might be there." Now, O'Reilly was chuckling, adding another layer of plausible deniability to Matt's scenario.

"Exactly," Matt said as he rocked back in his chair, his grin breaking into a full-blown smile. "Confirmation from one experienced pilot to another. What time is it, Sam?" he asked.

"11:30, Boss," she replied.

"This discussion has been very productive," he said, feigning a serious tone. "I believe it's beer-thirty. Anyone else thirsty?" he asked as he rose and headed for the outdoor fridge.

Everyone was laughing now, and I said, "We're from Florida, and as we say down there, 'It's five o'clock somewhere!'"

When Matt returned to the table with the cold beverages, Dimitri said, "Nice sidearm, I've always been a fan of Glocks."

As if noticing it for the first time, Matt looked down at the holstered weapon on his belt. "Oh, yeah, love them, she's been with me since my last tour in Afghanistan. I sometimes forget she's even there. Kinda second nature strapping her on, don't give it much thought."

"Until you need it," Doc added, smiling, nodding toward the large headless snakeskin tacked up on a plank.

Matt laughed, "Yep, it does come in handy at times."

Dimitri added, "Doc told us the story of your first meeting, nice shooting."

"Gracias," Matt replied. "I've had lots of practice over the years."

Reggie looked at the snakeskin, and then her attention was drawn to the apple tree when the watering system quietly kicked on. "Now that's something I didn't expect to see in the middle of the desert. That is one healthy tree and full of fruit. The plaque says in memory of your grandparents," she said somewhat questioningly.

Matt sat down and said, "Yeah, my parents were killed in a car accident when I was ten years old. My Gramps and Gram raised me. They lived in California. Gramps was an engineer and worked for a big aeronautical company, and Grams had her MBA and was head of finance for a large tech company. I went to high school, and they put me through college. I was in ROTC, so after graduating, I enlisted in the Army. I went right to helicopter flight school at Fort Rucker and have been flying them ever since."

"That's a nice memorial for them," Reggie commented, "Although a little unusual," she added.

"Well, there's a little more to the story than that. Grams was always the adventurous type, with a passion for scuba diving and motorcycles—she even had her own Harley. Gramps always supported her and often joined her, but he wasn't quite the risk-taker she was.

"So, when she came to him with what she thought might be a good investment opportunity in the early 80s on a new company that was just getting started, he was a little hesitant. Not Grams, she invested ten thousand dollars immediately. It took a bit of insisting on her part, but finally, a couple of days later, she got him to invest the same amount. She was one persistent lady. Gramps passed away on my first tour to Afghanistan, and just after I got home from my second tour over there, Grams passed away. I was glad I got to be with her during her last days.

"Since I was the only living relative, since mom and dad passed in a car accident, I inherited pretty much everything. Some went to charities they were involved in and environmental groups, but everything else came to me."

Sam was sitting there smiling as he continued. "So, I packed up everything, sold the house, took an early discharge, moved out here, bought this piece of property, and started Lone Wolf. I didn't want anything to do with the rat race."

Sam spoke up, "After I left the hospital in Afghanistan, where that mortar attack on the flight line took my legs, this guy followed my progress through Walter Reed and then paid for the additional rehab the VA didn't pay for. His friendship and support got me through some really tough times. He arranged for me to get these advanced prosthetics I'm wearing. They are state-of-the-art, and I can even fly with them. Then he offered me this job. I never thought I'd work in this field again with my physical situation. A little additional flight training, and here I am," she said with an obvious twinkle in her eyes.

"Hey, you were one helluva crew chief over there, and you loved it. When I got back, I couldn't see good talent going to waste." He returned her glowing smile.

"That is very cool, so he's kind of been your guardian angel through your whole recovery process," O'Reilly said.

"That he has been and more," Sam replied, smiling broadly, the twinkle still there.

"I do what I can," Matt replied rather quietly, his

smile revealing a deeper level of sincerity.

"And that's a hell of a lot. He supports the Wounded Warriors Association, programs for Vets with PTSD, and a lot more," Sam added.

Doc's eyes widened suddenly, as he said, "California, the 80s, the start-up company, your grandparents' memorial over there... that start-up investment was Apple Computers?"

Matt nodded slowly, "Told you Grams was a shrewd gal."

Joe let out a low whistle, "A twenty-thousand-dollar investment when they first went public has got to be worth...."

Matt stopped him with his comment, "A lot!"

CHAPTER 21

I broke the silence when I said, "You're a good man, Matt Madison, and I'm looking forward to our working relationship."

"As am I," Matt replied, tilting his beer toward the group in salute. It can get a little boring out here for Sam and me at times, although we like the solitude."

Doc had been quiet, sitting there, brow slightly furrowed for a few minutes. Finally, he got up and said, "You guys excuse me for a minute; I've got to make a call." He pulled out his phone and walked a little distance from the table. Questioning looks went amongst the team, but nothing was said. Doc finished his call and then asked me to join him. As the two talked, Dimitri said, "Well, it looks like now we're going to have two angels flying with us."

This brought a questioning look from both Sam and Matt.

Dimitri said, "When we were on one of our expeditions to Ecuador, O'Reilly flew into the mountains to rescue and pick up some seriously injured passengers from a bus that was about to fall over a 700-foot cliff.

"One was a very pregnant woman who was

banged up pretty bad, and her daughter, who had suffered a serious head injury, as well as the bus driver, who had broken ribs and a punctured lung. They all survived, and the baby was born right after arriving at the hospital, a healthy baby boy. Doctors said none of them would have survived if O'Reilly hadn't gotten them to the hospital so quickly. Of course, she managed to piss off the Ecuadorian Air Force in the process, but that's another story. Anyway, her being a redhead, the locals and press started calling her A'ngel Rojo, the Red Angel. It made all the news outlets and has stuck with her."

Now, O'Reilly was blushing, as Joe added, "That was some pretty kick-ass flying in the mountains, and then only to have room to put one skid on the road and hover over the 700-foot drop, hovering while we loaded the injured."

Now, Matt and Sam both looked surprised, exuding a new air of professional respect. Matt said, "That is quite impressive, O'Reilly, quite impressive."

"That sounds like the same kind of hero shit you pulled over in the sandbox, Matt. I think you two must have been cut from the same cloth," Sam added, laughing.

They were all laughing when Doc and I came back to the table and sat down.

"You guys having fun?" I asked.

"So, Colt, did you know we are in the presence of angels, and they both fly helicopters?" Dimitri asked.

O'Reilly said, "Just ignore him, Colt; he's just being his typical Dimitri wise-ass."

"No, it's true," Dimitri got out between laughs, "Matt's an angel too, even if he doesn't sport the look! Sam said so." Sam sat there smiling sheepishly.

"I'm sure there's more to this story, but I'll take all the angelic help we can get right now," I said. "We've got an update for you, Matt. There has been an interesting turn of events that you need to be aware of. It's true we did come here looking for Kincaid's cave, but since we got here, Zach has informed us that he has found out there's something strange going on at the solar energy research facility.

"Zach is a great guy; he has done so much for the residents of Fremont and the surrounding area. The locals love him, and he does a pretty good job keeping the tourists coming in and Fremont on the map," Matt said.

"Besides, I never did like the idea of that facility being built on Navajo land. Guess a lot of money had to change hands to get that approved," he added.

"Well, it turns out it is funded through a couple of shell companies owned by a Chinese weapons manufacturing conglomerate," Doc informed him.

"No kidding," Matt said.

"So, he thinks they're up to something dangerous?" Sam asked, now looking very concerned.

"He's not sure, but it is a possibility, and he's asking for our help to find out," I replied.

Matt looked at Sam, who nodded at him, and then to the team and said, "We're in, whatever you need."

Doc nodded, appreciatively adding, "Zach said you

would probably say that."

"Damn straight, with the Chinese weapons group involvement, we're talking potential national security implications. So, hell yeah, we're in," Matt replied emphatically.

"Not sure how things are going to progress, but we'll keep you informed as plans start coming together," I said. "One thing is for sure; we're going to need some aerial intel of the site—as close and as thorough as we can get."

Matt said, "Not a problem, just let me know what and when you need it."

"That's going to require some bending and even breaking the laws," Sam said, starting to laugh again.

Matt scrunched up his face and said, "Please, don't start that again, babe."

O'Reilly quipped, "Sounds like an inside joke going on here."

"Not so much a joke, but a story I'll have to share with you sometime over beers," Sam said.

O'Reilly, laughing, said, "I am definitely looking forward to it."

"Okay, gang, we're at a good stopping point. Matt, now that you're on board and we've brought you up to speed on what we know so far, we need to head back to Fremont and check in with Zach. We'll be in touch with any updates, and we can start thinking about the intel gathering mission. Keep us posted on any thoughts or ideas you may come up with," I said.

"Will do," Matt replied.

With that, we loaded up and headed back to Fremont to meet with Zach.

Doc said, "I think we've just added two valuable members to the team."

"Agree," O'Reilly added, "two very capable members."

Joe said, "From the way things are sounding, we'll need all the 'angelic' help we can get."

Dimitri laughed, "Two angels are always better than one. Especially if they shoot like Matt."

Reggie punched him good naturedly on the shoulder and said, "You and your guns."

"Hey," he retorted, "You know I'm right."

The car got silent.

She didn't respond because she knew he was right.

They pulled up in front of the trading post and met Zach inside. He asked, "Well?"

"They're in," Doc told him.

"I figured they would be," he said. "They've always been damn dependable, especially in an emergency."

"What about you?" Doc asked.

"All good here, I just had some business to take care of. You guys up for one of my cave tours tomorrow?" Zach asked.

"You bet, been wondering when we would get around to that," Doc said.

"What time?" I asked.

"Let's say 8:00 a.m., that's usually when I take my cave tours out. There's no sense in changing the routine, just in case someone is monitoring what goes on here. It will be just another one of my tourist activities, with a few added attractions."

"Good idea," I said. "We'll meet you here at eight."

"Anybody else hungry?" Reggie asked. "I'm starving."

"That sounds good," Joe said.

"Then let's adjourn to the restaurant. Zach, see you back here bright and early," I said.

"See you at eight," Zach replied.

Later that night, as Zach was falling asleep, the tinkling sound of a crystal chandelier in the wind woke him, and the familiar voice said, "Your help has arrived; trust them in all things. You will find the answer you seek to solve your problem."

He recognized the voice of the Protector and, without speaking out loud, responded, "I will." He fell into a deep, restful sleep, and the next morning, with a renewed sense of confidence, went out to meet Colt and his team.

CHAPTER 22

My team and I arrived at the Trading Post at the appointed time, and Joseph greeted us. "Morning, folks," he said cheerfully. "Zach will be here in a couple of minutes; he went to pick up the van. Coffee's on if you're interested." We availed ourselves of his offer, and just as we were finishing our cups of strong Navajo coffee, a van pulled up out front and the horn honked.

We thanked Joseph for the jolt of caffeine and went out to see a large white van with the words "Zach's Cavern Tours, Fremont, Arizona" painted brightly on its sides. He motioned for us to get into the large ten-passenger four-wheel-drive behemoth. Smiling broadly as we climbed aboard, he said, "Welcome to Zach's Cavern Tours." He had the A/C going full blast. Even this early, the sun was making its presence known as the heat reflected off the unforgiving desert sands.

Not knowing exactly what to expect, we came prepared for most contingencies. We each had backpacks with water, flashlights, climbing gear, and Doc had his med kit. We also carried enough firepower to hold off a small army.

Zach eyed our packs as we loaded up and said, "Well, it looks like you all came well prepared."

I replied, "We learned a long time ago it's better to have the gear and not need it than to need it and not have it."

"Well spoken, but I think you will find it unnecessary on this trip. This is going to be a cram course in world history, among other things," Zach responded.

"That would be extremely helpful. As we have discussed, while Jeannie did provide us with a lot of information, there were bits and pieces of information on the real history of things, and much of it was rather cryptic in its delivery," I remarked.

Doc chimed in next, rather excitedly, "I definitely want to hear more about your world and its diverse population."

"Not a problem, Doc," Zach replied, "and I think our varied population will be somewhat mind-blowing. But something to understand, we brought a major portion of our population with us when we migrated to this planet."

"So why did you leave your planet?" Joe asked.

The bumpy ride to the cave was about to get a heck of a lot more interesting as Zach answered.

"Our scientists detected our sun becoming very unstable and determined that a catastrophic solar event was imminent. Imminent to them was about two hundred years, so we began long-range preparations for a mass exodus from our planet. We had developed interstellar space travel some three thousand years earlier, so our task at hand became to build spacecraft large enough to handle the entire population of the planet."

After a pause, "That means you've had interstellar capabilities for hundreds of thousands of years," Doc stated, in awe.

"Yep, we've been hopping around the universe for quite a while," Zach said rather jovially as they parked next to the Zach's Cavern Tours sign, with the mouth of the cave looming darkly in front of them.

"But more later, follow me," he said.

They exited the vehicle and headed for the mouth of the cave, ready to enter Zach's underground world, or so they thought. As they entered the dimness of the cave's interior, Zach switched on his light, which illuminated the cave's craggy walls and continued down the passageway. As they came to a turn in the tunnel, Zach pointed out a niche in the wall and said, "You can stow your packs there; you won't be needing them. They'll be safe there until we come back."

We obliged him, and as our packs were neatly stacked, he said, "Okay, just a little farther. Now he had the only light, so we followed closely. In a few yards, he stopped and said, "We're here, you ready?"

Not knowing what they were getting ready for, I said somewhat reservedly, "I suppose so."

"Great," Zach replied, "there will be a slight change in atmosphere, but nothing to worry about," as he touched the gem on his bracelet, and a portal opened before us. He stepped through, and we followed into a warmly lit corridor that left us in stunned silence. Our eyes quickly adjusted to the lighting as it grew ever so slightly brighter, revealing more of the world we had just entered. Dimitri was the last one through, and the portal closed behind him.

Zach then said in a professorial voice, "We have the lighting set to start low and slowly increase in illumination so as not to shock your eyes coming from complete darkness into light." It worked beautifully, our eyes easily adjusting to the slowly increasing illumination, seemingly coming from all around us. A natural glow filled the area, emanating from no discernible light source.

As we took in our surroundings, we had to rethink our initial assessment of entering a corridor. We could now see it was much more than that. The vaulted ceiling, some fifteen feet overhead, and the highly polished natural rock walls and floor gave it a cathedral nave feeling. The variety of natural inclusions in the walls and floor provided a beautiful, almost artistic backdrop to our surroundings.

Reggie, eyes wide, said, "Man, this is not what I was expecting from what we've heard about Kincaid's cave."

Zach laughed, "Oh, this is not Kincaid's cave. This is part of our underground facility. We're five miles underground. The cave that he found was part of the very first creations by the indigenous people of the area, with some help from us. I guess I need to finish a bit more of the history lesson; walk with me, and I'll continue."

We started down the grand corridor, and Zach continued. "About 80 thousand years ago, our scientists detected a massive coronal buildup on the sun. We had detected those on our own sun and knew there would inevitably be a massive burst of coronal energy emitted, but we weren't sure when or how large it would be.

"The only thing we could do for the indigenous population of this planet at the time was to warn them and recommend digging underground sanctuaries. That would provide them with a minimum form of protection while our scientists began working on a more technological solution. Not many of the population at that time had the technological ability to do much more than that."

"There were large civilizations then around this world?" Joe asked.

"Oh, yes, many were very advanced; unfortunately, a number of those did not survive the solar onslaught," Zach answered. "And not all of them heeded our warnings. Our most advanced centers were spread out globally and controlled independently. We shared technology and communication, but left it up to the individual groups to use as they saw fit.

"As I said, our original mandate when we got to this planet was one of non-interference with the development of the indigenous life forms, unless absolutely necessary."

"What would absolutely necessary mean?" Doc asked.

"Intervention would only take place if something were happening that would negatively impact our colonies or people. Initially, we avoided human development as much as possible. We determined, however, shortly after our arrival, that socio-evolutionary development was going to need a little push to help the population move more quickly to an optimal civilized state if peaceful co-existence were ever going to be possible," Zach said.

"What does that mean?" I asked.

"The thing that a lot of your fringe science types have alluded to—genetic manipulation by an advanced alien race. That would have been us," Zach concluded, as we all tried to digest what he had just shared.

We had been walking down the magnificent hallway while talking and approached an open doorway on our left. Zach led the way into a huge room, and again, the subdued lighting intensified upon our entry.

"Welcome to my workshop," Zach said, spreading his arms expansively.

It was a breathtaking array of panels, tables, and racks, featuring a myriad of science-fiction-worthy equipment. None of it looked familiar, but lights were continuously in motion on almost everything, indicating they were all busy doing—well, whatever! In the center was an eight-foot-square tabletop surrounded by consoles of various sizes.

"This is very impressive," Joe said, "I'm guessing a lot is going on here."

"That would be an understatement," Zach answered, laughing.

Joe continued, "But how do you monitor what's going on?"

Zach walked to one of the consoles, waved his hand over it, and a holographic type of display appeared, hovering above, showing numbers and graphs. "Each of these devices has a similar display, and as they do their work, should an anomaly occur, the display activates, and I receive an immediate notification, no matter where I am." He touched another stone on his bracelet, and several machine displays appeared over it.

"So, the bracelet serves as your notification and control device," I said.

"Well, it's my mobile unit. I have a more sophisticated setup at the trading post. Together, the devices allow me to determine if I need to come here to rectify a problem or if I just need to be alerted to some activity. I have them," he said, sweeping his arm around the room, "all monitoring or working on different tasks that are important to the operation of my lab and the city."

"The city?" Doc asked questioningly.

Zach laughed again and said, "As the old saying goes, this is just the tip of the iceberg. You have a lot more to see and learn. But there will be time for that later. Right now, I need to see what our friends at the solar center have been up to," he nonchalantly said as he walked up to one of the consoles and activated its display. The display showed the currently active audio waveforms. Reaching into it, he manipulated a section of the display, and audio filled the room. It was in Chinese, and with another tweak in the display, the audio was in English.

"This is their encrypted communications network," Zach informed us. As they listened, a progress report was being given, stating that a location had been identified, the equipment had arrived, and drilling would commence within the next two days. The transmission then ended.

"Well, that's not good," Zach remarked. "Let's see where they are going to be working," he said, and he waved another hand over one of the other consoles. An X-ray image of the buildings appeared. He reached in, tweaked another area of the image, and the largest building floated above the console. We could see men moving about and equipment being set up.

"Wow," Joe exclaimed, "that is amazing."

"It's much like the device Jeannie gave you, only more sophisticated and powerful," Zach told him.

"I need to see the data they're working with and determine where their drilling is going to take them," Zach said as another tweak brought up numerical information, including GPS information and a display showing the projected location of the drilling and angle of descent.

"This is all real-time?" I asked.

"Yes, this is showing me exactly what they are looking at on their equipment. With it, I can add a geologic cross-section of the area and pinpoint where they will be heading with the drill."

"So, how close are they going to be to your power supply?" I asked.

"Luckily, I got the force field power leak stopped before they could really pinpoint its location, so now, they are using the old location data from '71. What little data they acquired recently to decide where to start drilling is close, but it will, however, put them into part of the natural cave system that runs about eight hundred feet above the power chamber."

"So, basically, they're guessing," O'Reilly said.

"Yes, but their guess will put them too close for comfort. Lucky for us, it is going to take them some time to get in proximity to the cave, but once they find it, that may be enough to entice them to expand their drilling, which becomes a huge problem for us."

"Then we have to stop them without them knowing they've been stopped by someone," Doc interjected.

"And therein lies our challenge," Zach said, his usual smile gone.

CHAPTER 23

"You said they were surveilling you, Zach?" I asked.

"Yes, but not just me, the whole area around the complex has extensive video surveillance. Here, check this out." Zach went back to the communications console he had been at before, and with a wave of his hand, it came to life again.

"Damn, that is so cool," Dimitri said. "It's just like magic."

Zach laughed, "To steal a phrase from a brilliant mind, 'Any sufficiently advanced technology is indistinguishable from magic,' so yes, it is a kind of magic, he intoned with a grin, as the video feeds from the research facility appeared before them. "The Chinese and their local hosts have surveillance both outside the perimeter of the compound and also inside. The range and resolution of their equipment are quite good. Trying to sneak up on them physically would be extremely difficult, if not impossible," Zach said.

"So, they've been operating here since they started with impunity," I stated.

"Yes, they have had no reason to believe that anyone is interested in or questions their reason for being there. They felt comfortable with their cover story," Zach responded.

"And they've been progressing at a rather rapid pace," I added.

"They have progressed unimpeded, except for the couple of little things I did to slow them down to buy me some time while I dug deeper into the real reason they were here, and who they actually were. I had to ensure that the issues I created all seemed to be natural problems that could occur spontaneously, such as equipment failures and communication issues. That's about it," Zach responded.

"How long would it take them to drill down to that cave you mentioned?" I asked.

"Since they just started, and they have good equipment, drilling 24-7, they could probably reach it in two weeks," Zach answered. "They'll be drilling through levels of andesite, basalt, granite, and a lot of volcanic material, so it could be slow going, but that still doesn't give us much time to come up with a plan," he added.

After a pause, I started grinning and said, "I think maybe it's time they had something to start worrying about other than just drilling. O'Reilly, how about you and your buddy Snake get busy doing some very visible aerial surveillance for starters? Let them know that somebody is interested in what they're doing and keeping an eye on them."

"That just might slow them down a bit, and at least make them more cautious in their actions," Doc added.

Zach said, "Sounds like you may have the

beginning of a plan, Colt."

I didn't say anything as I mused. After a few minutes, I said, "Don't really have a plan yet, but this may buy us some additional time to formulate one."

Shortly thereafter, Joe changed the subject and asked, "Zach, you said you were the planet's Guardian, just how does that work?"

Zach walked over to a console at the big tabletop in the middle of the room and waved his hand over it, bringing it to life. A large holographic image of the Earth, with the moon in orbit, appeared in the space above it. Surrounding the globe were thousands of red dots, a few larger white ones, and four large blue ones.

"This is the space junk currently surrounding our planet, including dead satellites," he said as the red objects grew brighter. He touched the top of the console, and the red images dimmed, and the large number of white ones grew brighter. "These are the current active satellites orbiting Earth." Beyond all the red and white images, much further out were four very dark blue, larger objects orbiting in an equidistant pattern around the planet. "And these are my satellites," Zach said.

Joe, looking surprised, said, "You have your own satellites up there?"

"I do," Zach replied, "they help me keep a close eye on things that my sensors might miss," he laughed and said, "which isn't much, but they do help."

"Aren't you afraid they will be detected?" Joe asked.

Zach said good-naturedly, "Come on, Joe... really?"

Joe realized he had fallen into an earth-centric state of mind and, blushing somewhat, said, "Right, I keep forgetting your technology is far superior to ours."

"Far," Zach underscored, "say by oh, I don't know, maybe over a couple of hundreds of thousands of years," he responded, laughing. "But they have been spotted on occasion when I had to change their orbits for closer observation of Earth. You've heard of the mysterious 'Black Knight' satellites reported in the fringe media?"

Joe replied, "Yes, they pop into the conspiracy media on the web now and then."

"Well, those are mine," Zach said, smiling. "I get them out of sight and back into their original orbits as soon as I'm done with my surveillance."

"So noted," Joe replied, "I have to keep reminding myself of the fact that you have advanced capabilities."

Now Dimitri entered the conversation, "So you say you protect the planet?"

"Yes, my sensors can pick up objects or junk that may be in an Earth strike trajectory. If they are small enough, I let them burn up in Earth's atmosphere on re-entry. If they are large enough to make it through the atmosphere and potentially cause damage or be heading toward a populated area, I help them disintegrate before landfall, making it look like natural occurrences."

"Damn, that's pretty cool," Dimitri exclaimed.

"And if I detect very large objects headed our way, I can nudge them and change their trajectory to make sure they miss us. If that doesn't seem feasible, then, as

I mentioned, I disintegrate them."

"What if our telescopes or systems spot that? Doesn't that raise suspicion?" Doc asked.

"My sensors can pick these objects up long before your technology can even detect them. So, your scientists never know they even existed," Zach replied.

"And you said you monitor the ISS too?" Doc added.

"Yes, I make sure there are no objects or junk that gets to them. That's a little trickier, but most of the stuff can be moved, and only now and then do I have to zap something."

"Well, your interventions don't seem to have been noticed," Joe added.

"Nope, all good so far," Zach said.

Dimitri had been staring at the images floating in front of them and finally said, "Can you show us how you zap that debris?"

"Sure, let's find something that's far enough out that nobody should notice," Zach said, while moving his hands over the console. Pretty soon, a red object in the furthest orbit had a glowing circle appear around it. Zach touched the top of the console, and it disappeared.

Dimitri said, "That's it?"

"Yep, vaporized, no extraneous debris or material left. Gone completely."

"And it's that way with anything you zap?" he asked.

"Yes, size or composition doesn't matter. I think

now you can see why this energy source must be protected. First of all, your current technology has no way of controlling it, and secondly, with the wrong hands messing around with it, it potentially could become a world destroyer," Zach warned.

Dimitri had moved next to Zach at the console and pointed to a series of white dots, lined up, wrapping around the planet, and asked, "Are these commercial communications satellites?"

"Yes, they are part of the network that has been launched commercially for internet communications."

"Part of that Star-thing network that got turned off over Ukraine a couple of years ago?"

"Those are the ones," Zach answered.

Dimitri looked at Zach and said, "So, if one or two of them were put out of commission, it would disrupt the area they are serving?"

"Yes, it would disrupt the entire network," Zach answered, now looking at Dimitri cautiously.

Dimitri had been watching closely as Zach had demonstrated the use of the device earlier. He slid his hand into place and brought up the aiming circle around one of the satellites, according to the Earth image in front of them, over Russia. Before Zach could stop him, he had targeted six of the satellites over Russia and vaporized them out of existence.

Zach made no move to stop him but said, "That may not have been a good idea," as Dimitri moved his hand away from the controls.

I said in a loud voice, "Dammit, Dimitri, get away

from there."

He stepped back with his hands up and said, "That's just a little payback, Boss."

I looked at Zach and said, "I'm sorry, Zach. Dimitri was fighting in Ukraine when the satellites were cut off and saw first-hand what that did to the Ukrainian military forces and the people when that happened."

Dimitri added, "It's personal, man, didn't mean to cause you any problems."

Zach's face was expressionless as he looked from me to Dimitri and then again to the orbs floating before them. His hand moved to the console, and the targeting circle came up again; seconds later, six more of the satellites had disappeared. Now, everyone was staring wide-eyed as Zach turned to Dimitri, smiling slightly, and said, "You missed a couple."

CHAPTER 24

"Isn't that going to cause a problem?" I asked.

"Oh, I'm sure it will," Zach answered, "but not for us."

"Somebody is going to get blamed," Doc said.

"Sure, they will, but who, and blamed for what?" Zach replied.

"Well, the satellites, they're gone," Doc said.

"True," Zach retorted, "but where did they go?"

There was a pause, and Doc said, "Well, what if they traced it back to you? Someone may have picked up the energy beam coming from here."

Now, Zach laughed out loud, "Your scientific community does not have the technology to detect the 'beam' as you call it, and even if they did, it didn't come from here."

Looking very puzzled, Doc said, "Well, where did it come from?"

Zach raised his arm and pointed at the moon image in the holographic display floating before them. Incredulously, Doc said, "The moon... You have a base on the moon?"

Zach, shaking his head slowly, looked at everyone

in the room and said, "I guess it's time for you to find out a little more about us. Remember when the Apollo 12 lander crashed back into the moon's surface after getting the capsule into orbit, and the researchers said the moon rang like a bell for two days, as if it were hollow?"

Everyone nodded in assent, and Joe said, "That made the headlines without any real scientific explanation."

Zach replied, "You're right, but their hypothetical comment was correct. It is hollow, well, at least some parts of it."

Eyes widened in disbelief, and stunned looks pervaded the room.

Smiling, Zach continued with his bombshell announcement. "It is actually our spacecraft that we parked in Earth's orbit when we arrived over 150 thousand years ago."

There was total silence in the room until Doc loudly exclaimed, "What?"

Joe followed with, "You're kidding?"

Everyone else stood there in stunned silence. Their faces showed varying levels of disbelief or incredulity, except for me, whose face displayed mild interest and an acceptance of the given fact.

"When we got here, the moon orbiting this planet was small by comparison, and its gravitational impact on the planet was minimal," Zach explained. "We removed it and positioned our ship in its place. Our ship was able to increase the gravitational impact on this planet, which had a positive effect on the tidal flow of your oceans. We were also able to increase the magnetic strength of the planet's core. That action created a more robust magnetosphere, thereby eliminating a lot of the harmful solar radiation that had been bombarding your planet.

"All of these changes had a positive impact on the Earth, and made it more habitable for a variety of lifeforms. Some were native here; others were the ones that came with us," Zach continued. "Our planet was twice the size of this Earth, and we were used to a much stronger gravity field than this planet had. When we landed, that fact initially made us seem quite strong, comparatively speaking. We were able to perform what might have been considered superhuman feats. Running, jumping, lifting heavy objects, and other physical activities. Although our physical size was similar to that of developing humanoids, our abilities far exceeded theirs, which was another reason we kept ourselves isolated from the developing population at the time. We helped our groups relocate to regions here on Earth that were similar to the ones they inhabited on our planet."

"So, our planets were very similar," Doc said.

"Absolutely, that's the main reason we chose Earth for our relocation. It was one of the planets most similar to ours in almost every way. We had multiple ships leave our planet, carrying as many of our inhabitants as possible before our sun went supernova."

"And so, all your people were able to find a suitable place to live here on Earth?" O'Reilly asked.

"Well, yes and no, but I think you are using the term 'people' too broadly," Zach answered. "If you are referring to species that look like we do.

"Our planet had a vast number of sentient beings that were included in our population, but not all had achieved space travel capabilities. Some had advanced technologically to varying degrees, but ours was by far the most scientifically sophisticated, having developed interstellar capabilities thousands of years earlier.

"We were only able to include a portion of the planet's population, about 250,000, on our ship. That's why multiple ships were built to evacuate those who wanted to leave. Some decided they would stay and accept their fate. It was their choice."

"Where did the other ships go?" Joe asked.

"We had identified a multitude of planets that could support our populations. Each ship was able to choose its destination—its place to start over. We chose Earth. The sun appeared stable, the planets in the system seemed to have potential for growth, and it was relatively close. In your celestial measurement system, it was only 150 light-years away. It took us two of your Earth weeks to get here."

If it were possible, the silence in the room grew. The information was presented so matter-of-factly that it had just shattered their notions of physics and space travel in an almost incomprehensible way. This was the stuff of science fiction, and now they were being told it was reality—but certainly not as they knew it. But here and now, our worldview just made a dramatic and unexpected "left turn."

In our conversation with Jeannie, the other member of Zach's origin, whom we had met in Ecuador, she had shared some mind-blowing information with us. But her revelations were usually rather cryptic and given in small doses. We were always aware that we were conversing with an advanced being, and I suppose our minds only grasped a superficial understanding of the information she shared. Even when we experienced some of her unique powers firsthand, it still felt easier to grasp on a science fiction level.

To date, our dealings and conversations with Zach had been conducted in everyday, very matter-of-fact terms that we could easily understand and accept... until now. His technology was mind-blowing, but we had grown somewhat accustomed to it after dealing with Jeannie. However, she never shared the real history of their arrival on Earth or the extent of their involvement in human affairs, unlike Zach. From our past adventures, we were only able to hypothesize their participation from the clues we uncovered. Zach had now pulled back the curtain.

I was lost deep in thought when Doc asked, "Well, Colt, where do we go from here?"

Breaking the silence in the room, I looked at my team and Zach and thoughtfully replied, "That, my friend, is the sixty-four-million-dollar question."

Zach, understanding our level of awe and amazement, said, "I think that's enough historical information sharing for now. You'll need some time to process this, and I'm sure you'll have a lot of questions, but we still need a plan to resolve our current situation. Let's head back to the surface and reconvene around the campfire tonight to discuss options for our next steps."

"I agree," I replied. We may have just hit information overload, and it could easily lead us away from the problem at hand. Besides, O'Reilly, you need to set up the surveillance routine with Snake as soon as possible and get that started."

"Right, can do, Boss," she replied. "As soon as we get above ground, I'll give him a call."

"The rest of us need to put our heads together and see what we can come up with. This is going to take some real creativity on our part."

Dimitri chimed in, sounding somewhat disappointed, "So, I guess going in with guns blazing is off the table?"

I chuckled... typical Dimitri, I thought, and said, "Well, at least for now." That qualifier seemed to cheer him up a bit.

"So, let's head back," Zach said, "and we'll reconvene later this evening." With that, he touched his bracelet, and a portal appeared. We stepped back into the cave chamber we had left earlier, picked up our gear, and headed back out into the Arizona sunlight with minds swirling and a daunting challenge facing us.

CHAPTER 25

During the ride back to Fremont, the vehicle was buzzing with conversation. Zach would occasionally add something, but, for the most part, let the discussions take their own path. He was aware that the team verbalizing the information would help them process the world-shattering recent information, so he let them ramble on until we all got back to the trading post.

As we exited the vehicle, Zach said, "See you around 7:30 p.m.?"

"Works for us," I replied as we headed back to our cabins. It was close to three o'clock, and we had been underground most of the day. Pangs of hunger were setting in, and we decided to freshen up and head to the little diner for supper and, of course, more discussion.

After a meal of country-fried pork steaks, roasted potato chunks, and a small salad, we all settled down a bit and were catching our second wind after the revelations of the day. We sat sipping the chilled apple cider, all lost in our thoughts for the moment when Reggie spoke. She had been quiet for most of the day. "I know I've said this before, especially after hooking up with you guys and our mind-blowing adventure in Ecuador, but this.... Never in my wildest dreams could

I have imagined that my joining this group would have led to my involvement in something of this magnitude."

We were all smiling at her comment, and I said, "I think it's safe to say that we all feel the same way. I'm pretty sure this is beyond anything we were expecting." Heads bobbed in assent around the table, and Doc added, "Colt is absolutely right, we have been thrown right into the midst of what seems like a science fiction movie of immense proportions. Only it's not fiction and it's not Hollywood! That's the crazy part—it's all fact. Our world of reality, for the most part, has just gone up in smoke and been replaced by something from *The Outer Limits*."

"And we have to operate in that new world," O'Reilly added.

Joe spoke up, "This is like one of those movies where the main characters find themselves having to function, operate, and survive in two different worlds at the same time."

"And while doing so, they have to save the world on top of that," Dimitri added. "Man, filmmakers would have a field day with this story."

Doc chuckled, "Either it's too bad or maybe a good thing they'll never know about it."

"Hey, if they did, that Rock guy could play me, rough, tough, and good looking," Dimitri said, grinning like a Cheshire cat.

"In your dreams," Reggie responded, you'd be lucky if they got one of those guys from the WWE to play you. One that's been hit in the head a few too many times and is just as out of touch with reality as you are!"

"Watch it, Reg, that kind of talk is fighting words," Dimitri responded laughingly.

"Bring it on, big boy," Reggie retorted, grinning, "I'll show you where the phrase 'Whoop Ass' came from."

We were all laughing uncontrollably now as these two got into a schoolyard squabble as they are wont to do. They both seem to enjoy the repartee and verbal sparring in jest.

I finally said, still laughing, "All right, you two, settle down or I'm going to have to put you both in a time out. Besides, we need to head to Zach's."

We left the diner and started our walk, passing the various buildings and businesses that lined the street. You couldn't help feeling like you were stepping back in time as the surroundings reflected a bygone era, when life was simple and serene. The locals, for the most part, were completely unaware of the strange dichotomy that lurked just out of sight and below the surface of their world.

We arrived at the rear of the trading post to find Joseph putting logs into the fire pit as the desert evening chill began creeping in. Zach was seated, and the chairs were arranged around the familiar circular pit. Soon, the flames began to crackle, and the sweet aroma of burning pine sap began filling the air. We all took our seats, enjoying the warmth that the fire was starting to provide, the setting sun, and the quiet of the evening, broken only by the snapping and popping of the burning resin-filled wood.

"So, you guys get a chance to absorb today's

history lesson?" Zach asked lightheartedly.

"As much as humanly possible, I guess," I replied. "That was one hell of a lesson."

"I know," Zach replied almost apologetically, "but we don't have a lot of time, and you really need a context to help figure out how we proceed from here."

"You're right," Doc replied, "As you noted, we have a million questions, but I guess they'll have to wait while we focus on the problem at hand."

"Exactly," Zach said, "but as we go along, I'll do my best to fill you in on many of the details you have questions about. A number of them, I'm sure, will be pertinent to our task."

"Thanks," Doc replied. "That will be helpful. Before we jump into things, I do have a question. You said Kincaid only explored a small portion of the underground network you created. In the newspaper article, he indicated that he had explored quite a bit."

"True, but he did exaggerate quite a bit. The part of the cavern system he discovered is the shallower section of the living area we helped create for the indigenous people. It was located a few hundred feet underground, and we tied it into some of the natural caves that were already present, making it large enough to house their entire population.

"The system we created started some sixty thousand years earlier and runs much deeper. For instance, the level of my lab is five miles deep, and it is located in the shallower region of the system. The more extensive parts start around 40 miles deep and continue downward."

"Deeper?" Doc exclaimed.

"The city begins around 200 miles deep and spreads out from there," Zach said.

"A city, 200 miles deep...?" Doc exclaimed again, incredulously.

Zach seemed to be enjoying the look of disbelief on Doc's face.

"Yes, we had a large number of subterranean dwellers on my planet, so a major part of our civilization exists underground," Zach stated.

"People are still living there?" Doc questioned.

"Thousands," Zach answered. "But we can talk more about that at a later date." Changing the subject, he then asked O'Reilly, "Were you able to contact Matt?"

"Yes, I called him and filled him in on our plan, and he said we could start the surveillance flights tomorrow, assuring me that he had just the bird for the job. I guess he doesn't want to use his shiny tour chopper, which is understandable," O'Reilly answered. "It would be easily recognizable."

"That was a big hangar," I added. "You said he had a Huey as well as the Bell?"

"That's what we saw," O'Reilly said, "but the full hangar doors weren't open all the way, so he must have had another bird in there."

"That could be to our benefit. If an unfamiliar helicopter is seen surveilling our 'friends,' that will add another level of the unknown to the mix. That should get them wondering and divert some of their attention away from their drilling," I replied.

"I've been thinking," O'Reilly said. "If we are in the mode of distraction for the moment to buy us more time to come up with a plan and maybe slow their progress due to increased scrutiny, what about throwing a good old-fashioned legal monkey wrench into the works?"

Doc chimed in, "Zach, do you think the people of Fremont would be willing to be named as plaintiffs in a legal action against that company? We could come up with environmental concerns or violating sacred land or something like that," Doc added excitedly. I could see things were falling into place, and I liked the direction they were headed. The team was brilliantly suggesting the germ of an idea for a permanent solution, but it would take some time to bring it to fruition, so slowing down the bad guys was just what this operation needed.

Now, Zach seemed to be picking up on the growing vibe. "Yes, I'm sure they would be willing to sign on for this. There has never been any love lost between the locals and that company. Plus, I've always thought some underhanded dealings took place to get the permissions necessary to build the facility in the first place on the reservation."

Doc turned to me questioningly, "Get Lawrence on the line?"

"With the time difference between here and Florida, we'll probably wake him up, but I want him on this right away. We'll need him out here ASAP." I added, "Do it."

I turned to Zach and said, "Lawrence is our team's resident legal eagle."

"Wine expert and ladies' man," Dimitri added, laughing.

"True," I acknowledged, "But he is a damn good lawyer, very well connected in the legal world, and he slings a mean legal monkey wrench, when necessary," I added, grinning.

Time had flown by as this discussion unfolded. It was 10:30 p.m. and had been a long day for all of us. The adrenaline would only keep us going for so long, and I knew, for my budding idea to work, I was going to need everyone on their A-game. I then chuckled to myself. What was I thinking? My team always brought their A-game to any challenge they faced, without fail. That's the way we roll.

A plan was coming together, but this was the easy part. I knew that. The hard part was yet to come, but I could see the potential for success growing, and that gave me pleasure. I would share my final idea with the team later; for now, "The game is afoot," as I like to say—a good place to end for tonight.

CHAPTER 26

The next day brought with it a flurry of activity. Lawrence had been contacted and was *en route* to Arizona. O'Reilly had headed out early with Joe to Lone Wolf Aero to meet up with Matt and start the aerial surveillance. Zach had scheduled a town meeting with the elders to inform them of the litigation plan. Dimitri and Reggie were reviewing our gear, ensuring we were prepared for any contingency or possible confrontation.

Doc and I were comparing notes on potential next steps. I told him I had a visit/dream from Jeannie last night. He cracked up laughing, as I sat there with a puzzled look on my face. He finally said, "Think about your comment; it just struck me as humorous."

I still didn't get it and said so. He chuckled, "Your communication last night, your dream... *I Dream of Jeannie*."

His obvious reference to the TV show of the same name finally hit me. I laughed and said, "Okay, I get it now, but I did have a communication, a dream, or something. She told me that she had informed Zach of all our activities and interactions with her and the Citadel that took place while we were in Ecuador.

"She said we all needed to be on the same page, so

to speak, moving forward."

"I'll go along with that; that's a good thing," Doc admitted seriously.

"I agree. Hopefully, it will make the flow of information moving forward easier and more efficient," I said.

"So, what next?" Doc asked.

"We get Lawrence up to speed when he gets here and then send him off to Phoenix to get the legal ball rolling. As soon as he gets the tribe's information from Zach and they formulate a legitimate-sounding complaint, we'll start the wheels of justice turning and see where it takes us," I responded.

"Surveillance and the courts, shaking the tree from two sides, I like it," Doc added. "That should certainly elicit a response from a group that is trying to keep a low profile on their activities out here."

"That's my hope," I added, "and that it will buy us enough time to put the third phase of my plan in place."

"And that would be…?" Doc asked.

"We can't drive these guys out with force without showing our hand. They would dig in and realize that something is being kept from them. They have the money and resources to be in this for the long haul, and people could get hurt. We have to motivate them to leave of their own volition."

"Well, they won't do that until they get what they're looking for," Doc said.

"Exactly," I responded. "So, we give it to them and convince them there's nothing more of value to them here."

Now, it was Doc's turn to look confused, "Are you crazy? Give them the power supply?"

I smiled, "Not at all, but we do give them a nice, fresh 'red herring.' I'll give the full explanation when we get everyone together. The lynchpin for this thing to work is going to depend on Zach and his technology. If it can't do what I need, then we're back to square one. We'll know one way or the other by tonight. But right now, let's make sure the other pieces are falling into place."

A little later, Zach met us at the trading post, where Lawrence, who had recently arrived, was at work on his laptop. He had spent a lot of time on the satellite phone and was entering data into his computer. There hadn't been much time for pleasantries; we had put him to work immediately upon his arrival. We were sitting at the table opposite him when he finally came up for air and said, "Hey guys, good to see you," as if just now noticing our presence.

"Lawrence," I responded, "Glad you could get here on such short notice."

"Hey, when the Boss calls, we answer," he replied, smiling—knowing I hated being called the Boss—a little good-humored jab that the whole team uses on occasion. "Things in Florida are moving along. I turned the legal wrangling we've been going through with the state over our last find at the Amelia Island site over to the law firm in Atlanta, which we used before. They are top-notch marine litigators and more than willing to jump in and keep things under control in my absence."

"Excellent," I replied.

"Well, Colt, I'm just waiting for some details from this Zach fellow and the plaintiffs in the case. I already have a colleague in Phoenix standing by to assist me with everything here in Arizona, including the Bureau of Land Management, the Bureau of Indian Affairs, the EPA, and the state attorney's office. I'm just waiting for the info and the 'Go' signal from you to kick this baby into gear."

"That's what I like to hear," I replied.

As if on cue, Zach entered the trading post and pulled up a chair. He had three sheets of paper and passed them to Lawrence. "Here you go, barrister. The town council of elders' formal complaint regarding this part of the Navajo Nation is presented in terms that the BIA, BLM, and EPA can understand. It includes the destruction of a Sacred Navajo religious site, the destruction of environmentally sensitive land, and the habitat for protected species. It raises questions about the legitimacy of leasing the land without the full approval of the tribe. Included is the list of all official signatories involved."

Lawrence had been reading the document and typing furiously on his computer as Zach spoke. By the time Zach was finished, Lawrence looked up from his keyboard and said, "Ready when you are, Boss," holding his finger over the Enter key.

"Do it," I replied, and the click of the Enter key filled the room. Lawrence immediately picked up the SAT phone and hit a speed dial number. Five seconds later, a voice answered, and Lawrence intoned, "Chet, it's coming your way. I'll be leaving here in a couple of hours and call you as soon as I get to Phoenix." A few words from the person on the line, and Lawrence responded, "Good, if you have any questions, you have my number; otherwise, I'll talk to you in the office when I get there."

Lawrence rocked back in his chair a bit, took a drink from the water bottle sitting on the table, and said, smiling from ear to ear, "Gentlemen, the wheels of justice are now turning."

Zach looked at me and said, "Did you happen to get a communication last night?"

"I did," I replied, "You?"

"Yep, she contacted me and filled me in on everything that went down in Ecuador. You were certainly busy down there," he responded, chuckling.

"That is an understatement," I replied, smiling.

"Well, I got filled in on all the details, so that's going to make it easier for us to work together," Zach said.

"I believe that was the whole reason for her contacting both of us," I said.

"Agree," Zach said, "What's next?"

O'Reilly and Joe pulled up to Matt's trailer, got out, and walked to the helo pad. Sitting there was not the shiny new tour bird or the vintage UH-1 Huey they had seen before, but a smaller OH-6 known as a LOACH or Little Bird. Its small size made it the perfect craft for doing recon. They had been used extensively in Vietnam and continued to be a favorite today for specialized jobs. It had a crew of two, could carry two passengers, and if necessary, it could be armed with a variety of deadly weaponry. Sam was doing a pre-flight walk-around, and Matt was talking with her as they approached.

"Damn, Matt, where did you get this little sweetheart?" O'Reilly said when they got to the helicopter.

Matt smiled and said, "My hangar is like a magician's top hat; you reach inside, and no telling what you can pull out." They had already removed the doors, and Sam was pulling off the "Remove before flight" streamers as Matt climbed aboard, followed by O'Reilly and Joe. Once everyone was strapped in and had their headsets on, Matt said, good-naturedly, "Let's go stir up some trouble," as the helo's turbine came to life. After a quick warm-up and a thumbs-up from Sam, the helicopter lifted off and headed toward the solar energy research facility. Joe had a video camera, and O'Reilly had a digital camera. They were going to conduct some real reconnaissance on these flights, as well as draw attention to themselves and ensure they were noticed.

O'Reilly keyed her mic for the intercom and said, "Matt, I need to let Colt know we're on our way."

"Roger that," Matt replied as he reached out and flipped a switch on the control panel and nodded to O'Reilly.

She keyed her mic again and said, "Colt, you copy?"

Seconds later, my voice came over her headset, "Good copy, O'Reilly."

She replied, "Good copy here, we're on our way."

"Copy, stay frosty," came my reply.

"Roger that, Little Bird out," she replied.

I set the radio back on the table and said to the group, "All right, folks, let the games begin. Zach, can you monitor their radio traffic from here?"

"Sure can, let's adjourn to the back room." Joseph had joined them, and Zach asked him to take care of the shop, as everyone, including Lawrence, went through the door into the private area in the back of the trading post. Zach went to a wall, extended his hand, and a section of the wall opened up, revealing a console much like the ones we had seen in his underground work area the day before. "Once they start transmitting or receiving, we'll be able to monitor it from here," he explained.

"Pretty slick," Dimitri commented, "You can work from home whenever you want."

"Within certain limits, I can," Zach responded, laughing.

"I guess we'll soon find out if this second part of my plan is going to work," I said.

"So, we have a plan now, Colt?" Zach asked.

"I believe we do, but the next part is going to be the most critical. It's a make-or-break scenario, and I'm afraid the success is going to be up to you and your technology, Zach," I stated. We heard the radio transmission loud and clear as it broke into our conversation, just as I was about to continue. It was in Chinese, and Zach said, "They've spotted the chopper and are wondering what it's doing." Zach did something at the console, and the rest of the transmission was in English.

"Let's see what they have to say, and I'll fill you in on the rest of the plan tonight," I said. The voice from the research center was a combination of interest and concern, wondering what the helicopter was doing, circling and hovering. One of the guards observed that the people in the helicopter seemed to be taking photographs. The control center ordered them to do nothing but observe for now. They asked if there were any identifiable markings on the helicopter. The report back said there were none.

I smiled. Now, we had their attention. Five minutes later, the guard reported that the helicopter was leaving. He and the other guards were instructed to remain vigilant for any additional suspicious air or ground activity. Then communications ceased.

Zach, looking at the group, said, "Well, it looks like that part of your plan is working. They now know they're being watched."

"Exactly what I wanted," I replied as I keyed the radio, "That's enough for today, O'Reilly, nice job. We just poked the hornets' nest."

"Copy, headed back to base."

"Lawrence, how long will it take before these guys find out they're being sued?" I asked.

"Depending on how hard I push, probably two to three days," Lawrence replied.

"Okay, why don't you take your time? I want us to have more flyover time and really get these guys worked up," I said. "Plus, I don't want them to draw a connection between the surveillance and the lawsuit immediately. They will probably do that at some point, but let's not make it too obvious."

"How about two weeks?" he said.

"Two weeks will be perfect," I answered.

"You got it, Boss. I'll head to Phoenix as soon as I get something to eat. I'm starving," Lawrence said, his stomach growling.

"I'll have Joseph take you to our diner here in town," Zach said.

"Great," he said, and with that, Lawrence packed up his laptop, grabbed his SAT phone, Zach closed the wall concealing his equipment, and he and Lawrence headed to the storefront section of the trading post.

Now, if Zach can pull off the third part of the plan, this just might work, I thought. I guess we'll find out the answer tonight around the fire.

CHAPTER 27

The wheels were turning, and I liked that; time was of the essence, so I needed things to flow smoothly, which I remembered rarely happened. But "hope springs eternal," I thought with a chuckle. The rest of the day was filled with a flurry of tasks being performed. I pulled Zach aside a little later and said, "I've got an equipment request I hope you can handle for me."

"Shoot," replied Zach.

"I need two four-wheelers for some desert surveying and surveillance. They need to be fast with desert camouflage paint jobs with long rifle scabbards attached, and I need them like yesterday," I said.

Zach laughed and said, "You don't ask for much," as he pulled out his cell phone and placed a call. It was late morning, and after a short conversation, he turned to me and said, "Tonight, right after dark. I'm guessing you don't want them to be seen being delivered here, so I'll send my box truck out to the main highway, load them up, and bring them behind the post. The truck comes and goes regularly, so it shouldn't draw any undue attention from our bad guys."

"Absolutely correct," I replied. "I think I'll have Dimitri and Reggie do a little additional ground surveillance. When they're spotted, that should really apply some additional pressure, especially if they're having to guess who is doing the surveilling."

"Pretty devious, Colt, sure takes the attention away from me."

"That's part of the plan; I've got a major task I'm going to need you to handle if we're going to make this thing work. I'll explain it tonight when we're all present. I'm going to need everyone's input to make sure I'm not missing anything."

"Lawrence said he will be hitting the road as soon as he's done eating, and I have a couple of things that need attending to, so I'll catch up with you guys tonight," Zach said.

The rest of us headed to the diner to see Lawrence on his way and grab some food as well. While we sat in the restaurant with Lawrence, I leaned over to Dimitri and Reggie and said, "You heard what I mentioned to Zach. You two up for some desert recon?"

"Hell, yeah," they both said in unison.

"Good, I'm going to need both day and night recon, so I want this to be somewhat visible but anonymous. So, camo, headgear, night vision, and face coverings. Dimitri, gear?"

"Everything and more," Dimitri replied. "And you said scabbards on the ATVs, so I'm guessing we go in armed?"

"Defensive only, but yeah, to the teeth," I replied.

Reggie and Dimitri looked at each other, grinning from ear to ear. They were like a couple of kids who just found out they were getting ponies for Christmas!

"Balaclavas and silenced weapons?" Dimitri asked.

"Absolutely, no one is to know our identities or who we work for," I told them. "Let's stir them up and let their alphabet imagination run wild." I added, "their choice, CIA, NSA, FBI, SOC, and anybody else they can think of. They'll have plenty to choose from, and that's just from the U.S. They won't know if other international agencies know about this and might be involved."

Lawrence had gotten up and was leaving, his parting comment being, "You guys should have fun with this one. You have a very devious mind, Dr. Burnett, very devious," a pause, and then he added, laughing, "and that's one of your finer qualities."

He left to peals of laughter, heading out to implement his part of the plan.

"I think that deserves a beer," I said, and a couple of rounds put a cap on the daytime activities and set the stage for what was to come later that night.

The team had gathered around the fire as had become the norm over the last week or so. There was an air of expectancy that permeated the evening. All were waiting for my big reveal of the final piece of my plan. The evening chill was setting in as the warmth and resinous aroma of the fire filled the air around them.

Zach broke the silence once everyone was situated. "Okay, Colt, let's have it. I'm anxious to hear what I'm in for with this master plan of yours."

I laughed, "Let me start by saying this is a work

in progress, so if anyone has suggestions or questions, don't hesitate to throw them out. We all need to be on board with the final piece of this plan for it to work. Agreed?"

All agreed, and I launched into the step-by-step explanation of my idea.

"Our goal is to help Zach protect his anonymity and that of his power supply and keep it out of the hands of these bad guys. Most importantly, we need to do that without drawing any additional attention to this area or the fact that there was outside intervention working against them, other than what we want them to worry about. Any overt confrontation would only serve to increase their resolve and interest in what might be hidden here. It could possibly motivate them to look much deeper into this mysterious energy reading from 1971.

"As I see it, the only way to get them out of here is to have them lose interest in this site, and the only way I can think of making that happen is to have them find what they are looking for and end their search."

"What?" Zach exclaimed.

"Hang on, let me explain. If they found what they thought was providing the energy reading and were able to remove it and take it with them, and then, finding no other indications of the energy in the area and believing that a reasonable single source could be removed, they would have no reason to continue their operation here," I explained.

"Okay, I'm confused," Zach said. I could see varying levels of confusion on the team's faces in the flickering firelight.

"This is the hard part, Zach, and you and your technology are vital to our success," I said. "Two critical things," I continued. "Zach, can you tell how accurate their information is on the location of the energy reading from '71, and how far they have gotten with their drilling?"

Zach, still looking puzzled, responded slowly. "The data they have is not terribly definitive except that the signal came from underground. So, they only have a general idea of a starting point, but since I readjusted the force field and the signal was lost years ago, they don't have anything new or specific to go on. Essentially, it's a guess by their lead physicist regarding the location, based on the 1971 data. As for their drilling, they are currently down approximately a hundred feet or so. They stop at regular intervals to take readings, but of course, they get nothing," Zach answered.

I smiled and said, "Then let's give them something."

Doc, who Colt had given a little more information on his plan earlier, said, "So, here's where the red herring comes in. Now, I get it," he said, smiling broadly.

"Exactly," I said. "Zach, you don't happen to have access to a nickel, iron meteorite, oh, about the size of a refrigerator, do you?"

Everyone sat there, trying to piece together what they had just heard. Then, one by one, you could see the idea behind the plan starting to make sense to them, including Zach. Now, Zach was the one grinning as he said, "A red herring, I get it!"

"But this is the hard part, the part that depends on you, Zach. You'll need to find a meteorite, somehow energize it with the same energy the force field emits, and then create a suitable ancient crash site, plant the red herring, and arrange for them to start picking up the signal again. Hopefully, their sensors are directional, so when we release some energy away from where they are drilling, it will draw them to the meteorite we've planted in the desert. We let them discover it, remove it, and when they continue to search, which we know they will, they will find no other energy readings in the area," I explained.

"Then, thinking they have found the sole source of the energy, they'll load it up and leave," Zach said.

"Bingo," I said. "But timing, discovery, and retrieval all have to be made believable for this to work. We must ensure they believe this is a one-time discovery. They will thoroughly search the area for any other meteorites, but the odds of there being more, in reality, would be slim, and we'll make sure there aren't any. Then, with luck and enough external pressure from our lawsuit, along with the pressure of outside surveillance and the discovery, hopefully, this will be enough to satisfy them and motivate them to get the hell out of Dodge before their whole endeavor comes under scrutiny from the media and becomes a high-profile nightmare. It could easily escalate into an unwanted international incident if the true nature of their company were revealed and if they think other government agencies are becoming interested in their operation."

"Now, that is one hell of a plan, Colt," Zach said. "But implementing it is going to be a monumental task."

I sat there smiling and said, "As my granddad always used to say, 'Ain't no mountain for a climber,'" to the groans of my teammates.

A little later, Joseph returned with the truck and the two ATVs. All of my requirements had been met. They were new, racing versions, and had leather long-rifle scabbards attached in locations that would provide the rider with easy access to the weapons; the camo paint job was excellent. They were unloaded, and I informed Dimitri and Reggie that I wanted them to begin daytime surveillance in the morning using camo desert fatigues and face coverings. I quickly outlined the area they were to cover, the route to follow, and the duration they should spend there. They confirmed the instructions and said they would be ready to start at daybreak.

Well, there it is, I thought, the plan is in motion, and the "operators" are in place. Now it's up to Zach and me to physically put the final pieces together and hope the logic I applied to solving the problem worked. Only time would tell....

CHAPTER 28

The following week saw everyone putting their assignments into motion. Daytime flights by Matt, O'Reilly, and Joe were going smoothly, following a varied flight schedule. Not setting up a routine kept the guards on their toes, as they never knew when the helicopter would appear.

Demitri and Reggie were doing their desert runs, keeping at a distance, being stealthy, but not so much that they weren't spotted, while giving the impression of not wanting to be seen. Lawrence was getting ready to make his big push next week. He had all the legal pieces in place and was ready to go.

Zach, Doc, and I had been visiting a new section of the underground facility. There was no need for additional tourist bus subterfuge, so the three of us would portal from Zach's back room straight to this new work area. It was just as impressive and amazing as everything else in this underground complex. Zach's resources did not disappoint; the room was huge, and our first visit found us staring at a large meteorite floating about four feet off the ground in the middle of the room.

Close to it were a couple of consoles, and a bluish glow engulfed the space rock. The two questions that immediately came to mind were, where did he get the meteorite, and how was it floating in the middle of the room?

Doc and I stared, and I turned to look at Zach, slowly shaking my head and said, "I'm not even going to ask."

He laughed and said, "I understand, Colt; not to worry, all things will be explained in due course. What's happening now is I'm slowly charging the meteorite with the energy field we want the Chinese to detect."

"No worries about it being detected during the process?" Doc asked.

"None, we're too deep for it to be detected for one thing, and as an added precaution, this area is completely shielded," Zach replied confidently. "Think of this process as a trickle charge on a battery. Once completed, the meteorite will emanate an energy signature that will perfectly match the one that was picked up in '71."

"Nice," I muttered, "I said I wasn't going to, but I do have to ask, how is it floating in mid-air? It must weigh a couple of tons."

"It does, but this is just one of many of our technologies you haven't seen yet. Levitating objects is child's play in our world. Everything in the universe vibrates, each with its own specific frequency. All you have to do is identify the frequency and then control or adjust it. You then have the ability to make the object do whatever you want. How do you think many of those huge megalithic structures from ancient history were constructed?

"I really get a real kick out of some of your so-called experts' explanations of those events. Logs, rollers, sledges, ropes, and thousands of men. Those are the scientists afraid to embrace other possibilities. Yes, we did provide assistance around the world in the distant past to a variety of your cultures as their civilizations grew and began to advance," Zach stated. "Now, I'm not saying we were responsible for all of them. Your ancient civilizations did have some brilliant engineering minds whose devices were created and used effectively over time. However, most of the truly massive or intricate structures of the ancient world, we did have a hand in, whether by building or guiding those who did.

"As your civilizations advanced, we were able to step away and let them progress on their own, with just an occasional nudge now and then," he said.

"And some of your fringe scientists or out-of-the-box thinkers are much closer to the reality of things than your so-called educated experts," Zach continued.

As we watched the meteorite continue to "trickle charge," he continued. "Your historical estimate of the age of some things is way off base, for example, the Giza pyramids and Sphinx are around sixty thousand years old. What the Egyptians did was repair a significant amount of the damage caused by the massive solar event. The Middle East got hit with the brunt of a very large plasma blast. Before that, the area was forested savannahs, rivers, and lakes. It also had multiple advanced civilizations thriving there. In a matter of hours, it was turned to ash. Rivers and lakes were vaporized, and a desert wasteland was created. Many of the civilizations had heeded our warnings and built underground refuges. For the most part, they survived and returned to the surface. Your archaeologists have found evidence of a number of them, but there are many more still out there, much deeper underground and very advanced."

During this history lesson, the radio transmissions from the bad guys at the solar facility could be heard in the background. The transmissions were in English, thanks to Zach's tech. The guards reported that the helicopter had returned and was checking specific parts of their compound. Once again, they were told not to engage with them but to photograph the helicopter, as it was imperative that they identify who was observing them. Matt and the crew spent the same amount of time as before, circling the compound and then bugged out—enjoying every moment of their flight.

"Real-time transmissions?" I asked Zach.

"Yep, and it sounds like those guys are getting a little concerned," Zach said.

"Just what I wanted," I replied. "Now, wait until Dimitri and Reggie do their land recon later this afternoon. That should put a bit of a spike in the tension meter at the command center," I said.

Doc said, "Sounds like your plan is having its desired effect, Colt."

"Now, we just keep turning up the heat and hope it continues to have a greater impact on these guys," I answered.

"This energy charging process is going to take

another day or so to make the signature convincing, so let's head back to the post. We really can't do anything more here," Zach said as he opened a portal to his back room at the trading post.

"A very convenient way to travel," Doc commented as he stepped through.

It was, indeed, I thought as we settled in at the table and Zach retrieved some chilled apple cider from the fridge.

"This doesn't happen to be from Matt's apple tree?" Doc asked.

"Actually, it is. He has a year-round harvest of apples that he shares with us, and we make the cider the traditional Navajo way, keeping him stocked with fresh cider as well. It comes out pretty good and is a nice, refreshing drink on a hot Arizona day," Zach answered.

"Agree," I replied.

Zach opened the door to the front of the store, and we found Reggie and Dimitri talking casually with Joseph, seated around the table. "Hey, Boss," Dimitri quipped. "Have a successful venture?" He knew we had been heading into the underground to check on the meteorite.

"As a matter of fact, we did," I replied. "And you guys?" I asked.

Dimitri looked at his watch and said, "Just killing a little time getting caught up on local history with Joseph here, until it's our turn to go out and shake the tree a bit."

I had decided we would space our surveillance

sorties between the air and land by around five hours. Dimitri and Reggie would take the ATVs on a route that Zach had laid out, which would keep them out of the town's surveillance zone by the bad guys and bring them in along the foothills east and south of the energy facility, covering their real starting point. Ingress from the east and egress in the same direction. This would not give away their actual starting point. With several possibilities in that direction, it would throw the surveillance team at the energy center way off on their point of origin.

Dimitri and Reggie would be out there for a couple of hours, pretending to stay hidden during their shift, but making sure they were noticed. All our radio communications were totally invisible to the bad guys, thanks to Zach's tech, except for one channel that had a low level of encryption that could purposely be easily broken into by their command center. This allowed us to feed them whatever bits of information we wanted them to have or hear—another piece of the plan to help make this whole operation more believable, I thought.

Picking up on an opportunity to learn more history, Doc said to Zach, "Since we have some time, would you mind answering a few questions I have regarding your whole migration to this planet?"

"Sure," Zach said, "Let's head to the back room where we can talk freely. Out here in the store is a little too open for those kinds of discussions."

Doc, Zach, and I went to the back room as Dimitri and Reggie headed out for their surveillance shift. Closing the door behind us and refilling our glasses with more cold cider, we took seats and got comfortable. Taking a sip of my drink, my eyes opened wide as I immediately said, "Whoa, this isn't what we had before."

Zach laughed and said, "Nope, I figured this discussion was going to require some of our special reserve hard cider."

"It has a bit of a kick to it, but it's still very tasty," I replied.

"That's the way we like it," Zach replied. "Now, Doc, you said you had some questions."

"I do, actually, tons of them; it's kind of hard to know where to start. So let me begin with, how did you make your ship look like a celestial body, the moon?"

A very matter-of-fact discussion ensued. "We have a process that we call planet reformation, kind of like what you call terraforming. We have a lot of options within our process, from comprehensive planetary reformation to targeted, smaller-scale operations. The planetary reformation is what we used to create the moon.

"Our process gathers particulate matter from space, and then we recreate it and apply it in layers to a planet or other formation we are working on. We actually used a lot of your original, smaller moon we destroyed to get started on covering our ship. It took about a year to create the first layer of the moon's surface. It was about five hundred feet thick. After that, we just kept adding layers until we reached the required thickness or depth that we wanted, which was five miles. Once we got there, we began directing small space objects into a controlled collision with the surface, creating many of the craters that you see. All the mountainous terrain on the surface and the really big craters are what we created."

Doc sat there with a "deer in the headlights" look on his face. I'm sure I had a similar expression. "We knew we wanted to have a robust protective skin and one that had enough mass to make the gravitational changes we needed on Earth. And yes, we do have access ports in some of the craters that allow us to fly our ships in and out, mostly on the dark side for obvious reasons."

"Next question?" Zach asked, smiling.

There was a lengthy pause as that information was digested. Then Doc simply said, "Amazing."

To which Zach replied, "Nope, just science."

Doc continued, "You said you transported around 250,000 individuals and spread them out around the planet."

"Yes, we had over 100 sentient species inhabiting our planet, but on our ship, we only carried a dozen. The rest were spread out amongst the other vessels. As I stated, our planet and yours were very similar in habitat and terrain, so we helped each group decide which location on Earth best matched their home area on our planet."

"A hundred sentient species?" Doc asked in amazement.

"I'm sure that's a little hard to comprehend since you think you pretty much have evolved as the unique intelligent species here on Earth and also become very ethnocentric." Doc took a long, pensive pause to digest what he was learning before continuing with his questioning....

CHAPTER 29

"Fascinating, and that's true," Doc pressed on, "but if you brought others with you, why haven't we found out about them?"

"Oh, you have," Zach replied. "As I said earlier, when we got here, we pretty much took an isolationist approach for tens of thousands of years. As *Homo Sapiens* became the dominant species, a number of our cultures established themselves in their own niche and, in many cases, flourished.

"It was inevitable that our groups would one day cross paths, and that's just what happened. As your numerous cultures evolved and progressed, many of us became known to you. Let me add this qualifier. The different physical characteristics of our planet's sentient inhabitants resulted in a wide variety of reactions from early Earthlings. Over many thousands of years, a large number of us had begun a slow assimilation into your cultures. Those of us who most closely resembled your physical appearance, that is.

"Those who looked vastly different were not able to do that. Many of them became the basis for your myths and legends, and in some cases, misplaced fear."

"What do you mean?" Doc asked.

"For instance, the Stynth, who were usually around 12 to 13 feet tall. On our planet, they were master builders, stonemasons, and miners. Here, they were considered by some to be monstrous giants merely because of their size and physical appearance and became feared."

"They were spread out over your world, and some co-existed peacefully with the local cultures. They utilized their skills and size to help construct many of the enormous buildings and temples that remain standing today. Others were hunted and killed. It became apparent to us that your mental development had not advanced enough to try to understand things that were different than you, even though they were sentient races. Fear became the driving force behind their lack of acceptance.

"As a result, we helped relocate our populations that were in danger, and many went into seclusion. There were some whose natural ability in self-preservation consisted of being able to camouflage themselves to the extent that you could walk right past them and never detect their presence. Others even developed a form of invisibility as a defense.

"The Illium were one such group. You call them the wee people, elves, leprechauns, and a dozen other names in other cultures."

Doc interrupted, "You mean the stories and legends about them around the world are fact?"

"They are," Zach answered, "and they are thriving to this day."

"Absolutely amazing!" Doc exclaimed, slightly

wide-eyed.

Zach laughed out loud and said, "If you like that, you're going to love the Zigarand."

"Zigarand?" Doc repeated.

Still laughing, Zach said, "More commonly referred to nowadays as Bigfoot."

"What...!" Doc exclaimed again in total disbelief.

"Yep, they can survive in a variety of extreme conditions and can be found in numerous regions on this planet. They are masters of camouflage, almost to the point of invisibility, and mainly a solitary species, peaceful, and quite happy to exist outside of today's world. That's why you never really see them. They have no desire for human contact and are content to live a secluded life wherever they are located."

"So, our legends are based on reality?" Doc asked.

"Well, not all of them," Zach replied, "As your various populations developed, so did your imagination. Many took grains of truth and turned some of them into epic tales. Going back to what I said earlier, we were only able to bring a small portion of the sentient races with us. However, there were other smaller groups with interstellar capabilities that came to Earth after we had settled here, adding additional species to the population, and not all were humanoid. That circumstance provided more fodder for your stories and legends."

"The stories and legends we have of gods and super beings, are they based on the races from your planet?" Doc asked.

"Yes, the large portion is. There is often a significant amount of fabrication on the part of the storyteller or chronicler, but much of it is fact. I need to qualify that a bit, since our world, for the most part, was a peaceful world, and we had reached a level of peaceful coexistence on our planet with no major conflicts or wars. Yes, we had our differences, but we found ways to resolve them without resorting to hostilities. It was not a utopia by any stretch of the imagination, but for the most part, we had a peaceful environment worldwide."

"That sounds amazing," I said, "something we continually strive for here but never seem to be able to achieve in any global sense."

"Another reason we have kept to ourselves," Zach added. "I will tell you, there are many enclaves where our technology is stored and used. Not all of our people have the benefit of our rejuvenation technology, so while they do have a longer lifespan than most inhabitants of this planet, they still age and die. Our history is passed down through a shared consciousness, so there are those out there who remember our beginnings. As such, we have worked over the millennia to establish ourselves in the spheres of power and influence worldwide. Not in any conquest or takeover sense, but in a more advisory and push-in-the-right-direction manner, striving for peaceful coexistence. Unfortunately, that is a concept your world doesn't seem to be ready for in any meaningful way," Zach said with a sadness in his voice.

Silence filled the room as the truth of his comments hit home.

"We keep striving for such an environment, but so

far it continues to elude us," I said.

"That is exactly why we do what we do. My network is worldwide and quite powerful, and we have not yet given up hope for this planet. We continue to work behind the scenes as much as possible to help your people achieve their goal of non-aggression someday. Until then, we will continue to protect this planet and use our influence and technology to achieve that global environment," Zach answered, now sounding more hopeful.

"Our history and legends have recorded some pretty bad stuff that some people or beings have done over the millennia," Doc added.

"Oh, don't get me wrong; we have had our share of, let's call them 'bad actors,' who were weak, and this feeling of superiority and power that your world provided them with led to perverse activities. This allowed some to be elevated to god-like status, and they have caused much harm. Meanwhile, others of our world intervened to mitigate their damage or negative impact on the population or planet. In some ways, their actions were subtle, while in others, they were drastic. Your legends speak of warring gods, Greek, Norse, Hindu, and Christian, among many others. Their battles on land or in the air, in flying machines or, more cryptically, as angels or celestial beings vying for domination, were halted by others from our civilization, who sought to maintain a positive equilibrium in the world's development. This required us to be ever vigilant and is an ongoing task to this day," Zach said.

"How is that even possible?" Doc asked.

"You are getting into an area that would take weeks to discuss and understand. For now, suffice it to say that not all natural disasters are natural, and not all accidents that impact the world are truly accidents. Individual countries experience technological incidents that we execute as setbacks to control the advancement of destructive technologies. In addition, we have provided scientific breakthroughs designed to benefit humanity and propel it forward. Once again, working to create sustainable worldwide peace."

"Good luck with that, Zach. I'm not too optimistic for our immediate future," I replied. "It's a goal we all hope for, but it's seemingly unattainable at this time."

"That may be true, Colt, but we've been working on it for millennia and will continue to use our resources to do so. There's another thing I suppose it's time to make you aware of," Zach stated.

"What's that?" I asked.

"Our advanced mental abilities and our use of telepathy," Zach responded without speaking.

Doc's head snapped up, looking first at Zach and then at me as I stared at Zach intently.

"You have telepathic capabilities?" I asked in amazement.

"Yes, among other things," Zach replied, not speaking as the jug holding the apple cider lifted off the table.

Zach was smiling now, and this time he spoke, "I didn't think it was time to reveal that to you yet, Colt, but in Jeannie's communication the other night, she said you needed to know this since you have the genetic markers giving you similar capabilities to mine. Not all have them to the extent that you do. Your abilities have been lying dormant until your contact with us."

The jug of juice slowly sat back down on the table to both my and Doc's amazement.

I am rarely left speechless, but now I was having a hard time finding the words to express my total shock at this revelation.

"This is rarely revealed to anyone. But Jeannie felt it was necessary since you have now become part of our inner circle. You have a very interesting education ahead of you, Colt, one Jeannie and I think you are ready to explore. We hope we have made the correct decision," Zach spoke out loud.

I had prided myself on being able to adapt to any situation, even the out-of-this-world ones of the last couple of years… but this, this just took it to a whole new level.

CHAPTER 30

Reggie and Dimitri had made their way to a line of large boulders that were in clear sight of the energy complex about two hundred yards away. They had parked the ATVs out of sight and taken positions that provided them with a clear view of the site. While feigning stealth, they were sure they had been spotted and were taking photographs of the area.

Dimitri keyed his radio, "Colt, you copy?" Using Zach's secure communication network, he was not concerned about using names in his transmissions.

"Good copy," came my reply.

"We're in position and pretty sure we were spotted."

"Roger that, we're monitoring the radio communication, and the guards have reported spotting you. There is some discussion as to how to proceed next, so stay put and alert."

"Roger that," Dimitri replied as he said, "Well," to Reggie, who was focused on the scope of her rifle.

"I can see at least two guys observing us through gun sights and another with binoculars. We do need to keep our heads down just in case one of those yahoos gets trigger-happy and happens to be a good shot."

"Not a problem," Dimitri replied, lying flat from his ground-level position. "I've got the guy in the guard tower in my sights. Anybody gets trigger-happy, and it's lights out for him first, and number two shooter right after."

"Oh, so you just leave me with the observer; that's not fair," Reggie replied playfully.

"Hey, if they decide to start a firefight, I'm guessing there'll be plenty of armed targets for both of us. Just remember, that's not why we're here. We're to be seen only and not engage," Dimitri surprisingly said.

"I know. I remember what Colt's orders were, but if somebody takes a pot shot at me, I'm not letting them get away with it," Reggie said firmly.

"You will if that's what Colt says," Dimitri replied in his "that's an order" voice.

"Okay, okay, I got it. I just don't like being one of those ducks in the carnival shooting booths. Just moving around, waiting to get shot at."

"Then keep your head down and eyes open. We just hang out here for a couple of hours and then head back to the hooch," Dimitri said, trying to console his petulant partner. She's always itching for a fight. But in the grander scheme of things, that's not necessarily a bad thing, he thought, smiling, at least he knew she was always ready.

The radio chatter from the energy center had set off a chime in Zach's back room, and Dimitri's radio communication had soon followed. Zach opened up his back room comm center, and we monitored what was happening. They were getting a little antsy at the "research" center and wanted to take action against the people they had spotted, but cooler heads prevailed, and once again, the guards were ordered just to observe and take no action. From the tone of their transmissions, you could tell they were not happy.

"Looks like things are starting to heat up," Doc said.

"They are," I replied. "Zach, how long before that meteorite is ready to go?" I asked.

"About this time tomorrow should be fine, Colt," he replied.

"So, our next big challenges will be to get it in place and figure out the best way to let them start picking up the signal in a very obscure way," I said.

"Getting it in place is no big deal," Zach said, "and I would suggest a seismic event that opens up a rift that would allow the signal to escape from underground."

"Is that something you can do?" Doc asked.

Zach laughed and said, "I wouldn't have suggested it if it wasn't doable."

"Apologies, Zach. I'm still having a little bit of trouble comprehending your immense capabilities," Doc replied.

"No worries, Doc, you've had a hell of a lot to digest in the last few days," Zach responded good-naturedly.

Laughing, Doc said, "Hell, in the last few hours!"

"True," Zach said. "It's time to put the history lessons on hold and get back to the immediate problem at hand."

"How long will it take to get everything in place?" I asked.

"We can be ready to go the day after tomorrow," Zach replied. "How deep do you want this thing? I'm thinking around thirty or forty feet. We don't want it to be too easy to get to, but we also want them to be able to get to it and get out of there pretty quickly."

"Good point," I said. "How often do you have seismic activity in this area?"

"Not too often, Colt, but it's not unheard of," Zach answered.

"So, we should pick a location, say, kind of in line with where they are drilling, but out in the desert toward the mountains. Then we create a tremor the day before we open a rift and then a larger tremor a couple of hours later, releasing a bit of the energy signal, and then maybe one more, opening the rift wider, which will release a stronger signal for them to detect and follow."

"That I can do. We can dig into the location with my equipment; I can place the meteorite there and then use the planet reformation tool I was telling you about to refill our tunnel and cover and re-bury the meteorite, making it look completely natural when it is uncovered from the surface."

I was smiling broadly and said, "Now that, Zach, is one hell of a plan!"

"So, to recap," Doc said, "it will take us three days to place the rock and start the seismic activity. It'll probably take them two days to locate the site, another two days to dig down to it, and at least another two to three days to transport the necessary equipment to remove it. Then it will take one more day to conduct a thorough sweep of the area, looking for additional energy signatures, and finally another day to arrange for the transportation of the meteorite out of the area to who knows where. They may even fly in a heavy-lift chopper to remove it from the ground and move it, rather than trucking it out, but that could draw a lot of unwanted attention. So, from the time of placement to departure, maybe ten days?"

"That sounds about right," I replied.

"During this time, are we keeping the surveillance going, Colt?" Zach asked.

"Yes, if anything, we step it up a bit to keep the pressure on them."

"What if they start to get more aggressive toward it?" Doc asked.

"If they're smart, they won't, since that would draw a lot of unwanted attention to what's going on out here. But if they're stupid enough to try something, then we'll respond in kind."

"Okay, just wanted the rules of engagement to be clear, so we'll let the rest of the team know tonight," Doc replied.

"Good, we've got our work cut out for us, and I suggest we get started." I picked up my SAT phone and dialed Lawrence, who was waiting for the go command. He picked up on the second ring, "Okay, Lawrence, you have a go. File the lawsuit and put pressure on to have these guys notified right away."

"Roger that, Colt. First thing in the morning, the wheels of justice will begin turning. The state should have some branch of law enforcement deliver the official paperwork to them within 24 hours."

"Excellent, keep me posted on progress and their response."

"Will do, Colt, turning up the heat here!"

The call ended, and I thought, well, the plan is totally underway now. Let's just hope these yahoos respond the way I think they will. But there was a little niggling in the back of my head that said, "Better be prepared for the unexpected." Luckily, that was my team's mantra!

Aerial and ground surveillance kept up as we prepared for the placement of the meteorite and the "Big Reveal," as it were. The intensity of communications within the energy center and among its security personnel was growing increasingly agitated. On the second day of our preparations, we were underground when Zach said, "Hey, Colt, you better check this out." A notification chime had gone off on Zach's video feed as he drew my attention to the video monitoring activity at the energy center. Two black vans had just passed through the gates, parked around the side of the building, and six men in tactical gear had exited, each one carrying large duffel bags.

"Well, that looks rather ominous," I replied.

"Doesn't look like they're preparing for a low-key exercise," Zach said.

I turned to Doc, who was with us, "Better alert the team that these guys have just upped the ante with additional personnel and weapons. We continue business as usual, but stay extra frosty out there. We don't want them to know that we know what they're up to."

Doc immediately got on the radio and communicated the information and orders to all team members.

O'Reilly came back, "What if we're fired on?"

"Tell them to bug out and head back to base, and tell Dimitri not to fire unless fired upon first. If this thing escalates and gets out of hand, we don't want to be seen as the aggressors. We're just defending ourselves."

Doc relayed the message, and we resumed our preparations. We had a schedule, and I didn't want to deviate from it if at all possible. We were getting ready to move the meteorite into place later that afternoon when the video alert chime sounded again. This time, the screen showed us three vehicles at the center's gate. One was a tribal police vehicle, another the local county sheriff's vehicle, and the third was a black SUV. The guard at the gate did not let them in but notified someone inside, while an officer from both law enforcement agencies stood by and waited along with a civilian in a dark suit. Moments later, two men came from the building to meet them. We could hear the audio as the men were introduced, and the man in the suit handed them a folder, informing them that they were being served with legal notification of a lawsuit brought by the Navajo Nation against their operation. They had 48 hours to respond officially in person at the federal building in Phoenix. The recipients signed a paper, and the three men returned to their vehicles and left.

There were a few moments of silence as the document was quickly read, then all hell broke loose. Shouting, arm-waving, finger-pointing, and several expletives were expressed as the two men returned to the building, gesturing and speaking loudly.

I turned to Doc and Zach, who were both grinning broadly, and said, "Well, I guess now the hornet's nest has been officially kicked."

"I think that is putting it mildly," Zach responded. "Let's get back to it and really shake things up," he said, followed by, "Pun definitely intended."

That afternoon, we hit them with the first tremor.

CHAPTER 31

"Well, it sounds like things may start to get more interesting," Matt said to O'Reilly as the Little Bird was headed back to Lone Wolf Aero.

O'Reilly said, "I just hope they don't get stupid and start taking pot shots at us out here."

"It shouldn't be a problem if they do, at least not for us. This little gal has a ballistic plastic windscreen and lightweight Kevlar panels for her body. It would take a direct hit by an RPG to do any real damage, and even then, it would be survivable."

"Damn, sounds like she's combat-ready," O'Reilly quipped.

"Old habits are hard to break. I know in most civilian circumstances it's overkill. But Sam can be pretty persuasive, and we have the resources, so why not?" Matt said.

"True enough, I have to admit that I've run into some very unexpected situations flying for Risky Business in what we would call civilian encounters. I agree; you can never be overprepared. Our team's mantra is 'Expect the unexpected.'"

"Words to live by... literally," Matt replied as he

brought the Little Bird in for a smooth landing on the helipad. Sam was waiting for them as usual and conducted a quick post-flight walkaround, asking us how it went and if we had encountered any issues.

"None," Matt informed her, "she performed beautifully."

"That's what I like to hear," Sam replied and continued her inspection, getting the tow bar and four-wheeler ready to take the bird back to the hangar.

"Guess I'll see you tomorrow. Let's go for around 10:00 a.m. just to mix things up a bit," Matt said.

"Sounds good to me," O'Reilly said, as she threw her gear into the vehicle and headed back to Fremont.

Matt had walked back to the "office" table, grabbed a beer on the way, and was sitting in the shade when Sam joined him. She had also gotten herself a beer out of the fridge. Matt was sitting there with a furrowed brow, slowly sipping his beverage, when Sam said, "I heard the radio transmission from Doc about the additional troops that showed up today."

"Yeah, that's not a good sign," Matt replied. "Can't say I expected that."

"You don't think they would be stupid enough to start some kind of armed confrontation, do you?"

Matt paused before answering, running the possible scenarios through his head. "I hope not, babe. It would definitely be a stupid move on their part. But they do have the cover of being a private corporation with a private security force, and if they felt threatened or said they were fired on first, it's feasible things could get out of hand really quickly."

Now, Sam shared Matt's furrowed brow as she took a drink. "They've brought in a lot of extra dudes, and you know they didn't come empty-handed. That would be a lot of firepower for Colt's team to try to handle. What do you want to do?" she asked.

Matt slowly shook his head as he took a long pull of his beer. "Never thought I'd have to say this, especially out here, but how's your aim?"

"As good as it ever was," Sam replied, her lips tightening into a smile.

"Then I suggest we get ready, just in case," Matt said with a level of resolve in his voice.

"Copy that, Boss, I'll start tonight. That way, if needs be, we can be ready to go in ten mikes."

Matt got up from the table, went to the fridge, got two more beers, handed Sam one, kissed her on the forehead, and said, "You're the best."

She smiled at him, gave him a tilted bottle salute, and said, "Damn right I am." They relaxed for the rest of the evening, both pondering the potential of what might possibly lie ahead.

Doc, Zach, and I had moved the meteorite into place. Zach had covered it and filled in the tunnel they had cut to put it into position. It all looked completely natural. Zach double-checked everything and assured them they were ready to deliver the seismic event that would open up the rift tomorrow and release the energy signature to be detected by the bad guy's equipment.

Back in the main work area, Zach asked if we

would like to hear what was happening in the energy center building. There was no surprise this time. We had gotten used to Zach being able to do almost anything with his technology. Of course, we said "yes," and with a few adjustments, voices could be heard in multiple discussions in Chinese. Seconds later, the same discussions were heard in English.

My plan was working; a low level of chaos was running rampant in all the discussions. The aerial and ground surveillance, as well as the lawsuit, were all going according to plan. The lack of progress in finding the energy signature only added to the palpable frustration in the voices.

"I do believe the stew is coming to a boil," said Doc. "Just wait until they have the energy signature to deal with tomorrow. Me thinks the pot may boil over," he finished.

I was extremely pleased with the events so far, but my level of concern for my team and the locals was growing, as I didn't know just how much that situation would eventually escalate. The arrival of the new troops greatly concerned me. I feared they were preparing for a more hostile approach to their current situation.

Dimitri and Reggie were prepped for a night recon mission, and as the sun was setting, they had moved to their entry point in the area a mile or so east of their designated observation post. They would likely be observed entering that area if thermal detectors were in place at the facility.

The two of them would ride with no lights, using night-vision goggles to navigate, and hope that darkness would conceal their movements. They had gotten the message about the arrival of additional troops and had no real idea of how they would be equipped or what the deployment plan might be. They would have to rely on communication from Zach and me for any updates.

They were moving stealthily into their positions, using their thermal gear and augmented night vision to observe the facility, when their secure coms squawked.

Shortly, they heard my voice, "Hey, nightbirds, heads up, a Jeep is leaving the facility with four tangos, and it looks like they're some of the new dudes that arrived today. They have night vision gear, and I would guess thermal too, so take appropriate precautions."

"Roger that," Reggie replied. She turned to Dimitri and said, "Nightbirds, I like that."

Dimitri snorted and said, "You would." He keyed his mic and said, "Don't see any action in our area."

"Roger, they seem to be doing a general perimeter sweep, so I don't think your position is compromised. If it looks like things are getting too close, bug out or go to ground if necessary, but do not engage."

"Copy," Dimitri answered.

Among their gear, they had lightweight thermal blankets that would cover any heat signature their bodies would emit, plus their fatigues featured the latest camouflage pattern, making them almost impossible to detect with night vision. They settled in and kept an eye on the facility. The Jeep came into view, but it was at least a mile away and making no moves in their direction, so they relaxed while the hours slipped by uneventfully, except for the scorpion that tried to take up residence in Reggie's hair and the rattlesnake that thought snuggling up to Dimitri was a great place to spend the night. Neither of those creepy critters would live to tell their kids about that night in the Arizona desert.

At three a.m., they packed up their gear and headed out of the area, this time making sure they were spotted leaving. They wanted to ensure that the people at the facility knew they were under constant surveillance, which would add another level of concern about the seriousness of the ongoing surveillance.

It worked; Reggie and Dimitri were spotted, but too late for any intervention, as they disappeared into the rocky terrain over a mile away, heading east. Zach and I were monitoring the facilities' surveillance and took note of the level of concern and frustration being expressed by the "bad guys" in the chatter there at not having spotted some observers earlier and not having any idea who they were. More fuel to the fire as the pot continued to boil, I thought.

CHAPTER 32

At 6:30 a.m., Zach unleashed the next tremor. This was the one that was going to break open the earth enough to allow a small amount of the energy signature to escape and hopefully be detected. Now that I knew we could monitor the live chatter at the Chinese-occupied command center as well as the radio communications, I was paying close attention to the audio. Zach's tech did a great job of separating the radio transmissions from the interpersonal chatter that was going on in the command center. There was a distinct separation between the two, so it was easy to follow what was being said.

There were obviously a lot of unhappy people there. Tension was rising, and tempers were beginning to flare, especially with the leader of the new group of personnel that arrived yesterday. He was obviously a military type and wanted to take decisive action against the individuals surveilling them. Zach did say that one of the encrypted messages sent two days ago notified headquarters personnel that they were under surveillance. The response was that they would be sending additional security.

The project head, I assumed, had exerted pressure

through his rank and pulled the others into line, explaining the need to maintain an extremely low profile during this operation. Failing to do so could have dire consequences, both locally and potentially globally, if the real reason and support for this operation were to become known by the United States government.

Significant differences of opinion began to emerge among those in power at the facility. It was hard to say just how much clout this new player had, but he was certainly exerting it in a very aggressive way. He was still being overridden by the man in charge of the scientific team, but it was becoming increasingly obvious that a power struggle was brewing.

Listening to their conversations, it became clear that on-site personnel were taking their orders from two different individuals or departments that were not in agreement on how things should proceed. While the chaos it was creating within the organization was beneficial, the possibility of it turning ugly, and in a physical sense, was rising. The main group was very scientific and research-oriented, with the American physicist leading the charge. This new group seemed more security-focused, militaristic. This could spell trouble for the Risky Business team in a big way.

A few moments later, an excited voice came over the radio from the drilling site. They had picked up the energy signal, very faint, but they had a signal. They noted it had not come from the drilling site but from further out in the desert. The discussion centered on whether or not the location could be pinpointed and how quickly.

I gave Zach a nod, and a much stronger second

tremor occurred; this is the one that would open the rift wide enough to allow a much larger energy spike to be released and easily pinpointed. The excitement at the center was off the charts. Computer comparisons were being carried out to confirm it was the same type of energy reading as in '71. An Immediate confirmation came back, and the whole place switched into pinpointing the location of the point of origin.

Zach grinned and said, "Let the games begin."

"Zach, a question," I said. "When I gave you the go-ahead for the big tremor, I didn't see you do anything with your equipment."

Zach smiled as he replied, "We never got to finish our discussion from last night. Remember me telling you all things vibrate, and one of the things we've done is learn how to control those vibrations?"

"Yes, you said your equipment allowed you to do a variety of things with the manipulation of the frequencies," I responded.

"It does, but you remember the jug of apple cider on the table?"

As I was about to answer, my eyes got wide as it hit me like a freight train.

"You didn't need your equipment. You did it with your mind," I said, both a statement and a question.

Zach spread his arms wide, smiling, bowed at the waist, and stood back up, like a magician at a carnival responding to his audience after pulling a rabbit from his top hat. "Now, you're getting it," he said more seriously. "Not all our advancements have been in technology. You still have much to learn, but you're getting there," he said.

My radio squawked, and O'Reilly's voice said, "Leaving the nest now, headed your way. ETA 15 mikes."

I keyed the radio, "Copy that, be advised there is quite a bit of new activity out there. We kicked the hornet's nest pretty hard. Proceed with caution. The new arrivals are pushing to play a little rougher, think they are military or merc types, so stay frosty."

"Roger that, we felt the tremor over here. You guys are giving a whole new meaning to shake and bake," O'Reilly added.

"Sounds like they're gearing up for a recon op to locate the signal," Doc said. He had been listening to the radio chatter and the discussions in the center.

"If they're any good, it should only take them a couple of hours to locate the source. Once they do, they'll have to decide how to proceed. That's going to take a while," Zach said.

"I saw a backhoe in their compound work area, so my money is on them starting to dig," I said.

"True, but the science types are going to want to be careful, so they'll take it slow. Once they discover the meteorite, they're going to have to lift it out. I think that the backhoe may have the lifting capability to move it. However, they don't have the truck or trailer to put it on and move it, so they will have to make arrangements for that. That's going to take some time," Zach said.

"You know they're going to work around the clock to get it out of here as quickly as possible, so what would take a normal crew five or six days to get it, they will try to do in three," I said.

"Yeah, Colt, maybe two if they push it, and we really don't want to slow them down, but we still need to maintain the sense of an external interest notion to keep our little charade looking real," Doc added.

"So that means we keep surveillance going and the pressure on," I responded. "But with these new guys, we need to be careful, since it sounds like their boss is itching for a reason to start something. I don't know how long the science dudes can keep him under control, and I don't know how long of a leash his real boss has on him. This is going to be really dicey. We've got some unknowns that could make this thing turn out fine or get out of hand really quickly, and that would be no bueno," I said.

"You've got that right, Colt, and this is a fight I may have to keep my dog out of," Zach cautioned. "I have to be invisible in this one, but I'll help where I can. It looks like it's going to be up to you and your team."

Doc laughed and said, "You can't make yourself invisible, can you, Zach?"

"Nope, sorry, Doc, that's not one of my abilities—darn it," Zach answered.

"Okay, with what we've seen and learned about you in the last couple of days, I just had to ask," he responded good naturedly.

We all had a good laugh at Doc's comments. That went a long way in easing some of the tension that had been building around this operation.

"Let's get back and brief Dimitri and Reggie before they head out for their night recon. I think this one may be a little different than the past few. I'm pretty sure we're going to have more eyes looking for them than in the past, especially when they locate the source of the energy reading. They will, for sure, post guards around it, and I would bet that roving patrols will increase as well. The kicker is, the location we selected for meteorite placement is a lot closer to the cover Reggie and Dimitri have been using, so that's going to have to change. We may not want to get that close to the site. I don't want to take a chance of instigating any kind of detection or confrontation," I added.

They portaled back to the trading post and Zach's back room; it was 6:30 p.m. Dimitri and Reggie were getting ready for their recon shift when I called them into the back room. "Here's an update for you guys, things are moving along as planned, but faster."

No sooner had I said that than Doc said, "Hey, Colt, they're moving the backhoe out to the site." He had been monitoring the video feed from the center. "Looks like they have trucks loaded with large lights, and one of them is pulling a generator."

"Guess they're planning on working all night," Zach added, "It's going to take a while for that backhoe to get to the site as slow as they are, but once they start digging, that means they'll probably reach the meteor by early morning. I guess all the pressure we've been applying has really motivated a sense of urgency with these guys."

"Colt," Doc interrupted, "They're also loading up more security people in two Jeeps and a pick-up truck.

That's going to put the security force at about 20 strong. Whoa!" Doc exclaimed. "They just added another vehicle, a Humvee, don't know where that came from. I haven't seen it before at the compound, and it looks like it has a .50 caliber gun mounted in the rear. These guys are going out loaded for bear."

"I guess the vehicle was always there in the big warehouse shed they have for equipment, but I'll bet the new guys brought the artillery," I said as I turned to Reggie and Dimitri.

"This definitely adds another wrinkle to things. It looks like you'll need to gear up for a little longer stay out there and be prepared in case things go south. That's a lot of manpower and firepower that I hope doesn't come into play."

"Can do, not a problem," Dimitri replied, looking at Reggie, who nodded in agreement. As they left, I gave my signature advice, "Stay frosty out there."

CHAPTER 33

As we watched the video feed from the site, I felt a level of apprehension growing that hadn't been there before. This new player, who had arrived with his men, added an ominous undertone to the entire operation. I had been hoping for a low-key resolution to Zach's situation, and it looked like we were on that path until now. This new guy was definitely a wild card thrown into the mix, and he has come in with either a dangerous attitude or orders that, in a geopolitical situation like this, didn't make sense.

The only thing I could fathom was that this was a rogue operation not actually sponsored or supported by the governmental powers that be, in which case, all bets were off on possible outcomes. We had been operating under the assumption that this was a foreign government-supported operation, and as such, specific actions and events could be politically anticipated. If it wasn't, then all bets were off. We could be playing by a whole different set of rules, which meant there might not be any rules at all.

I explained my concerns to Doc and Zach, who were both surprised that we hadn't thought of that sooner. The communications that Zach had monitored gave us no indication that this was anything other than a foreign government-sponsored activity. Nothing pointed to a potential terrorist operation until now. "This new player and his actions and attitude toward the scientist types are what tipped it off for me. He definitely comes across as the man in charge now and the one calling the shots," I said. "Look at the firepower he's deployed in the open. I don't think that's something a government would do, especially at this juncture in the operation."

"Too radical for a government to take that action, knowing the potential political ramifications it could have. I think you're right, Colt; this is a rogue terrorist group in action," Zach said, "so what now?"

"We still want them to get out of here with the meteor to dispel any future investigations or searches, so nothing has changed there, but now, if we're fired on, we respond with extreme prejudice," I said as I keyed the mic on my radio and repeated that same message to the rest of the team. "How copy?" I asked after I finished my new revelation and orders.

"Good copy, Snake is in," replied O'Reilly.

The sun had set, and Dimitri and Reggie had made it to their surveillance position. "Hot damn, good copy, Colt," came Dimitri's reply, "we're ready." I couldn't believe how happy he sounded, being that they were outmanned and outgunned; well, actually, I could believe it, and I knew Reggie was feeling the same way. The odds didn't bother them at all.

They had taken up their positions about twenty feet apart in the rocks with a good view of the personnel at the site. Reggie had positioned herself about ten feet higher than Dimitri. She had a good angle and a clear line of sight on the dig site. She laid her desert camo-wrapped Remington next to her, using her night vision scope to scan the area. They already had the generator running and the big lights on, so it looked almost like daylight where they were digging; there was no need for night vision there. It was the shadows and dark areas surrounding the work site that she wanted to keep an eye on. Their nemeses had security posted on the perimeter and had mobile patrols roaming farther out into the darkness. She kept her eyes on all approaches to their position.

The drone of the generator could be heard rolling across the desert landscape as the backhoe removed bucket after bucket of dirt covering the meteorite. Slowly, it was making progress, digging deeper on its way to the final prize.

"It's going to be a long night," Dimitri said quietly into the mic connected to his earpiece, speaking to Reggie.

"That it is," she quietly replied. "Why don't you grab a few Zs? I'll take first watch and wake you in two hours."

"You don't have to twist my arm on that one," he replied, pulling his .50-caliber Barrett sniper rifle, also wrapped in desert camo netting, closer and resting his cheek against its stock, the barrel of the beast pointed in the direction of the backhoe and dig site. The night was long and uneventful, as everyone waited with high anticipation to see what the morning would bring.

It was around 5:30 a.m. when Dimitri's voice woke

Reggie, "Time to wake up, sunshine. It looks like they've found the meteorite, and there's a lot of excitement going on."

Reggie wiped the sleep from her eyes and immediately surveyed the scene through her scope. Sure enough, four men in hazmat protective gear were using the bucket of the backhoe to be lowered into the large hole that had been dug overnight. They were armed with indistinguishable handheld electronic devices. About an hour or so later, the bucket had brought one of the men back to the surface. He had taken off his protective hood and was relaying something to the other workers.

Dimitri keyed his mic, "Colt, you seeing this?"

"Roger, we have a good view from here," Zach, Doc, and I had spent the night in Zach's underground. I guess you could call it a control center, monitoring the video and radio transmissions of the workers. Zach had actually positioned one of his "Black Knight" satellites overhead, and they had a crystal-clear view of what was going on. He zoomed in on the hole with the meteorite and could see the other men there taking off their protective gear.

"They've determined that the energy it's emitting is not harmful," Zach reported, "which it's not. So, they can work freely now to remove it," he added.

The radio transmission from the crew in the hole confirmed that assumption and requested that men with shovels be sent down to help dig around it so some sort of lifting strap could be placed under their discovery. They also reported its size and approximate weight based on their preliminary assessment of its composition.

The radio discussion now centered around the backhoe's ability to lift the find out of the hole. Extension ladders were brought in, and another six men with shovels entered the pit. In the meantime, the head of the scientific group had been on their encrypted radio frequency requesting a large truck and trailer to remove the energy source from the area, once they had extracted it from the hole. It was around 8:30 a.m. or so. Things were moving rapidly.

Confirmation was received that arrangements were being made, stating that they should have a vehicle on-site within a matter of hours. The person on the other end of the communication questioned if they had spotted any more surveillance, and the boss had replied no. He was then instructed to have the security team conduct a sweep of the area to ensure no one was watching. Also, during this time, technicians accompanied by security personnel were spreading out, carrying what appeared to be energy-detecting devices, and checking for additional signatures in the surrounding areas. They covered a wide range, some as far as a mile or more away, and came dangerously close to Dimitri's and Reggie's location, but the two were never spotted.

As planned, no additional energy readings were detected, and this information was relayed to their superiors by security personnel. In their radio communications, they began discussing this find as potentially a one-off event, and if there were other similar meteorites, none were known to be in this area.

That was precisely the conclusion we had hoped they would come to, and hopefully vacate the area as no longer useful or of any interest.

Large lifting straps had been dropped into the hole as the meteorite was wrapped and secured for being brought to the surface.

The Arizona sun was high in the sky when the truck and trailer finally showed up. The desert around the site was not particularly soft, given its proximity to the mountain range, but the recovery team had brought out a bulldozer from the compound. In the hours leading up to the arrival of the truck and trailer, they had leveled a makeshift roadway for it, compacting the ground at the site even further.

As we watched from underground, Zach commented, "These guys know what they're doing. They obviously have done something like this before, and some of them must be trained construction workers."

"Well, they were out here for a drilling operation to start with, so it makes sense that you'd have trained heavy construction people running that part of the operation," Doc said.

"True," I said, "let's just hope they can get out of here without a snag," as the truck and trailer arrived.

I then got on the radio and contacted O'Reilly, who had been waiting at Matt's for their next recon flight. "Okay, O'Reilly, these guys are getting ready to load the rock, so let's give them a little added incentive to move things along quickly."

"Roger that, Little Bird on its way," she replied as

Matt brought the turbine to life, lifted the OH-6 off the ground, and headed to the site. "ETA 10 minutes."

CHAPTER 34

The backhoe had been moved into place, and the bucket dropped down to be connected to the meteorite. Slowly, it began its lift of the two-ton rock. It was a heavy lift for this medium-sized machine, being that it wasn't one of the larger ones that could have easily extracted it, so it was straining a bit to raise the huge "rock" out of the ground.

While this was happening, the security personnel were expanding their search area and conducting sweeps more frequently. The Humvee with the .50 caliber machine gun mounted had positioned itself between the scattered piles of boulders at the base of the mountains and the work site, the gunner on a slow swivel, covering the area surrounding the site. The van had been brought out with additional men, and cases had been removed and opened, revealing additional weapons.

Dimitri was watching this closely as Reggie monitored the slow progress being made in lifting the meteorite out of the pit. It was then that Matt and O'Reilly arrived on the scene, and the security personnel went into high gear. Obviously, their orders had changed since they began to fire on the helicopter immediately.

"Well, this is a new challenge," Matt said to O'Reilly and Joe over the helicopter's com as he made a hard bank to get them out of the line of fire. They had come in at about 1,000 feet, not making for an easy target, but within range of the weapons these guys were using. He immediately began to climb as a couple of lucky shots pinged off the bird's skin.

O'Reilly was on the radio with me. "We're taking small arms fire," she reported, as another couple of lucky shots hit the helicopter, not doing any damage.

I replied, "Okay, you guys get out of there."

"Copy," O'Reilly responded.

"All right, these guys have pissed me off," Matt said over the chopper's com.

"Joe, you got a good shot?" Matt asked.

"Better than most," he replied.

"Good, open that big bag on the floor back there and let me know when you're ready," Matt said.

The radio squawked again. This time, it was Dimitri, "Colt, they're launching drones. I've seen them put up five so far. They're fanning out in all directions, mostly headed our way—checking out the cover and boulders over here."

I felt helpless as I watched the scene unfolding before me, not being out there taking part in the operation as I usually did. "Can you guys ex-fil?" I asked.

"No way. This area is starting to get crowded, and with these drones overhead, we'd be spotted in a New York minute. We're stuck here and about to have to engage these guys; they're getting really close."

Reggie broke in on the radio, "They got the rock out and are loading it on the trailer now," she reported. "Science guys are freaking out at the gunfire, and I've got a drone overhead. We've been spotted." Two seconds later, the blast of the Browning 12 gauge broke the silence as the drone disintegrated into pieces.

Reggie looked toward Dimitri, who was lying on his back, grinning, holding his shotgun. "Just like shooting skeets," he said.

"Well, they know we're here now," she replied.

Back in the helicopter, Joe let out a low whistle and said over the com, "Nice selection, Snake, give me something else to shoot at." In the bag, there had been an assortment of weapons. Joe had chosen an M249 SAW (Squad Automatic Weapon), sitting in the open doorway as Snake brought the little chopper around and gave Joe his targets. Joe opened up on the surprised group of fighters on the ground, who were not expecting return fire.

O'Reilly spotted the Humvee changing its location. She pointed and said to Matt, "Looks like they're bringing in the heavy artillery."

"Well, that's not good for us," adding, "this little gal isn't built to handle that," as he banked hard in the opposite direction and said over the radio, "Sam, you copy?"

"Copy," came her reply.

"We're a go," he answered. "Be back in 10 mikes."

"Roger that, we'll be ready, Snake."

Not sure what was going on, O'Reilly turned to

Matt with a questioning look.

"When we get back, I'm setting down on the opposite side of the hangar. You take over and return to the site, providing as much support as possible to Dimitri and Reggie. I'll catch up to you." Nothing more was said.

The little bird touched down, and Matt jumped out as O'Reilly took the pilot controls and lifted off, heading back to the dig site. The radio came alive; it was Dimitri, "Hey, guys, could use a little help over here. They have identified our position, and we got about a dozen baddies headed our way." They were dropping them one at a time, but Dimitri and Reggie knew they were in trouble. They were slowing them down, but they kept moving in.

"Hang on, big guy, we're headed back to you; be there in five mikes," O'Reilly said over the radio.

"Just hurry it up," Reggie said as she dropped another bad guy.

Matt sprinted around the corner of the hangar and had the helo pad in sight. He smiled as he continued his sprint. Sitting there with the rotor turning slowly in all her kick-ass glory was his sweet twin-turbine Super Cobra. He could see Sam in the back seat, helmet on and strapped in, grinning from ear to ear. As he climbed aboard and slipped his helmet on, he thought, It's great what you can buy at these army surplus sales.

His headset came alive, "'Bout time you got here, she's warmed up and ready to go," Sam said.

Matt eased into the throttles, and the turbines began their howl as rotors spun, and he lifted off. "She sounds good," Matt said over the com.

"She is good," Sam responded, "Just like me," laughter in her voice.

"How's your trigger finger?" Matt asked.

"Itchy," she replied.

"Good because we've got a 'technical' with a .50 in back that needs to go away," Matt said. Technicals were the name they gave to pick-ups or any vehicle with a heavy machine gun mounted on it that the Taliban would use for heavy firepower when they were over in the Sandbox.

"Just point me in the general direction, and I'll take care of the rest," Sam replied.

He was nose down about twenty feet off the desert floor, hauling ass. "O'Reilly, got a copy?" Matt called.

"Roger that, good copy. Where the hell are you?" she asked.

"Headed your way, stay away from that .50. I'll take care of it when I get there," he replied.

"Roger that," she replied, "just trying to keep bad guys away from Dimitri and Reggie now, but that big SOB keeps trying to get an angle on me to get a shot."

"Joe's switched to the M-60 back there; you sure have quite the arsenal in the back seat," she said.

"I know, redundancy is our friend. Got you in sight, coming up on your six, bank hard left, and climb. I need a little room to work, Snake 1 out."

O'Reilly didn't question his order as she made a hard bank to the left and pulled the nose up in a steep climb. It wasn't until she banked that she saw the Cobra. Her eyes wide, she keyed her radio, "Snake!" she said in an unbelieving voice.

"At your service, decided to give you a little help with your pest control problem," Snake replied. "We're going to take care of that technical first, then we can go after the ground troops," Snake said. "Get to a safe distance, O'Reilly, and enjoy the show, Snake 1 out."

While he had been talking, the Humvee had moved out of rocky concealment and stopped as the .50 rotated to get a bead on the Cobra. One of the security personnel jumped out of the passenger's side and ran around the front of the vehicle, loading an RPG. He stopped with his back to the driver's side window as he brought the rocket-powered grenade launcher to his shoulder, aiming at the new, unexpected threat. The machine gunner had rotated and was taking aim as well.

The radio squawked as Dimitri said, "I got the RPG."

Reggie then said, "I got the gunner," as the Barrett .50 caliber and her Remington both barked at the same time. The machine gunner dropped instantly, with part of his head gone. The chest of the RPG dude exploded, as did the head of the driver of the Humvee. Dimitri's .50 caliber round had penetrated the RPG guy, the window in the Hum Vee, and the head of its driver, leaving the running vehicle rolling aimlessly with the lifeless driver slumped over the wheel, his foot still on the gas pedal.

"Nice shooting, guys, now my turn," Snake said

over the radio. "You got the tubes loaded, babe?" Snake said to Sam.

"Sure do," she replied.

"Then the Humvee is all yours," Snake said.

Seconds later, two of the 70mm rockets left the launching tubes mounted on the Cobra and obliterated the vehicle.

"Now, let's go give O'Reilly an assist and take care of Dimitri and Reggie, too," Snake said as he banked hard and lined up on the ground troops that were now scrambling in disarray. "Bring the rain," he said as Sam opened up with the two 134 mini guns attached to the hard points on either side of the Cobra. Belting out a potential 6,000 rounds a minute, she devastated the troops below.

While the firefight was taking place, the scientists and workers attended to the loading of the meteorite. A cover had been thrown over it, and the whole thing was strapped to the trailer. The truck and trailer were headed to the main road, followed by a small number of energy center vehicles that were still operational, filled with workers.

Doc, Zach, and I had been observers from underground, and even though I was itching to get into the middle of things out there, I knew that wasn't possible, so I continued my role as "quarterback." I keyed the radio and said, "O'Reilly, Snake, do not engage the non-combatants. If they don't have a gun, let them go, and don't interfere with the truck's progress. We need to make sure it gets away."

"Roger that," came the reply from both

helicopters. There was no movement on the ground below at the dig site as the vehicles barreled down the makeshift road, heading for the main road out of Fremont.

CHAPTER 35

My radio came alive as O'Reilly said, "Colt, we're hovering over the research center, and the techs are loading up two vans with computers and stuff. It looks like they're getting ready to make a run for it. What do you want me to do?"

"Nothing, let them go. They are no danger to us," I replied.

"What about the black SUV at the tail end of the convoy? Pretty sure I saw a black uniform get in the driver's seat."

I turned to Zach, "We need to check that out. We don't want the military types reporting what happened. The geeks were so shaken, they probably won't be able to get any details right, but this guy might be more of a problem. We need to identify who's in the vehicle."

"I think I can help with that," Zach said as he got on the radio and said, "Snake, can you get a close-up of the driver of that black SUV?"

"With all this dust, it might be a little tough, but I'll see what I can do," Snake replied.

The trail of vehicles was kicking up such a tremendous amount of dust that you couldn't see the vehicle in front of you or the one behind, making it so all they had to follow was a brown cloud. Snake dropped in at window height, about seventy feet away from the SUV, and turned his gun camera toward the vehicle. He had no idea that Zach had patched into his video feed, and we were seeing the same thing he was. With a couple of adjustments, Zach cleared out the dust from our video image, and we could see an American in the passenger seat and identified him as the physicist who had sold the government SR-71 information to whomever these bad guys were, a traitor. The driver was the head security dude who had brought in the additional troops the other day.

"That's good enough," Zach said over the radio. He looked at me, and I knew what he was thinking; I nodded in affirmation.

"Snake, these guys are two of the top bad guys and can't get away; they need to be taken out with extreme prejudice."

"Copy that, guns hot," came the reply. With all the dust being kicked up by the trucks and the rotor dust, the driver hadn't even noticed the helicopter as Snake pulled another twenty feet away, rotated the Cobra, and started crabbing sideways with his nose gun pointed at the vehicle. The 20mm M-197 in the nose of the Cobra only had a capacity of 750 rounds, but he knew that would be enough as he sent one burst of all 750 rounds through the driver's door and into the passenger's compartment.

Death filled the compartment as the vehicle flipped in midair, the entire front end ripped to pieces. No one in the dust-filled sky being created by the trucks in front even noticed. Snake turned back and started a slow climb, clicked his mic, and said, "Mission accomplished."

As he flew back over the dig site and saw the smoldering vehicles and bodies lying around, Snake's first thought was that somebody was going to have one hell of a mess to clean up. Radio traffic got a little hectic as Dimitri came on and said, "We've cleaned up our area and are heading back."

"Roger that," I replied. "No need for stealth, just head straight back to Fremont, shortest route."

"Copy, on our way. We checked for survivors; there are none," Dimitri reported.

"Copy, see you back at the trading post," I replied.

"Colt, the truck and all the associated vehicles have made it to the road out of town and are headed toward the main highway," O'Reilly reported. "And they are in a hell of a hurry."

"Copy, let them go, head back to the nest and meet us at the trading post."

"Roger that," she replied.

As Doc, Zach, and I surveyed the video image of the carnage at the dig site, I said, "That's going to be one hell of a mess to clean up. We sure don't want any law enforcement types showing up, seeing that, and starting to ask questions."

Doc nodded, adding, "That would be disastrous."

Zach walked to the console by the big table in the room. We had been watching what was happening in real time from his Black Knight satellite feed. Now the view shifted slightly as he manipulated the console.

He zoomed in a little closer to the scene. Next thing we know, a white circle appears around the smoldering Humvee and the SUV Snake had just destroyed, lying on its side. A second later, they both ceased to exist, as did the shot-up Jeeps, as the targeting circles appeared around them. Another adjustment and circles began to appear around each of the bodies on the ground simultaneously; then, the bodies disappeared. Another adjustment, and all the weapons and the multitude of spent shell casings were gone. Doc and I stared at the scene before us; no evidence remained of the gun battle, only a large hole in the ground with a backhoe sitting next to it.

"I couldn't really do anything earlier during the firefight, but now that it's over and there are no witnesses to see what happens, I can help with the clean-up," Zach said.

A few more minutes passed as Zach made a close visual review of the site. Satisfied, he made a few more control adjustments, and the view changed to a more global perspective as he repositioned his satellite.

"So, what happens now that they have the meteorite?" I asked Zach.

"Let's check. My guess is they have a cargo plane waiting at the old airport about 50 miles from here, and they get the rock out of here as soon as possible." Another console adjustment and an aerial image appeared of an old, abandoned airstrip with a medium-sized cargo plane sitting on the end of a runway, which was covered in weeds and sagebrush, that had obviously been recently cleared away. It had a loading tailgate/ramp in the down position, ready and waiting to receive the arrival of the truck, trailer, and its cargo.

"You got that one right," Doc said.

"I've been following the chatter on their encrypted communications since the meteorite was discovered. These individuals, whoever they are, must be very well-connected and have unlimited resources, which allowed them to initiate an exfiltration plan on very short notice. I'm going to dig into that and see who these guys are really working for, but for now, I just want to follow the rock," Zach said.

"And of course you can do that," I said, smiling.

"Of course I can, Colt. I made sure I could track it wherever it goes, worldwide," replied Zach, "and they will never know they are being tracked."

"Good, because now that we know this was a terrorist operation, I want to learn more about them. Who they are, where they operate from, who's funding them, and figure out their master plan and next move."

"That won't be a problem," Zach said with confidence. "It may just take a little time."

"Let's head back to the trading post. The rest of the team should be arriving soon, and I think we all could use some time to catch our breath after the events of the last 24 hours," Zach said as he opened a portal to his back room.

"I agree completely," Doc said, emphatically, as we stepped through.

We had all taken seats at the table in the main store area. Once everyone had arrived, Zach put the closed sign on the door and pulled the shades. Joseph was there, and Snake and Sam had joined us at Zach's request after having put both choppers back in the hangar and shutting things down. Dimitri and Reggie had shed most of their tactical gear and left their long guns on the ATVs, under cover in the back of the building. Joseph had brought out three large jugs of cold cider and placed them on the table, along with glasses for everyone to use. As he stepped away, he said, "Oh, by the way, that's the good stuff."

Doc and I knew what he meant and looked forward to the bite of the hard cider.

As Zach poured the cider, Snake/Matt looked around and said, "I haven't been here in a while, Zach. I like what you've done with the place."

Sam added, "It looks great." There was something a little surreal about this normal, everyday conversation taking place, I fleetingly thought.

"You two need to get out a little more and stop by; we're always ready to throw a fresh chunk of meat on the grill," Zach said as he graciously thanked them. When we all had full glasses, Zach raised his and said, "To a successful mission with the help of good friends, new and old."

A chorus of "Hear, hears" went around the table as the glasses were drained. This, of course, was followed by a bit of coughing and a few exclamations.

I had forgotten that not everyone had experienced the hard cider like Doc and I had the other night, so we knew what to expect.

"Wow!" O'Reilly exclaimed. "That is some good stuff!"

"Outstanding!" Dimitri said as he and Reggie both raised their drained glasses for refills. Just having spent almost twenty hours in the desert, concealed amongst the rocks in their hideout and surviving a hell of a firefight, they deserved it, as Zach gladly refilled their glasses. You could tell the adrenaline-filled atmosphere in the room was starting to ease as people leaned back in their chairs, and discussions and quips, followed by laughter, slowly began. It wasn't long before Snake/Matt finally said, "You guys know we were glad to help out in this situation and would do it again if requested, but I'm still not sure I completely understand the details of this mission."

We knew a plausible explanation would be necessary for him, so O'Reilly jumped in and explained that Doc's search for Kincaid's cave was legitimate, and it just so happened that her old CIA connections had been raising questions about what this international group, seemingly funded by the Chinese, was actually doing out here in the middle of nowhere USA, supposedly studying solar energy. The CIA's covert sources determined that, in reality, this suspect unidentified group was working on a directed energy beam weapon, and O'Reilly was called back into service to find out more about it. In reality, Risky Business and the CIA utilized Doc's actual hunt as a means to gather more information, confirming that the potential development of a new type of weapon by our adversaries was indeed accurate.

Since this was an extremely sensitive political situation, they thought the government should not be directly involved. Moreover, since the CIA does not officially operate on American soil and did not want to involve the FBI, our government needed a covert intervention. As it turned out, O'Reilly discovered, without divulging Zach's involvement, that the nemesis was a terrorist organization and not a Chinese government-sanctioned operation, so she was asked if she could intervene.

All of which was mostly true, except for the part about CIA involvement. O'Reilly said she had agreed to the assignment and, as it turned out, was able to enlist Zach, Snake, and Sam for the operation she had planned. All this was accomplished without divulging Zach's actual level of involvement or his real identity, which, of course, they were able to conceal and pull off successfully.

Matt and Sam had been listening intently. After a few quiet minutes, Matt finally said, "So what did they dig out of the ground?"

Now, O'Reilly's acting skills were put to the test. "We're not sure," she smoothly replied, "but it was something that was part of their project taking place within the fenced-off compound, and I was told to let them get away with it. Once it had been determined that it was going to be taken out of the country, the CIA could officially become involved and take over the operation."

The room was silent as Matt and Sam digested the truths, half-truths, and little white lies. A level of apprehension grew as we waited for their response. Finally, Matt said as he raised his glass, "In that case, I'm glad we could help out." The sigh of relief was almost audible as others raised their glasses for refills and another toast to a successful mission. "Besides," Matt continued, "it gave Sam and me a good reason to bring the old girl out of mothballs and shake the dust off her. Sam and I haven't flown together nearly as much as we used to, and I've missed it. Let's not let that happen again, life's too short," he said as he leaned over and kissed her fervently and unabashedly on the lips.

Joe nudged O'Reilly, who was smiling, leaned over, and quietly said, "Told you so," with a huge smile on his face.

CHAPTER 36

After finishing all three jugs of cider, everyone went their separate ways and took a much-needed break for showers, clean clothes, and a good meal at the diner. Some then went to their rooms for a little rest, but Doc and I headed back to the Trading Post. It had been ten hours since the action at the dig site, and we were anxious to get any updates that Zach might have.

"Well, they changed planes somewhere in Mexico and are headed out over the Atlantic, destination unknown," he informed them. "I'm sure they'll be taking their find to a research facility of some sort. We'll just have to keep an eye on them for now. I'll be contacting the tribal police and local sheriff tomorrow to inquire about any information they may have regarding the site. The gates are wide open, and it seems like everyone is gone."

"That should increase your level of plausible deniability to anything that happened there," I said.

"It's going to be interesting what they determine in their investigation," Doc added.

"Very. Since no one has shown up, I'm guessing our firefight uproar didn't draw any attention, and with only a big hole in the ground, who knows what conclusions will be drawn," Zach replied. "I'm sure it will have both agencies chasing their tails for a bit before just letting it go."

"That reminds me, I need to call Lawrence tomorrow after you report the situation to the authorities and see what's happening on the legal front," I said. "We may just want to drop the case."

"No, let's let it ride for now. We involved the Office of Indian Affairs and the BLM in the suit. There may be something that comes out of it, even though the major party listed in it has disappeared. There could still be some dirt in both departments that needs to be cleaned out. Let's wait and see what happens," Zach said.

"Fine by me," I replied.

"The elders were pretty adamant about their feelings toward these two departments, and rightly so; they've been screwed over for a long time. Let's just see what happens."

"It will keep Lawrence busy for a while doing something other than maritime law," Doc replied good-naturedly.

"You know, Zach, I still have more questions," Doc said.

"Well, now that we have a little breathing room, I guess we can get back to those, plus Colt, you and I also need to have a chat back down in my facility. How about let's all get a good night's sleep and be fresh tomorrow?" Zach said.

"Sounds good to me," I replied, wondering what Zach had on his mind.

Whatever it was, it didn't keep me up wondering. I had a good night's sleep and woke up refreshed and ready to go. Local law enforcement was notified of the strange situation, and I made a call to Lawrence, who informed me that some interesting developments were happening at the BIA and BLM, and he would keep me updated if anything further developed. Their inquiry, as part of the lawsuit, seemed to raise some questions in both departments.

Zach took the whole team to his underground workshop in the morning and showed them some new areas with artifacts that they could explore without any chance of them destroying the world, as long as they didn't let Dimitri touch anything, he said, laughing as he left them.

He and I then went back to a room adjoining his big lab area. It wasn't a large room. There was a console against one wall, and four comfortable-looking high-back chairs with headrests were arranged in the middle. The lighting was subdued but not dim. "Have a seat," Zach said as he sat in one of the chairs. The atmosphere in the room immediately induced a feeling of relaxation and well-being.

"This is great," I commented, "I need a room like this."

"The room is designed to enhance one's ability to learn," Zach said. "I'm going to be helping you learn a few things you may not know about yourself. First, most humans have at least one alien genetic marker in their genome. You have four, which is a very rare thing. I don't know why you have them, but they do give you certain abilities not available to most people.

For instance, one is your ability to communicate with Jeannie and me telepathically.

"I thought it was some kind of a dream state or something like that," I said.

"But then you realized you could have a conversation with her, as short and cryptic as it was, you could ask questions of her and sometimes receive answers," Zach said.

"Yes, that happened just recently, a couple of times."

"You were learning," he replied. "I'm going to help you enhance those abilities. You won't be able to communicate with everyone, but there will be a few, such as Jeannie and me, that you will be able to converse with more clearly."

"Lay your head back, relax, and listen to my voice."

"This isn't one of those hypnosis things, is it?" I asked, laughing slightly.

Zach laughed, "No, not even close. Just relax and listen."

I did as he instructed and immediately felt a sense of calm and well-being coursing through my body.

"What you are feeling is normal. Relax, and let it engulf you. Open your mind to nothing, let it wander, don't focus on anything. We are helping the untapped synaptic pathways open and connect in new ways. Some of yours had already started to access these abilities; we're just helping them open wider and faster."

The next thing I remember was a feeling of bliss

before hearing Jeannie's voice. "Welcome, Colt, I'm glad to see you have finally arrived."

"Wow, Jeannie, this is amazing—a new experience, for sure."

"Enjoy your journey, Colt; this is only the beginning," followed by her angelic laugh.

I opened my eyes, not realizing they had been closed, and saw Zach still sitting across from me, smiling.

His thoughts were crystal clear as he echoed Jeannie's statement, "Welcome, Colt, your journey has begun," I heard him say, but without moving his lips!

I started to speak, and his thoughts said, "No need for words now, Colt."

I thought, "So now, I can communicate with you and Jeannie this way?"

"Anytime, anywhere, and there is much more you will learn over time, but for now, this will suffice."

"Learn," I thought, "like what?"

"In due time, Colt, it is a process. A marathon, not a sprint, don't try to rush it."

He stood up and spoke this time, "Let's get back to the others; we don't want them getting worried."

I stood and looked at my watch, realizing that two hours had passed since we entered the room, which seemed like only five minutes. I followed him out, saying nothing, still trying to wrap my head around what had just happened—and again, I heard Jeannie's angelic laugh and could physically feel her humor.

I asked Zach if the communication was going to be like this all the time, and he said, "No, you can control access to your thoughts if you want to. Like closing a door for privacy, but if you want to communicate, the pathway is wide open."

Well, at least I can have some privacy, I thought.

Immediately, Jeannie's voice came back, "If you desire it, Colt."

"This is going to take some getting used to, you guys," Colt thought.

Both responded, "It is and a lot of practice, but it will come and become second nature to you in no time," followed by laughter from both of them.

"This is going to be like watching a toddler take his first steps," I thought, but before there could be an answer, I thought, "Okay, guys, closing the door now."

No more comments came, but Zach turned back to me as we were walking to join the group and said, "Now you're getting it."

The group was standing in the polished hallway as we came out of the lab, and Doc said, "There you are; we were about to come looking for you."

"No problem, Zach was just giving me an in-depth tour of my brain," I answered jovially.

Dimitri quipped, "Boy, I'll bet that was a scary trip," breaking into full-blown hilarity.

Reggie pounced, "Not as scary as if it were yours."

Doc looked at Zach and said, "Can we check and see where the rock is now?"

"Sure thing," Zach nodded, and we headed back to the lab. Within minutes, the world globe was floating in front of us again, this time without all the space debris. As it slowly rotated, a large red dot appeared in France.

"It looks like they've stopped in France for now." Zach zoomed in and found a small airport outside of Rouen, north and east of Paris. A cargo jet was parked on the apron, being refueled.

"Well, there they are, but it looks like they haven't reached their final destination, since they are refueling. We'll have to continue to keep an eye on them. We'll check again later. Besides, I've got something to show you," Zach said as he turned and started walking down that amazingly beautiful hallway. We got to a small alcove on the left, and Zach stepped in, motioning for us to follow. We did, and next thing we knew, we were moving downwards in what I can only describe as an elevator without a door or ceiling.

We stopped within a few seconds, and Zach led the way into another hallway, coming to a halt in front of a large, closed door. Standing next to it, what I first thought was a statue turned out to be a human giant, at least 12 to 13 feet tall, standing at attention in a guard's stance. The figure was as breathtaking as the other statues we had seen; his skin tones looked real, and the muscles visible to us were perfect, worthy of a Da Vinci diagram. What stopped us in our tracks was when he turned his massive head and looked down at Zach, saying something in a language foreign to the others but not to me.

My mouth dropped open as I understood every word he said as he spoke, and said, "Welcome back, Guardian." This "statue" was, in actuality, alive. Everyone stopped dead in their tracks. The giant was clothed in a thick leather tunic with short sleeves and pants, his feet covered by large leather boots. His huge, muscular arms protruded from his sleeves. Arms to his side, with the head resting on the floor, was a huge hammer in his right hand, while in his left hand, in the same position, was a massive pickax.

Zach said something in response that I missed. The giant's head returned to his forward stare, saying nothing more. As Zach approached, the door opened on its own, and lights came on in a completely different type of room—large but with a more rugged feel, lacking the shiny cleanliness of the other rooms we had seen. As the group walked past the guard, standing unmoving at the door, all stared as they passed, and Doc muttered, "Zach?"

That is Stilgard, one of the last Stynth in this part of the complex. His job is to guard this room, which he has done for thousands of years. Still in awe, it took us a few minutes to scan the interior of the room we had entered. It was long, maybe ninety to one hundred feet, and at least eighty feet wide. "This is our gold processing room," Zach told us.

It was then that we saw, down to our right, the large machine against the far wall. He explained that the machine processed the raw ore and smelted it into ingots in a matter of minutes. To its left, stacked in neat rows reaching the end of the room, were gold ingots—three deep and each the size of a typical building brick.

The stacks were at least eight feet high. The gold wall must have been fifty to sixty feet in length.

In front of it, maybe ten to fifteen feet toward the middle of the room, were stacks of smaller ingots, approximately half the size of the larger blocks. The rows were ten blocks wide and seven feet high, and also extended the length of the room. Dimitri, eyes wide, said, "I feel like I've just walked into Fort Knox."

"This is one of the ways we fund our ongoing operations."

Doc immediately jumped on Zach's phrase, "You said 'our' operations?"

"Yes, over these many thousands of years, our original settlers have worked to establish a worldwide network of organizations. We have operating centers globally. In many of the centers, they have operations similar to this, although this is the oldest. Gold, silver, diamonds, and other rare commodities are gathered and stockpiled and used as needed to fund our many operations," Zach explained.

"You must have trillions of dollars then, globally," Doc said.

Zach laughed, "Sorry, Doc, the actual dollar figure far exceeds your level of comprehension."

"What kind of operations are you talking about?" O'Reilly asked.

"The kind that keep mankind from destroying this planet," he replied cryptically.

Continuing with his lecture, Zach said, "When this site was being constructed some ninety thousand years ago, as we reached the ten-mile-deep depths, we came across huge veins of gold and silver. Pushing a little deeper into the ancient volcanic layers, we came across pockets of diamonds and other gems. This whole area is mineral-rich, but the depths prohibited your surface-dwelling ancestors from detecting them. We began harvesting these riches and stockpiling them, knowing that in the future, they would become valuable commodities."

"But what exactly does your network do with resources like this?" Doc asked again.

"That is a discussion for another time," Zach said as he turned and headed for the door.

CHAPTER 37

As we walked toward our doorless elevator, Joe asked, "How deep are we, Zach?"

"This level is seven miles below the surface, my lab is two levels above us, five miles below. The mining operation spans another three levels below. Each level is approximately one to two miles deeper than the one above; they vary according to the location and depth of the resources. Our mining is no longer exploratory. We have found the deposits we need and will continue to work them until there is a need to move on, which I don't see happening anytime soon," Zach said.

We stepped into our elevator, I guess we'll call it that, and were whisked to the level of Zach's lab. When we entered the lab, it was clear that something was happening, as the lights were blinking and the holographic displays above the consoles were displaying various types of data. The large Earth globe was suspended over the table, minus the moon image. A bright red line had traced its way around the globe and was currently stopped. The large red dot at its end was glowing brightly.

"So that's the current location of our meteorite?" I asked.

"Yes, it is, and I guess we have our answer as to who these guys were working for," Zach said, as the image grew in size and the dot appeared, stopped almost in the middle of Iran.

"So, it was the Iranians who were behind this," Dimitri spat out with an intense level of distaste.

"Well, if not behind it, they certainly are involved," Zach replied. "They were not on the top of my list of perpetrators," he added.

"Zoom in and let's get an exact location," I said.

The image grew larger, and we could soon make out the region, which had a yellow and black circle marker on it, with the red dot sitting on top of it.

"Uh-oh," Zach said. "That's not good."

"What do you mean?" Colt asked.

"That yellow and black circle marks one of Iran's nuclear facilities, and that is Natanz, the largest one in the country. It's located deep underground. We don't know how deep, but it's bunker buster bomb proof—even tactical nukes can't get to it supposedly," Zach answered.

He was busy making adjustments on the console, and a video image appeared. He had obviously repositioned one of his satellites over the area, and the image provided a large section of the countryside around the facility marker in the center, showing us about a ten-mile radius.

He checked additional data on a screen next to the video feed and said, "Well, it's been there for two hours, so my guess is they've unloaded it and are positioning it into one of their big labs. We need to keep an eye on this," he said with a level of concern in his voice. On the other side of the room, a large image of one of the international news channels appeared with the volume low. Next to it appeared another large image, this time of the Al Jazeera news channel.

"What's going on?" Doc asked.

"I'm pretty sure these guys are about to get real stupid," Zach replied. "To bring an object emitting an unknown energy signature into a nuclear facility that size is not a smart move, I don't care who you are."

They had been staring at the screens for the better part of an hour. Nothing but run-of-the-mill news and propaganda was being spewed on the television channels. Zach checked his data again and noted that the meteorite had been at the site for a little over three hours when I finally asked, "Okay, Zach, you're obviously waiting for something to happen, what is it?"

Quite bluntly, Zach said, "I didn't want these bad guys messing around here ever again, so you might say I included a little surprise package for them... he didn't finish his sentence as the red dot of the meteorite turned purple.

On the video screen, the satellite image seemed to jitter for a few seconds. Then the ground for about two hundred yards subsided, dropping maybe ninety feet before a huge fountain of dirt, rock, and debris exploded from the center of where the yellow and black circle had been located. It looked like the entire countryside for miles around it bulged, expanding upward by hundreds of feet. It reminded me of how the old aluminum foil containers bulged when the popcorn we used to pop on the top of the stove filled them. As quickly as it appeared, the explosion "imploded," taking the surrounding countryside with it into the huge crater it was forming, expanding swiftly, much wider than our field of view.

Zach quickly broadened the satellite image by miles, and still the huge crater was expanding. Secondary explosions continued until the crater expansion finally stopped, reaching almost two miles in width. From our vantage point overhead, the center of the crater appeared bottomless.

We were all standing there, staring at the screens, and within five minutes, the TV feeds went nuts with breaking news bulletins about an accident at one of Iran's nuclear facilities. The next breaking news was the reporting of earthquakes with magnitudes of 9.6 and higher around the country.

I turned to Zach, who was standing there, arms crossed, staring at the big screen with a wry smile on his face.

"What?" was all I could say.

Zach turned and looked at me, and straight-faced said, "Guess they didn't read the sticky note I put on the meteorite that said, 'Don't scan this rock.'"

Looking back at the satellite feed from above, the gaping crater continued to expand, and the beginnings of a small mushroom cloud were forming, rising from the center of the crater.

Zach turned to look at the rest of the team and then back at me and said, "This is why we keep our energy out of the hands of your people. If you could measure it, there was less than half a thimbleful of our energy infused in that two-ton meteor. That's how it reacted to the use of their scanning technology. Of course, the explosion was amplified tens of thousands of times over, going off in that nuclear facility. That's what caused the real problem. Now you can see the outcome if the two are somehow ever combined."

The news reports continued to come in, describing initial assessments of the extent of the devastation. The next breaking news banner was that massive earthquakes had damaged two more nuclear sites. The death toll continued to rise.

Reports continued with the detection of radioactive fallout beginning to appear, spreading to the surrounding cities and countryside.

"Those freaking idiots," Zach said angrily, as he worked over the holographic displays of his consoles. Finally, he said, "There, I've just created a containment bubble a mile around the sites and dispersed the radioactive material in the air to a non-lethal level. I hope every one of those bastards responsible for this was in the lab when they scanned the meteorite."

Zach was mad... no, he was extremely pissed as he sat down on one of the stools in the lab. Finally, he said, "There will be a lot of collateral damage from this event, and I am responsible for some of it. But those who are working on weapons of mass destruction are always trying to make them more powerful and more lethal, and are really the ones to blame."

I walked to him and said, "Zach, as I see it, your

role in this, as unfortunate as some of the outcomes will be, fulfilled your job as planet Guardian. If we hadn't stopped them from getting access to the power supply, the possibilities of that outcome are even more horrible to imagine. Once we provided a solution, stopping them from getting their hands on it, what they did after that is on them."

Doc chimed in, "Colt's right, Zach, their final actions were out of our hands, and like you said, they got really stupid."

He took a deep breath and said, "I know you're right, but this type of destruction pains me deeply."

Zach got up and watched the news feeds headlines for a couple of minutes, then went to the table, pulled back the satellite view, and moved the global view to include all of Iran, so that the two-mile-wide crater was visible from space. He made a couple of adjustments, and white lines appeared, emanating from the crater location and spreading outwards, and showing up in various regions. "Those are the quake lines that formed," Zach said. Some were larger and longer than others. "The blast has impacted the natural fault lines that already existed in the area, providing the energy to make them active."

On the floating Earth globe, he zoomed in on the northern region of the country and also brought up the satellite image of the area, showing the city of Tehran. Examining the white lines that had appeared, some had emerged in the city, although they were smaller in scale.

By now, an hour had passed since the explosion, and aftershocks were still being felt as Zach zoomed in on the image to a clear view of the city buildings below.

He turned to us and said, "This is one of those times in history where, as Guardian, a series of events has occurred, and an unplanned opportunity has presented itself for global change for good. A decision that falls squarely on my shoulders, as it has for many thousands of years, and the occurrence of events, large and small, must be made. The ruling military government buildings and the supreme leader's headquarters filled the screen as Zach made an adjustment at the console. The image began to shake, and a fissure opened up in front of the multi-block-long complex. As it opened, the buildings started collapsing, falling into it as the rend tore through building after building. Smaller buildings around the area also collapsed. The earthquake lasted two minutes and, in that time, the political nature of that ancient country changed forever.

After a few moments of silence, Doc said, "It looks like a series of self-inflicted events is going to have a significant impact on the future of this entire region."

Zach turned off all the images in the room and said philosophically, "Time will tell, as it always does." He opened a portal to his back room at the trading post, and we all departed this underground nexus for change.

CHAPTER 38

Over the next two days, what had started for us as a mystery to be solved about some long-forgotten explorer, his purported discovery, and a potential treasure hunt, had turned into a geopolitical global reorganization with *Outer Limits* overtones. All this… through no fault of our own.

Local law enforcement had shown up investigating the disappearance of the entire solar energy research organization and the mysterious hole in the ground, and left scratching their heads, telling Zach they would get back to him.

Lawrence had contacted us with the court ruling that the agreement with the solar group was illegal and therefore null and void. Additionally, a couple of the administrators at the BLM and DIA were under internal investigation when large sums of money were found in their personal accounts from a questionable corporate entity.

The local tribal council had submitted a request to remove the fence around the facility and assume ownership of all equipment and buildings left behind by the center. It had been approved by the court within twenty-four hours, thanks to Lawrence and his group of lawyers in Phoenix and their aggressive approach to the situation.

Iran had announced with other Middle East countries that they were ending all nuclear programs for the foreseeable future, while denying governmental responsibility for the massive calamity. There were also communications among the other nuclear countries concerning new talks on ending or at least additional control and monitoring of these types of programs. It appears that our "event" had a significant impact on attitudes toward the limitations and control of nuclear programs worldwide. I mused that it would be safe to say that the two-mile-wide crater and the collateral destruction had scared the "beejezus" out of everyone involved, as well as their global neighbors.

Zach had gotten past his angry mood and was getting back to his old genial, taciturn self, explaining to me that massive destruction had happened many times before, recorded in myth, legends, and biblical references, but he had never gotten used to the death and destruction that often accompanied these major world events or changes. With a shake of his head and genuine sadness on his face, he acknowledged that catastrophic happenings are something that a Guardian learns to deal with. I reassured him that, pragmatically speaking, some very good things came out of the event, even though there were also horrific negative aspects. Nodding, Zach added that there are both upsides and downsides to living a very long life.

Things were wrapping up as Zach mentioned he had more information to share with us. The team returned with him to the underground, and he showed us more of the facility. Of special interest was a room that used holographic displays introducing us to all the inhabitants of his planet, not just the few species they were able to bring on their ship. Doc noted that he could see how many of them were the basis for a large number of religious and supernatural legends passed down through historical records worldwide. Zach concurred and provided us with many examples of this happening. He also showed us how the planet reformation had begun on Mars before the major solar events destroyed much of it, driving the settlers back to Earth or underground, where enclaves were still active today. The biggest problem they faced was that the solar storms had stripped away the planet's atmosphere. Now the inhabitants had to live in sealed sections of their underground cities, providing another jaw-dropping "Zach moment" for us.

Along with that came the confirmation that yes, there were UFOs, and we continue to be visited and observed by other space-faring civilizations. Most were of an inquisitive nature, but not all were harmless beings. Zach said he has had to intervene a few times over the millennia to protect Earth from these visitors with "ill intent," as he called them. Most of those types had gotten the message after he had to destroy one of their large ships back in the 1900s over Siberia, Russia. He said our scientists refer to it as the Tunguska event and attribute it to a large asteroid that exploded just before it hit the ground, creating an air blast.

In reality, it turned out to be a ship from a planet about 300 light-years away whose warlike civilization was based on planetary conquest and control. He luckily destroyed/vaporized the ship before it could land. That sent a clear message to others with similar intentions that Earth was off-limits, and it had the means to defend itself if necessary.

Zach said to the group, "I realize this is a lot to take in, but you have to understand you are now part of something greater than anything you could have imagined, and it must be kept secret. I think from what you've seen, you all understand that. This crash education course could have been provided to you differently under other circumstances, as we have learning processes that deliver information directly to the brain. It is quick, painless, and quite effective.

"But your group has been exposed to my world in a very unorthodox manner through firsthand life experiences. I felt that continuing to show you firsthand would be the best way to complete your necessary introduction quickly. The big details are what you need to know for now. As you might suspect, there is much, much more, but additional information will be provided as necessary. You are a unique group of individuals with skills that complement my own. In many instances, such as this most recent one, you are capable of doing what I am not and have performed most capably. That is why you are being included in this sharing of information. I feel that I may have need of these unique skills in the future, and want you to be aware of the global implications that may be at stake should that need arise."

I was standing next to Zach as he continued, "This is the first that Colt has heard of this. I wanted you all to hear it from me at the same time. None of you are being forced to take part; if you choose not to, we have painless ways to remove memories and wipe the slate clean, as it were, of anything you have learned or experienced while here. There would be no negative outcomes from that decision. Should you agree to join me, then all your information and communications will come from Colt." He turned to face me, smiling, and said, "I already know Colt has agreed to join."

Colt realized Zach had read his thoughts as he was thinking, hell yeah, I'm joining, replying to Zach, "That was a little sneaky, man."

"Just a little," Zach replied, still smiling.

He turned to the rest of the group and said, "It is totally up to you, your decision alone," and waited.

The team members, a little awe-struck, turned and looked at one another, silent for a few minutes, then almost in unison said, "I'm in."

Zach turned back to me and said, "Welcome to the family."

Almost immediately, Dimitri's hand went up, and Zach said, "You have a question, Dimitri?"

"Yeah, does this mean that now I get to shoot that space ray gun thing again?"

Replying in a deadly serious-sounding voice, Zach said, "Only if Colt says it's okay." He got it out before breaking up laughing, saying to me, "You do have a leash for him, I hope."

I just shook my head from side to side and said, "I try," as the whole room broke out in laughter.

Except for Dimitri, who looked around and said, "What?"

Once the laughter had subsided and conversations had begun amongst the team members, Zach leaned to me and said, "Jeannie agreed with this decision. Just wanted you to know."

Stepping away, Zach said to the group, "Follow me, I've got one more thing you need to see. He led them to another room that almost resembled a theater, with about fifteen chairs in it. As they all took their seats, the large wall in front of them lit up with a three-dimensional forest scene, slowly pulling back to reveal a broader view of a huge city that resembled the Citadel they had found in Ecuador. Its architecture was majestic and breathtaking. As their viewpoint slowly changed, moving around the cityscape, they could discern people at street level and vehicles in the air. The aerial view pulled back even further, and in the distance, a large body of water could be seen, with mountains in the background. The room was silent as everyone soaked in the beauty of the scene.

Zach spoke, "That is my city. It is approximately one hundred miles below us."

As the team was digesting that bit of information, he walked over to me as I was standing at the back of the room.

"Colt, you need to get Dr. Worthington here as soon as possible," Zach said.

That startled me. Tess was aware of all the goings on with Jeannie and the history of her advanced civilization and its connections with the history of our planet and its development, but she had never been to the Citadel in Ecuador, nor had she met Jeannie, and certainly knew nothing about Zach and this part of the story. With a puzzled look, I agreed to get in touch with my favorite archaeologist immediately.

CHAPTER 39

Knowing Zach would not make that kind of request unless it were of the utmost importance, I pulled out my SAT phone, looked at my watch, and saw that it was about 10:30 p.m. in Cairo. I hit speed dial on her name, and the phone rang. Zach's tech ensured that all satellite and cellular communications worked perfectly, regardless of their location, above ground or below, making communication very convenient.

She picked up on the fourth ring. "Hello, Dr. Worthington," I said.

"Colt," an excited and surprised voice said, "Well, hello."

"Hope I didn't catch you in the middle of anything," I replied.

"No, I just got home from the museum a couple of hours ago, ate something, took a shower, and was having a glass of wine."

"Sounds nice," I said, "have an extra glass?" I asked.

She laughed, "Well, of course I do, where are you?" she asked.

I pictured the living room of her apartment in Egypt and touched the stone on my bracelet. A portal appeared, and I stepped through into her living room, saying, "Right here."

She was sitting on her couch and almost dropped her wine glass when I appeared standing next to her.

"Oh, my God, I swear I'll never get used to that," she said as I leaned down and kissed her forehead.

Still reeling from my sudden and unexpected arrival, she pointed to the wine rack on the counter. I retrieved a glass and returned to the couch, noticing that the bathrobe had partially fallen open, revealing a significant portion of her silky, white leg and thigh. Smiling, I put my arm around her and gave her a proper, passionate kiss on her lips. "Guess she missed me, too!"

It was one of those take-your-breath-away, full-of-promises kisses, and she responded in kind, pressing her body against mine. The moment held until I slowly broke away and said, "How quickly can you get a bag packed?"

Her eyes widened, not expecting that kind of response to their kiss.

I grinned that boyish grin she loved so much and said, "We're going to Arizona, so pack accordingly and lightly. I looked at my watch and said, "You've got ten minutes." I tossed down my glass of wine and poured another as I said, "I'll wait here."

She looked at my face and saw both the humor and seriousness in it. She knew what that meant as she finished her wine, jumped up, and headed to start gathering a few essential travel items without hesitation. "You're not kidding, are you?" came the voice from the bedroom amongst the rustling of clothing being dealt with both on her body and her small duffel bag. "How long?" came the question from the other room.

"Three, four days tops," I replied, "and it's hot during the day and cool at night."

"I know Arizona this time of year, silly boy. Where?" came the next question.

"Northeast Rim of the Grand Canyon," I replied.

"Roughing it or...?"

"No, we have accommodations, rustic but nice," I replied.

"Got it," she replied, "five minutes."

"Great, I've got time for another glass of wine," I said.

"Since I have no idea what we're doing," Tess said, "better pour me one for the road too."

He did and had it sitting on the table when she came out: khaki six-pocket shorts, casual hiking boots, a beige tank top with a long-sleeve cotton shirt over it, sleeves rolled up, and shirt tails tied at the waist, her keffiyeh around her neck, her hat, and her backpack slung over her shoulder.

I looked at my watch as Tess picked up her wine, tossed it down, and said, "Ready!" Ten minutes exactly. This woman is amazing, I thought as I stood up, kissed her again, and with my arm around her shoulder, I mentally envisioned Zach's lab and touched the blue stone on my silver cuff. The portal opened, and we stepped through it together.

I didn't quite get the kind of reaction expected. Maybe I suppose because stepping into a room full of electronic consoles with lights blinking doesn't have the same effect on someone who has been accustomed to opening royal burial chambers filled with riches, fit for a king or queen, as it would have on an everyday person.

Tess turned to me and calmly said, "Well, I guess we're not in Kansas anymore, Toto," looking around the room once again. None of the holographic images were on, so I guess the room looked like any other high-tech computer lab to her.

It's all about context, I thought, and immediately got a response from Zach saying, "Very true, Colt," as he entered the room, walking up to my companion and casually saying, "Tess Worthington, I'm Zach Fremont, a colleague of Jeannie's, and very pleased to meet you," extending his hand.

She accepted it and returned a firm handshake that made him smile as she said, "Always glad to meet Colt's friends."

"I must apologize for the abrupt circumstances surrounding your trip here, but it was rather important, and Colt was kind enough to oblige," Zach answered.

Tess, doing her usual detailed inspection of her surroundings again replied, "Although I'm not really sure where 'this' is, but Colt said we would be going to Arizona, the Grand Canyon area."

"Oh, let me assure you, that's exactly where you are, only five miles below the surface," he replied.

This revelation elicited a reaction from Tess, who looked quizzically at me, somewhat surprised, and said, "Underground, five miles?"

Zach stepped right in and said, "I'm sure you have questions that will be answered, but right now, I believe we have some folks who are going to be happy to see you, so please, follow me."

When we entered the immense, beautifully carved hallway, I could see a sense of inquisitive wonder appear on her face as Zach led us to the room where the rest of the team was gathered. They looked up from their seats as we entered, and a mild level of pandemonium arose as choruses of "Tess" broke out as they left their chairs and converged on her. Greetings and heartfelt hugs were shared as a feeling of a gleeful reunion filled the room.

Zach, still smiling, pulled me aside and said, "We're going to have to bring her up to speed quickly on what has happened and where she is. It's important that she understands the significance and gravity of the situation."

"I agree," I said as the reunion continued. "But that's going to take a little time," I said.

"Not as long as you think," Zach replied, with a wink.

The questions were flying fast and furious from everyone in all directions.

"Where have you been? How did you get here? What is this place? What are you guys doing here?"

Zach interrupted the information melee that was

occurring and said, "Hey, guys, I need to borrow Tess for a few minutes, and all this will be much easier for everyone," as he took Tess by the arm and motioned me to follow them back to his lab area.

Tess, now looking totally bewildered, went along as Zach led us both into the small room that just days earlier had been the location for my "mind expansion treatment"—or whatever you call it.

"Please, have a seat, you too, Colt," Zach said as he sat down.

"I know you are familiar with Jeannie," he said, "and who she is, although you two have not yet met." He turned to me and said, "That will be changing very soon."

Tess replied, "Yes, I am very familiar with Colt's experiences and Jeannie's history and their activities."

"Then you understand how advanced the civilization Jeannie and I come from is compared to Earth and some of its involvement in your history and prehistory," Zach stated.

"Yes, I do, although I'm sure there's a lot more to learn," Tess replied.

"Good, then what we are about to do is, I guess you could call it an update for you. Colt has recently received new information that extends his understanding far beyond his previous limits. What I am about to suggest is that you allow me to educate you both to a much fuller extent. Colt, this will benefit you as well; that's why I would like you both to go through the process together."

"So, what you're referring to is that rapid learning process you talked about a couple of days ago," I said.

"Yes, this will take you both to the same level of understanding. Jeannie thinks it is imperative for all our futures. If you agree, it will take about an hour. This will give your brains time to absorb the information and open new synaptic pathways in them without causing any harm or discomfort."

Tess looked at me now wide-eyed with huge question marks in her facial expression.

I smiled reassuringly and said, "I've been through this process, and look at me. I'm fine."

This brought a wry smile to her face, and she said, "I'm not sure I'd call it fine, but okay, I'm game." Looking back at Zach, she said, "And he will be with me the whole time?"

"Yes, he will, in fact, you will even be able to converse during the session."

"Oh, great," I quipped, "So no tranquility, peace, and quiet like I had before?"

This drew a hard punch in the arm from the chair next to mine, "You cretin," she said, eliciting a big smile from Zach.

CHAPTER 40

An hour later, we both opened our eyes, and Tess turned to me and said, "Oh, my God, I had no idea."

"Pretty amazing," I replied, only slightly more prepared for the experience than she had been. It was much more expansive than my previous session, and I was visibly impressed. "That was more than I expected," I said to Zach.

He nodded and said, "It is a major expansion of your learning experience. There's more, but for now, you are prepared and both on equal terms in the knowledge of our extraterrestrial race and history."

Tess commented, "I feel surprisingly refreshed. Not what I would have guessed or expected after having that much knowledge dumped into my brain."

I said, "Too many Sci-Fi movies," giving her the hitchhiker's thumb sign.

Zach laughed and said, "We don't do exploding brains or people running around screaming in pain with their hands on their heads."

"That's a good thing," Tess replied. "Boy, do I feel good," she continued.

"Another benefit of the process is a major dose of

the rejuvenation energy one gets. It gives more energy, vitality, good health, and longer life," Zach replied.

"Really?" Tess asked.

Zach nodded, and getting up from his chair, said, "I need to get the others back to the trading post, but you two stay here. You're not done yet. I'll be right back," and he left the room.

"What did he mean by that?" Tess asked.

"I have no idea," I replied.

Zach returned after a few minutes and sat back down, placing his fingertips together in a thoughtful pose before speaking.

"Let this be your final lesson for today. There is something out there that is part of everything we do. The universe and galaxies are all part of a cosmic connection. Everything is connected; how or why, we have no idea. However, over the course of our existence spanning hundreds of thousands of years, it has become increasingly apparent to us that this is true. One of your great scientists once said, 'We are made of star-stuff. We are a way for the universe to know itself.' It was his way of highlighting our intrinsic connection to the cosmos, and he was correct." Colt and Tess both recognized the Sagan quote, as Zach continued, "Everything happens for a reason, most we can't or don't understand. So, civilizations try to put these events into a frame of reference their minds can comprehend and accept, when all they are doing is fooling themselves and refusing to accept this universal truth.

"Man has found many convenient ways to

categorize the unexplainable. In religions, it is a belief in the will of whatever supreme being guides you. In everyday life, we have a multitude of names for these unexplainable events: luck, fate, serendipity, coincidence, the list is long. Few have the ability to acknowledge that it is a cosmic event, something that beings experience whether they like it or not. As humans, we want to feel in control of the world around us, but in reality, we move and act at the will of the unfettered cosmos.

"Advanced beings gave up trying to understand it long ago. If it is meant to be, it will. Many would call that a fatalistic approach, once again, trying to frame it in a reference they can understand. I would say it is a plane of existence approach. There are macrocosmic connections out there that are made every day, every hour, every minute, and every second. Be open to them, listen to them. If your gut seems to be telling you something, be it good or bad, or you have a dream or a feeling about something, listen to it! The star system is sending you a message, and it's up to you to decide how you will react. Sometimes these messages seem loud and clear, and at other times, much more subtle. Be open to them all."

Zach stopped, waited a couple of minutes, then stood and said, "Come with me."

Without hesitation, Tess and I followed him into the hallway and then turned into a small adjoining hall that we hadn't noticed before. At the end of it were two large doors, devoid of any design or ornamentation. As Zach approached, the doors slid open, and he stepped aside, revealing a dark room. He motioned us to enter;

we did, and the doors silently slid closed behind us. Zach remained outside.

Standing in complete darkness was disorienting, but after a few seconds, a shaft of golden light came from above, illuminating a large dais in the middle of the room. It was maybe four feet high, five feet wide, and seven feet long. We could make out that it was intricately carved, but what caught our attention was the top, as our eyes were drawn to a large, ornate sarcophagus glowing in a light that was slowly getting brighter.

We began walking toward the sarcophagus when the carving on the end of the dais revealed itself to be a large carved cartouche inlaid with gold. As we got closer, Tess gasped and grabbed my arm, trembling. She was frozen in place, her breathing had stopped, and then suddenly, she exhaled and raised her other hand, pointing at the large golden cartouche and whispering... "It's her."

It was then that I recognized it, the cartouche of Cleopatra!

Now, my heart began pounding as we slowly approached the dais together, and the unbelievable craftsmanship of the sarcophagus became clear. Gold was everywhere, and the colors were striking. The blues were carved sapphires, and the greens were emeralds; there were also white diamonds and inlaid silver. The black stones were polished obsidian, and the reds were rubies. As we reached the side of the dais, its engraved hieroglyphs inlaid with gold became visible.

Tess began translating out loud, "Here is the final

resting place of the Pharaoh Queen of Upper and Lower Egypt, Cleopatra. Last of the Ptolemaic Dynasty and ruler of all Egypt. May she find eternal peace in the afterlife."

Tess was now leaning against me, her arm around my waist for both the physical and emotional support she needed at this moment, tears running down her cheeks.

I pulled her closer and quietly said, "You did it; you found Cleopatra."

It was then that we saw, still partially shrouded in darkness, the golden throne. Beautifully engraved hieroglyphs adorned the golden surface, and brilliant-cut jewels were set into the surface. Without thinking, Tess had reached out and placed her hand on the sarcophagus. In an instant, the throne was bathed in the same golden light, and a human form began to materialize. Within seconds, Cleopatra, in all her majestic pharaoh's regalia, sat on the throne before us.

We were both stunned when, unbelievably, she began to speak in a language we did not understand, yet we heard her words clearly in our minds.

"Welcome, I have been expecting you for some time. You have been the one selected to discover my final resting place. I know not how, but I had a vision long ago that you, Tess, would be the one," Cleopatra softly intoned.

I had to wrap my arms tighter around Tess to support her as her legs gave way, thinking for a moment that Tess had fainted, but then realizing that the shock of hearing this apparition mentioning her by name had startled her so that she almost collapsed. Now that I thought about it, I felt myself getting a little shaky too. We both regained control and stood firmly again as the image continued to speak.

"I have chosen this as my final resting place among my new, yet ancient family. I have traveled far, and I am no longer a pharaoh or a queen, just a woman who has found a new home. I left that life behind me and do not regret it. My only regret is that I lost the love of my life too early. You are strong and destined to do great things, but do not let the same heartbreak befall you that I have suffered. During life, the loss of one's true love cannot be reclaimed. Therefore, I implore you, never lose yours. Having delivered my message, I can now join my Anthony with a full heart in the afterlife. Thank you for fulfilling the prophecy that has consumed my every waking moment for so long."

The image began disappearing slowly as the light over the throne dimmed. Soon, it was bathed in darkness again, but the light over the sarcophagus seemed to glow brighter and then slowly began to dim. As it did, the room's walls took on a soft glow. We stood in that dimly lit space for I don't know how long, entwined in each other's arms, Tess softly sobbing again as I felt my sight growing blurry from the dust in the air... I told myself.

The soft crying subsided, and Tess, still holding me tightly, looked up with tears still in her eyes, said, "Never," and raised her lips to mine in a kiss I will remember for the rest of my life. I knew then that this was one of those cosmic moments Zach had talked about as I returned the kiss with every fiber of my being. We stepped away from the dais as the glow over the sarcophagus continued to dim and the doors to the room opened on their own. As we started to walk away, Tess turned for a final look at the sarcophagus and said, "I didn't find her... she found me."

We walked slowly toward the open doors, stopping at the entrance, looking back at the dark room when Tess turned to me and slowly asked, "Did that really happen?"

Looking into those glistening eyes, I responded, "I hope so."

We left the room, and the doors silently closed behind us. Standing in the main corridor, I turned to Tess and said, "That had to be what Zach was preparing us for."

Tess, her normal self-assured tone returning, replied, "It had to be; I'm sure it was!"

Zach's message came loud and clear in my mind, "Meet us at the Trading Post."

Now, holding Tess's hand, I said, "We have to go," and opened a portal to the back room of the post, and we both stepped through.

The team was seated around the table. Zach was standing waiting for us as we walked into the room. He looked at us expectantly and then was pleased when Tess said, "Amazing."

That had obviously been the response he had been waiting for as he smiled broadly and pulled up two more chairs. The cider was back on the table, and the glasses were full. He picked one up and said,

"Colt, you and your team have performed in a manner beyond expression. Your self-description as a treasure hunter far understates your singular and collective actual abilities. Words cannot adequately express my gratitude for your help in resolving this operation. Therefore, I salute you and your team," he said, raising his glass.

"And since you all profess to be treasure hunters, it wouldn't be right for you to leave empty-handed." Zach nodded toward Joseph, standing by with a rolling cart covered in blue velvet. Pulling the cover off revealed several wooden boxes, one of which he placed in front of each team member. Removing the lids, they found two gold ingots and a small velvet bag inside. When the bags were opened, an assortment of multi-colored, priceless gems poured out.

"Consider this a small personal token of our gratitude for your help."

The gold from Zach's mine was 24 carats pure. That amounted to about three thousand dollars an ounce, making each five-pound bar worth around two hundred and forty thousand dollars each, and there was no way to put a price on the gems in the pouches.

"Also, if I could ask all of you, please, to stand," Zach intoned, which we did. Joseph then approached Zach with a black box. He opened the lid as he approached the ladies first, asking for their right hands. Reggie was first, and as she extended her hand to Zach, he removed a large gold ring with a blue stone and a diamond on either side of it. He took Reggie's hand and slid the large ring onto her finger.

It looked huge, and as she was about to say something, the ring shrank in size until it fit her finger perfectly. The same thing happened with O'Reilly. The stones were exquisite, and they sized themselves to be tasteful and not the least bit ostentatious.

The men's gold rings were slightly larger and expressed a more masculine feel. He reached Tess and uncovered another section of the box, removing a ring with a blue stone completely encircled by diamonds, as well as two red stones set among the diamonds on either side of the center blue stone, and slipped it on her finger. It fit itself the same way as the others had. She went to pull her hand back, and he stopped her, holding it and removing a solid gold ring from the box. There were no stones on this one, but it had a flat surface with a finely carved cartouche on it. He slid it on her little finger, and it fit perfectly the first time. Her eyes widened as she recognized Cleopatra's cartouche. He leaned forward and said something to her that I couldn't hear. Her look of astonishment grew.

My turn came, and I held out my hand. Zach removed a large gold ring, but this one was different. It had a red stone at its center, surrounded by diamonds, with two small blue sapphires positioned on either side of the red stone. It sized itself, and Zach smiled and said quietly so only Tess and I heard, "Fit for a king—or whatever you two imagine."

After a few moments of stunned silence, Dimitri said, laughing, "Colt, you'd better get on the phone and tell Mac to get the jet ready to come pick us up. I don't think we would pass security with this on a commercial flight," pointing to the wooden box with the gold bars in it.

Stepping back as everyone stared at their newly delivered riches, Zach said, "I do believe this calls for a celebration, so I have had the grilling experts in the town busy at work preparing one of our famous Fremont cookouts. I've already put a call in to Matt and Sam, who will be here along with everyone in the town. We are set up out back, and the food should be ready in a couple of hours. I suggest you prepare yourselves for some culinary delights, courtesy of the residents of the town."

I realized now that the aroma of outdoor fires and grilling meat was, in fact, evident. In all the excitement, I hadn't noticed it before, and I also hadn't realized how hungry I was, as everyone began professing to be starving as well.

Three hours later still found us all behind the trading post, sitting at the homemade picnic tables, enjoying the best barbecue ever. All the residents of the town showed up and participated in one way or another in the preparation of the feast. Matt and Sam had brought over a case of the famous hard cider for the adults and another case of the regular cider for the kids.

It was our last night in Fremont, and it turned into one hell of a celebration.

We were thanked repeatedly for our help in ridding the town of the energy center and returning the land to the people. It was a good feeling to have been able to help in that regard. As the night grew late and people began cleaning up in the firelight of the many small fires that had been built, Matt and Sam took me aside for a private conversation. Matt said, "I never dreamed that accepting the job to fly Doc, O'Reilly, and Joe around the canyon would turn out to be such an adventure."

Sam agreed and said getting back into the cockpit and flying with Matt was a wonderful and unexpected event. As they stood there, Matt's arm around Sam's shoulders, it was clear they had found something that they may have both thought was lost, and that made me feel good.

He also assured me that if I ever needed an additional pilot, all I had to do was call. No matter where or when, he would be there. We embraced as brothers and, receiving a kiss from Sam, said our goodbyes.

The evening was filled with handshakes, embraces, and tearful farewells. We had put in our call to Mac, the pilot of our corporate jet, who said he would be landing at the airport late tomorrow afternoon to pick us up. The cleanup had been completed, the fires were put out, and the team, including Zach, Joseph, and a fresh bottle of hard cider, had retired to the back room of the trading post.

The mood was somewhat somber as we sat around the table, probably for the last time, with our glasses of cider. Tess had her head leaning against my shoulder as we sipped our drinks. Finally, Zach said, "It has truly been an honor working with all of you. What started as a problem to which I had no solution turned into not only a solution to my problem but a series of events that have had unforeseen positive global outcomes and new friendships."

"I think it's safe to say there were cosmic influences at work here," Doc added. "I wouldn't be a bit surprised at that."

Tess looked at me and then back at the group and said somewhat softly, "I wouldn't argue with that. One never knows," raising her glass in a toast as the others did too. "To the cosmic threads that tie us all together," she said as everyone nodded and took their drink.

Zach spoke again, "Now, you all know something of my world and what is going on unseen, and its importance and its need for secrecy. I have no doubts it will remain safe with you." There was another lifting of glasses in positive acknowledgement. "I will say this, Colt, Tess, Doc, Joe, O'Reilly, Reggie, and Dimitri, we will see each other again, I have no doubt. I know not when, but I feel our paths were destined to cross, as I am sure they will again. I have new friends, a new family, and I am looking forward to what the future will bring."

It was then that a long, lone wolf howl filled the evening stillness. Zach smiled as we all did, and Doc said, "You don't think...."

Dimitri laughed and said, "I guess Woofie agrees." That indeed in itself was cosmic.

We left the next day. Departing with memories, experiences, and the feeling that this was not the end of something, but only the beginning—of what we didn't know, but were sure the future had plans for us, and we would discover them in due time, as we always did.

EPILOGUE

The following two weeks were hectic, as I played catch-up at the office back in Florida. Within a day, I received an update from Lawrence that there had been a serious shake-up at the BLM both locally and at the national level. The same was true with the Bureau of Indian Affairs. New leadership had been put in place, and things were looking good.

Oh, and Lawrence also loved the ring that Zach had sent him, since he was an integral part of the team as well. Fremont had taken control of the old energy center and converted it into a school, serving students from Kindergarten through 9th grade. They also established a tech center for hands-on trades in welding, building construction, and heavy equipment operation, utilizing the equipment left behind by the center's previous occupants. They also expanded the medical clinic that was left behind. It was now a well-stocked, "no cost" medical facility for local residents.

On a more global scene, the twenty-something-mile-wide crater and nuclear explosions in Iran had gotten the attention of world powers and the United Nations. Serious meetings were being scheduled, and discussions of control, disarmament, and the end of testing and development of enriched nuclear material were on the table. Additionally, a significant positive regime change was underway in Iran, as a democratic movement was gaining momentum and gaining traction. Removal of the radical religious/morality police squads was taking place all over the country. Their local offices and headquarters were stormed by partisans, often without mercy.

A new, more tolerant government was being discussed and gaining strength as a genuinely democratic vote was planned for the election of new leadership. To the entire world's benefit, Zach's radioactive containment fields were holding at the blast site and limiting radioactive contamination. He had assured us that he would be able to decrease the levels of radioactivity within six months to safer levels, without wanting to do it too quickly and raise questions about how that could happen.

Tess had returned to Cairo, where she caught up on her current projects and put all future ones on hold for the time being, agreeing to meet me in Switzerland later in the month. We both agreed that we had a lot to discuss. The team had dispersed as they usually do after one of our, shall we say, "unusual," expeditions. Each was going their own way to blow off steam as they saw fit and relax, and no one was surprised to learn that Dimitri and Reggie were "vacationing" together.

All this ran through my mind as I sat in front of the roaring fire in the large fireplace, with its big eight-foot-tall windows on either side, offering Tess and me a beautiful view of Lake Lucerne. I had leased a quaint chalet for a month in the little town of Gersau, Switzerland, not far from the city of Lucerne. The snow was beginning to fall heavily as the sun set behind Mount Pilatus, and the sparse lights of houses on the dark mountainside across the lake began blinking on like fireflies in the night sky. Tess had insisted: no sand, no beaches, and no hot weather, and no arm-twisting was needed.

Tess joined me on the couch in front of the fireplace, holding a fresh bottle of wine, wearing the familiar bathrobe she had on when I had whisked her away from Cairo five weeks ago. Pouring the wine and handing me a glass with her right hand, I took it, then held onto her hand, kissing it gently and admiring the gold ring on her little finger, the cartouche plainly visible.

"That's a beautiful reminder of our experience," I said.

She smiled and replied, "Did you hear what Zach said when he gave it to me?"

"No," I replied, "I saw him lean close and say something, but couldn't hear a thing."

Tess held her hand up again, "He said it was hers."

"What?" I exclaimed. "That was actually Cleopatra's ring? That's amazing!"

Tess set her glass down and picked up a large Art History book she had brought and began paging through its illustrations. Carvings, tile works, and fresco paintings were featured in full color throughout. She finally stopped at a page with a beautiful painting, labeled "Anthony and Cleopatra circa 30 BCE, artist unknown," in which Cleopatra was standing behind Anthony, her hands resting on his shoulders. He was seated in a large chair draped in purple cloth of some type. Both were dressed in regal finery; she in her gown and jewels, and he in his military uniform, with his ruby-red cloak over his shoulder and sword at his side. A magnificent painting, I thought, the detail was amazing for being that old. Tess then took her finger and pointed to Cleopatra's right hand on Anthony's shoulder, and there, visible on Cleo's little finger, was the gold ring that Tess now wore. I gaped in amazement

and said, "Unbelievable."
Next, Tess drew my attention to Anthony's right hand resting on the arm of the large chair. There, clearly visible on his ring finger, was a large gold ring with a red stone at its center, surrounded by smaller white stones, with two small blue stones on either side of the red one. I was speechless and sat there in silence. "It couldn't be," I finally said quietly as I looked at the ring on my finger. Tess closed the book, placed it on the table, and said, "Maybe not," as she took my right hand in hers, both rings now side by side. "But, maybe, just maybe it actually is."
Still in shock at this revelation, I sat staring into Tess's eyes as she said, "Zach has shown us that the cosmos has its own plan and only reveals it to us when it feels it is time for us to receive it."
I put my arms around her and pulled her close, saying, "Then I believe it's time," and kissed her with the same passion as our kiss in Cleopatra's chamber, as the snow continued to fall and the fire crackled. Together, we sat there feeling the warmth of each other's bodies as we stared into the dancing flames in the fireplace, each pondering what the cosmos might have in store for us next....
But for now, we had each other, and that was enough.

**The Risky Business Chronicles Will Continue
More mystery, adventure, danger,
and treasure await them.**

ABOUT THE AUTHOR

Hep Aldridge

Hep Aldridge is a certified scuba diver, cave diver amateur archaeologist, and retired college administrator whose main area of interest in PreColumbian cultures of the Americas has expanded to mysteries of ancient civilizations worldwide. He has led or been part of archaeological expeditions to Mexico and Honduras, making discoveries that have been reported in National Geographic Magazine. Hep's related interest in space and "things unknown" was fueled by his time living in New Mexico as a teenager when he began to question the many strange andunexplainedthings he saw in the the night sky in the mid 60's. Some years later, chance meetings in Florida with well-known treasure hunters, Art McKee and Kip Wagner developed his interest in salvage operations for lost undersea treasure. The combination of these interests led to the genesis of the Risky Business Chronicles, a series of books which now spans five distinct sagas with a recurring memorable cast of characters. Hep is an Air Force veteran and resides on Florida's Space Coast.

To be the first to hear about news, new book releases and
bargains from Hep Aldridge

GO HERE TO SIGN UP TO BE ON THE VIP LIST
http//mailchi.mp/b0c291dd854f/hep-aldridge

Learn more about Hep and his background on his webpage

http//hepaldridge.com

You can write directly to Hep and connect with him online.
EMAIL: cxburnett@gmail.com
FACEBOOK: https//www.facebook.com/hep.aldridge7
X: https//x.com/AldridgeHep
INSTAGRAM:https://www.instagram.com/hepaldridge/

BOOKS BY THIS AUTHOR

Sunken Treasure Lost Worlds-Book 1

From the depths of the Atlantic off Cape Canaveral Florida, searching for sunken Spanish treasure, to the Andes mountains of Ecuador chasing the legend of a lost golden library, Dr. Colten X. Burnett and the Risky Business team are on a quixotic adventure.

While trying to make an honest, well sort of honest living, searching for remnants of the lost 1715 fleet, Risky Business Ltd. becomes entangled in a mystery that
covers two continents and may rewrite history.

The lure of uncovering a lost civilization, as well as the secrets it holds, motivates the team on their dangerous journey into a cosmological unknown.

Revelations: Sunken Treasure Lost Worlds-Book 2

As the mystery deepens from the peaks of the Andes to the ocean floor off Florida's Space Coast, Colten X. Burnett, and the Risky Business team are confronted by new perils and discoveries in their extraordinary quest for both treasures and what might be explosive, historical findings.

New friends and new adversaries make their quest a suspense-filled thrill ride.

Will they find the elusive treasure galleon, is the legendary golden library in Ecuador real?

Encounter: Sunken Treasure Lost Worlds- Book 3

This final installment of the #1 bestselling Risky Business Trilogy finds Colten Burnett and his intrepid team of adventurers in the jungles of Ecuador in search of the elusive Golden Library.

Pursued by multiple enemies, the team uncovers jaw dropping otherworldly treasures linked to a mysterious lost civilization that has the potential not only to enrich them but to save the planet Earth from self-destruction.

Buried Treasure : Lost Worlds, A Search For Aztec Treasure-Book 4

In 1521, the Aztec empire fell to Spanish Conquistadors in bloody genocide. The Aztec ruler, Montezuma, was murdered, and his treasure... disappeared. Legend says the treasure was spirited away by Montezuma's elite Eagle warriors, headed for an unknown desert location in the southwest of what is now the United States. It has never been found.

Dr. Colten X. Burnett and the Risky Business team have a lead. Will the unexpected map they now have in their possession guide them to the long-lost treasure in the land of the Mescalero Apache?

Hidden Treasure : Secrets Of Cleopatra's Gold-Book 5

Cleopatra: Rich, powerful, seductive, cunning. She is perhaps the most historically recognized ancient Egyptian ruler, but to this day, Cleopatra's burial tomb has yet to be found. In this adventure, Colten Burnett's Risky Business team takes on the daunting and dangerous challenge of recovering stolen statues that may hold the secrets to the famous pharaoh's life, death and fortune. Criss-crossing the middle East, the adventurous team of highly skilled men and women encounter antiquity smugglers and dealers, looters and even otherworldly beings as they race to uncover one of history's most enigmatic mysteries.